Lawrence Earle Johnson

Death Line

a novel

ARCHWAY
PUBLISHING

This book is a work of fiction. Places, names, characters, and incidents are solely the product of the author's imagination or are used fictitiously. Any resemblance to actual events, locations, or persons, living or dead, is coincidental.

Archway Publishing books may be ordered through booksellers or by contacting:

Archway Publishing
1663 Liberty Drive
Bloomington, IN 47403
www.archwaypublishing.com
1 (888) 242-5904

Because of the dynamic nature of the Internet, any web addresses or links contained in this book may have changed since publication and may no longer be valid. The views expressed in this work are solely those of the author and do not necessarily reflect the views of the publisher, and the publisher hereby disclaims any responsibility for them.

ISBN: 978-1-4808-2022-7 (sc)
ISBN: 978-1-4808-2023-4 (hc)
ISBN: 978-1-4808-2024-1 (e)

Library of Congress Control Number: 2015945421

Print information available on the last page.

Archway Publishing rev. date: 08/18/2015

*"Things are not
As they appear."*

Acknowledgments

To Jennifer Tacbas for her incredibly talented and infinitely patient work on my author photos (www.jennifertacbas.com);

To Katherine H. Downie for her artistic skill and amazing talent in marketing and graphic design (www.katherinedownie.com);

To Karen Moeller also for her valuable assistance;

To Jeremy Johnson for his keen editing eye and for his support and encouragement;

To Linda Downie for her sharp editing skills during final edit;

To Ryan Johnson and Nathan Johnson for their faith in my efforts;

To my mother and father who encouraged me in all my endeavors and made me what I am today;

But most of all to my infinitely patient and understanding wife, Cindy, without whose continual support, masterful editing, and insightful perspectives this book could not have been written.

Prologue

Kevin screamed for hours before he died. The thin man stood over his lifeless body. "He wanted to know more about ELF," he said to the scientist in the white lab coat. The scientist looked up, but said nothing.

"Amazing, isn't it," the thin man continued casually, "how much pain can be inflicted on a human body without leaving a mark—without touching the body even once."

"It wasn't warranted," the scientist said tersely.

"Oh. But it was. We needed proof. Now we have it."

"You didn't have to kill him," the scientist said, his contempt for the man undisguised.

"A necessary casualty," the thin man said, his smile totally devoid of warmth. "Besides, we can't have one person stand in the way of national defense—now can we?"

The scientist shook his head and looked away. The thin man's smile faded, his eyes cold as steel. Another weak link, he thought, as he turned and left the room.

Marquette, Michigan, August 18, 1981

chapter 1

Clayton Wolfe squinted as spikes of light from the midsummer sun reflected off the cold, blue-green waters of Lake Superior. Adjusting his fisherman's hat down over his eyes he cast again into the depths, hoping to catch a lake trout heading for the warmer waters near shore as autumn approached.

He breathed deep the fresh scent of pine and pure air that was the trademark of Michigan's Upper Peninsula. *God's Country*, he thought. That's what the locals called it. And to Wolfe, Marquette was just that. Moving his feet to get a better perch on the jagged rocks of the breakwall, he cast again into the spray, narrowly missing a seagull doing his own style of fishing.

Wolfe cocked his head as he heard an unusual sound. At first it seemed to be part of the wind—but it was more than that. Then he recognized it. It was the sound of someone crying. Wolfe looked to either side of him. Seeing no one, he finished reeling in his line and climbed to the other side of the breakwall. There on the rocks, waves and spray soaking her clothing, a young woman sat crying.

He looked around to see if someone was with her. Seeing no one, he quietly climbed over the rocks behind her.

"Can I help you, Miss?" he asked as he touched her shoulder from behind. Startled, she jerked her head around, nearly losing her balance. Wolfe grabbed her arm to keep her from falling, and lifted her to a higher position away from the spray.

"No," she said after she got her composure. "I'm all right. You just surprised me. I didn't hear you come up."

"It's no wonder," Wolfe said smiling, "what with all the wind, waves and crying going on."

"I wasn't crying," she said defensively. "Not really. It was just the water stinging my eyes."

Wolfe took a good look at her. Even dripping wet she was attractive. Her reddish hair hung down in curly streamers while her hazel eyes challenged him. Her white top was plastered to her chest, its wetness inducing a transparency Wolfe couldn't help but notice. "Hadn't you better get out of those wet clothes?" he finally said, returning his gaze to hers, which had now turned icy cold.

"Oh, I think you've already taken care of that by the looks of things," she said sarcastically as she pulled her blouse away from her chest.

"No," he interjected. "I mean that even during summer the breeze is cool. You could catch a chill if you're not careful."

"I know exactly what you meant," she snapped. "And I'll thank you to keep your thoughts to yourself. Good-bye."

Her white sneakers squished as she climbed the remaining rocks and headed back down the breakwall toward shore. Soaking wet, her jeans revealed an enticing figure. Wolfe couldn't keep his eyes off of her. Taking a pair of binoculars out of the case he had slung over his shoulder, he focused on the old powder-blue Mustang she got into. Then he pulled out a waterproof notebook he had stuck in his L.L. Bean tan canvas shirt pocket, and wrote down the license number as she drove away.

Wolfe paused, looking down at the paper. I shouldn't be doing this, he thought. I have a mission, and this isn't it. She's definitely attractive, and it's been a long time. But the mission is critical, and she's not part of it. But what if she was? She *was* crying. And angry. Something surely upset her. Trouble with a guy, most likely. He'd certainly handled enough domestic disputes in his past life. Still, he had no leads regarding his mission, and she was the only enigma he had at present. He knew it was thin, but he had nothing else to follow up on right now. He decided to go for it.

Wolfe walked into the Marquette County Sheriff's Office, and saw Sergeant Maki sitting at the desk in the center of the greeting area. Maki was in his forties, five-eight in height, and trim build. "Hey Wolfe!" Maki greeted. He was one hundred percent Finnish and a lifetime resident of Michigan's Upper Peninsula.

"Maki!" Wolfe responded. "Good to see you."

Maki jumped up from his desk and extended his hand. "Good to see you too, *Wolfeman.* So where the hell ya been? Gone over a year and not even a peep from you, Wolfe. Not even a *postcard.*

"Yea, I know. Sorry about that. It was just . . . something I couldn't talk about. Still can't. Nothing to do with you." Wolfe hung his head and looked at the floor.

Maki look chagrined, but nodded. "OK. I guess I understand." He paused a moment, then said, "Well anyway, good to have you back."

"Thanks, Maki," Wolfe said. Then he turned to Maki who was making his way back to his desk, and said, "Could you do a favor for me??"

Maki stopped and turned. "Sure. What is it?"

"Can you run a license plate for me? It's not official but I'm checking into something and I'd like to find out who the owner is. No big deal, really. But I would appreciate it."

"No problem," said Maki, who walked over to the computer

terminal with access to the DMV and punched in the information. "Comes back to a Terri Ann Sommers," Sergeant Maki said with mock gravity. "Sixty-three forty-four Lakewood Lane, Chicago, Illinois. White female, red hair, hazel eyes, height five-six, weight one-twenty-five, date of birth November 5, 1954. Speeding ticket in '75, ten over, and expired license in '78. That's it. What do you want her for—gangland slaying or somethin'?"

Sergeant Maki's attempt at humor left something to be desired, but Wolfe laughed anyway. He had gotten to know most of the Marquette County Sheriff's Department personnel over the years between his clandestine activities, and showed himself to be an avid fisherman and also an expert with firearms. He had ingratiated himself with Maki and the sheriff, by offering to help their pistol team improve their combat shooting. This was important to the sheriff as he desperately wanted to win some competitions and raise the status of the department among the other law enforcement agencies, who viewed the deputies as a bunch of buffoons. That attitude did not sit well with the sheriff, and he was out to change it.

"Not really," Wolfe replied. "Just curious."

"You know I could get in a lot of trouble for doing this, don't you?" Maki said.

"And I owe you one for it, too," Wolfe said, waving as he took the printout and left the sheriff's department. The ritual was always the same. But Maki never collected, and Wolfe always showed him the best fishing holes and trout streams that crisscrossed Marquette County.

Maki grumbled to himself. "Shows *me* the best fishing and *I* was the one born here. *I* should be showing *him*. After all I grew up here!"

Wolfe looked at the printout. The Chicago address would do him no good. She was obviously visiting Marquette, and it would be tough finding her just driving around. It looked like he was out of luck. Anyway, he thought to himself, why should he care so much about this girl he just met? Maybe something about a damsel in distress, he thought. Wolfe gave up wondering, and headed for his favorite restaurant.

chapter 2

The light was dim, but that was fine with Terri Sommers. The Little Italy restaurant cloaked its patrons in dark reds and black, instilling a sense of comfort and isolation from the cares of the world—something she desperately needed. The wine she had already consumed helped some, but it couldn't numb the shock of her kid brother's sudden death. How could it have happened? People in perfect health just don't drop dead for no reason. But that's what the coroner said. Cause of death unknown. She couldn't buy it. People die for reasons, and she was going to find out how he died.

Her order came, the waiter placing the steaming plate of lasagna and garlic bread on the table in front of her. After refilling her wine glass, he asked, "Is there anything else I can get you, Miss?"

"Not now, thank you," she said, and began to break off a piece of the bread. She started to take a bite, then put it down as she realized she had no appetite.

"Then may I join you for dinner?"

"Excuse me . . . ?" she started to say as she looked up at the waiter for the first time. Her eyes tried to focus, then recognition set in. It was the man from the breakwall.

"What are *you* doing here?" she said, annoyance replacing surprise.

"I saw you by yourself," he said, sitting down. "I asked Johnny—the owner—to let me serve your dinner. I wanted to apologize. And offer my assistance."

"Assistance for what?" she said, glaring at him.

"For whatever's bothering you," he answered, leaning forward. "What do you say? May I join you?"

Terri looked at him closely for the first time. A shade under six feet tall, he had a strong build, sandy hair and large, brown eyes which seemed to draw her to him. Though his face was handsome, it had a certain character only years and pain could have produced. But the eyes convinced her. "OK," she said reluctantly, "but don't get any bright ideas. This is only for dinner. I still don't trust you, Mister . . ."

"Wolfe," he said, a broad smile on his face. "Clayton Wolfe."

"Now there's a name that inspires confidence in a woman," she said with more than a trace of sarcasm.

"Don't judge a book . . ."

"Please," she cut in. "Spare me the clichés." Terri poured the last of the half-liter into her glass, took a large swallow, and looked at him. "Why haven't you asked me my name?"

Wolfe couldn't tell her about the illegal license check. He stalled, looked into her eyes. They seemed soft and inviting. Yet there was something there—something that whispered be careful. He would have to remember that.

"I knew you'd get around to it sooner or later," he lied.

She sized him up for several seconds. "Terri Sommers," she said finally, offering her hand. "Pleased to meet you—I *think.*"

"The pleasure's all mine," he said, taking her hand.

Suddenly she had second thoughts. "This is ridiculous," she said, pulling back. "I'm not sure this is such a good . . ."

"Give it a chance," he said before she could finish. "I think you could use some company, and I'm a good listener. I'll behave myself—I promise."

"All right," she said, sighing heavily. "I'm too tired to argue. Maybe you're right. Maybe I do need someone—anyone—to listen. Lord knows I haven't been very successful on my own."

"Good. Now tell me your problem, and don't spare the details." Wolfe ordered another bottle of wine and a glass, and pulled up a chair next to her. The red and white checkered tablecloth, the ambience of low lights, dark curtains, Sinatra playing in the background and wine, loosened Terri's inhibitions a bit.

"OK," she began, leaning back in her chair. "About two weeks ago I had just gone to bed when I got a phone call from my kid brother, Kevin. He was attending Northern Michigan University, and was working on a master's degree in environmental sciences. He said he had been working on an environmental hazards project and he'd made a startling discovery—something about *elf* waves, he said."

Wolfe poured some more wine in her empty glass. Terri took a sip. "I researched 'elf waves' and found that elf stands for Extremely Low Frequency waves of the electromagnetic spectrum—those waves under 100 cycles per second."

"Interesting," said Wolfe. He took a sip of his own wine, pondering what she had said. Then he said, "*Was* attending the University?" jumping back to a previous statement of hers. "You mean he's no longer in school?"

"No," she began, tears welling in her eyes. "He's no longer in school. He's dead."

Wolfe offered his napkin to Terri. "I'm sorry," he said somberly. "What happened?"

She wiped her eyes, then continued. "He wouldn't talk about it—said it was too important to discuss on the phone. He promised to tell me about it if I'd meet him here. Since our parents passed away, I'm the only family he has. So I made arrangements and came to Marquette to see what he'd found."

"Were you concerned about his safety at that time?" Wolfe asked.

"Not really. He is—was—a very intense individual. When he got into something, it was all or nothing. I guess I'm the same way, come to think of it. It wasn't unusual for him to call me on the phone wherever he was and talk about something that excited him. But I must admit there was something different this time. Something in his voice . . ."

"Did he say anything that might indicate what his discovery was?" Wolfe asked, trying to jog her memory.

"Not really, other than the fact that he was working on an environmental hazard project when he made his discovery. Whether or not it was related to that, I don't know."

"Then what happened? After the phone call, I mean," Wolfe said.

"I told him I'd meet him at his apartment last Thursday—three days ago. When I got there he was gone. No one knew where he was. And no one in the building could remember having seen him for several days. It was then that I began to worry. Kevin was adventurous, but not irresponsible. He would never even think of missing an appointment, especially with me. He was always considerate—always on time. I knew something was wrong."

"Then what happened?" Wolfe pressed.

"I went to the sheriff's department, the city police, and the state police and reported him missing. There were no reports of finding a person of his description on file, so I went back to the motel and waited while they tried to locate him."

Terri took another sip of wine, the pain of remembering evident. "The report wasn't long in coming. A hunter found his body near a logging trail about ten miles northwest of here. That was yesterday. The coroner said he had been dead less than twenty-four hours.

That means he had been alive but missing from campus at least two days before he died, and probably longer."

"So the question is," Wolfe summarized, "where was he during that time?"

"Yes," she agreed. "And why did he die?"

The rest of the conversation yielded nothing regarding the situation, so Wolfe suggested they visit the coroner's office the next morning and see what they could find out. He followed her to her motel room at the Ramada Inn and bid her goodnight.

Seeing her safely tucked away, he sat in his modified Jeep Wrangler, thinking about the case—for in his mind it was now a case—probably murder. The wind had picked up and rain had started its staccato dance on his windshield. The temperature had dropped precipitously, and Wolfe knew it was going to be a nasty night. The damp chill in the air seemed to portend future events, not an encouraging sign, thought Wolfe. He had a feeling—a bad feeling—that things were about to take a serious turn for the worse, though he couldn't put his finger on how or why. Did his assignment have anything to do with Terri's brother? If so, how? If not, what happened to him?

His thoughts ran back to 1975, when the Edmund Fitzgerald left Duluth, Minnesota, with a load of taconite iron ore heading to Detroit. Lake Superior has been known to be a treacherous lake, with waves coming from all directions during rough storms. Captains would much rather traverse the oceans than Lake Superior. And on that fateful November 10th of '75, the Lake proved its fateful reputation. The Edmund Fitzgerald sank before it could reach Whitefish Bay, taking with it its entire crew of 29 souls.

Gordon Lightfoot memorialized the tragedy in his song, "The Wreck of the Edmund Fitzgerald." Wolfe hoped that whatever he was getting into, would not be memorialized by Gordon Lightfoot. Or anyone else, for that matter.

The rain was getting worse and the wind was now howling.

Wolfe snapped out of his reverie, put the Wrangler in gear, and headed to his cabin in the woods. He hoped a fire in the rustic fieldstone fireplace would take the chill out of his bones tonight. Somehow he doubted it.

chapter 3

The next morning the storm had passed, and the mood of the sky was completely changed. A full sun was warming the bright, clear blue, cloudless sky and Wolfe's mood was markedly better. He was on his way to pick up Terri, having agreed that there was no point in taking two cars to visit the coroner's office.

Terri opened the door and Wolfe's heart skipped a beat. Her long red hair was sparkling in the sun and her face had a blush that bespoke a healthy outdoors lifestyle. She wore a black pull-over top with a green windbreaker, and well-fitting jeans of some kind or another. From the looks of things, the brand didn't matter, thought Wolfe. Gray sneakers finished off her ensemble. Wolfe was enjoying it all when he looked at her eyes and saw her watching him check her out.

"Meet your satisfaction?" Terri said with a trace of sarcasm.

"Oh. Uh, sorry about that. Instinct."

Terri began walking towards the parking lot. "Sure," she said, with a slight smile. "I think I know what your *real* profession is. Wolfe *hound.*"

Wolfe decided to put the shovel down and stop digging. He was in deep enough.

When they got in the car, he tried to change tacks. "What about you?" Wolfe said. "What do you do for a living? Or are you married?"

"That's cute," Terri said. "Are you saying married women don't work?"

"Of course not," he said, trying to recover. "I meant, are you a working woman?"

"You want to know if I'm a hooker," she said, deliberately being difficult.

Wolfe let out a low growl of frustration as he gripped the steering wheel tighter.

"You already know too much about me," she said, guardedly. "Let's hear a little about you first."

"There's really not much to tell."

"Let's start with what you do for a living."

Wolfe looked a little uneasy. "Oh, a little of this and a little of that."

"Now that's informative," she said, shaking her head.

"Honestly," he said. "I don't have a full-time job, per se."

"Well then, what do you have, *per se*?"

"I write a little. History of the region, mostly. Not much money in it, though. So I teach part-time at the University, and do some investigative work now and then for law enforcement agencies in the area. It keeps me busy."

"What do you teach at the University?" she pursued. "Have you published any articles or books?"

"What is this? An inquisition?" he said, looking over at her.

"Eyes on the road, chum," she said. "Just answer the questions."

"I teach criminal investigation," he continued. "And yes, I have published a book or two. Satisfied?"

"Not really," she said, running a comb through her hair. "I'll feel better when I see your name on a course listing or a book cover. Got any?"

"Well, actually, it's been a long time since I taught. And I write under a pen name," he said, knowing this would not fly. It didn't.

"Sure you do. You use a pen name so as not to interfere with your other non-job," she said, the sarcasm undisguised and unrelenting. "What schools did you attend? Where did you get your training to teach? To conduct criminal investigations?"

"Writing an article on me?" Wolfe broke in.

That stopped her. "What? You know I'm a writer?"

"I do now," he said, smiling.

"And how . . ."

"Elementary, my dear Terri," he cut in. "By the questions you're asking, you're either a cop, or a reporter. Since you don't seem to have the constitution to be a cop that just leaves reporter."

"What do you mean, I don't have the constitution to be a cop?" she challenged.

"Well, do you?"

"I suppose not," she said slowly, calming down slightly. "But . . ."

"Your reaction to your brother's death," he continued. "Had you been a cop, believing what you believe about his death, you would have been hounding those law enforcement agencies mercilessly, if not conducting your own personal investigation. You did neither."

"I did everything I could," she said defensively.

"I wasn't being critical," he said. "I'm sure you did. Maybe together we can do more."

Silence found them as they approached the coroner's office. The building was typical of the Upper Peninsula of Michigan. Fairly old, with white clapboard siding and a black shingled roof. It was rectangular, wider than it was deep, and had an austere, almost clinical look to it. Basically, it looked to be what it was, thought Wolfe. A place for dead bodies and refrigerated compartments.

Terri gave a little shiver as they got out of the Wrangler, not altogether due to the chill in the air.

They walked up to the entrance, but saw a notice on the door that the coroner's office was closed. Wolfe left a note in the door explaining the basics, and that he'd be in touch the next day. He turned to Terri and said, "Well, not much we can do right now. What say we take a look around? I'll give you the grand tour, since I imagine you haven't done much of that since you arrived—recently I assume."

"Right," said Terri, looking for any sign of ulterior motives. Sensing none, she continued. "Might as well. Will do me good to get a lay of the land that my brother called home, however briefly." Her eyes misted slightly, but then the sun shone again and she strode confidently to the car.

Wolfe gave her a tour of Marquette, a small city of about 20,000 people, including 8,000 or so students at Northern Michigan University. Then he took her on a somewhat perilous drive up Mount Marquette. It was not a high mountain, but was steep and with twisty roads in poor shape. At one time drivers came here from all over the world to compete in the Press-On-Regardless (POR) rally, and one of the stages was Mount Marquette. It took quite a toll on the vehicles, which ranged from Jeeps and Subarus, to Porsches and Ferraris, and everything in-between.

He took her to Presque Isle, which reached out into the sometimes hostile waters of Lake Superior. A marina there was tucked in a protected cove that was sheltered from the wind and waves. This was also one of the stages of the POR rally, and the cars flew around the one-way road around Presque Isle at speeds that caused some of the drivers to catch air as they went over small undulations in the blacktopped surface. But away from the traffic the Isle was surrounded by jagged rocks that protected it from the fierce wave action of the lake.

Wolfe then left Presque Isle and swung over onto route 550, Big Bay Road, and headed north.

chapter 4

Terri was impressed, and surprised that Wolfe had so much knowledge of the area. "How do you know all this?" she asked, turning to look at him as he was driving.

Wolfe kept looking straight ahead. "I'm around here a lot when I'm working, and when I'm not, I vacation here because there is so much to see and do."

"Are you from here? Have family here?" she asked.

"No. I just like it here. The locals call it 'God's Country.'"

"So, if you're not from here," she asked, "just where *are* you from?"

Wolfe knew this question was coming, and he had time to prepare an answer, but that didn't help him. He couldn't tell her the truth, and he really didn't want to lie to her, though that had never been a problem in his line of work.

His silence drew a strange look.

There was a long pause.

Finally he turned to her.

"I can't answer that, Terri," he said. "I wish I could, but I'm not able to, and I can't explain why. Some things are unknown, and some are unknowable. My life falls into the latter, I'm afraid. I hope you can understand."

His eyes back on the road, it was her turn.

"You don't make sense," she said. "You're a part-time this, and a part-time that, you know a lot of people and a lot about the area, but you're not from here, and you can't tell me where you *are* from." She paused, looking at him intently. Then finally, "are you a spy or something?"

Wolfe took a deep breath and slowly let it out. This was worse than anything he had done in the past. He concentrated on the scenery as they headed for Big Bay. Pine trees lined the narrow, two-lane road, and the road took on a strange aura as they left civilization behind. There were strange things that went on up in these woods, things legends are made of.

Wolfe's mind wandered back to his past, as feelings and events began to crowd his mind. This drive always did that. There was something mysterious here. It was almost like going back in time. In fact, it drew him there. Wolfe didn't like not being in control. Normally he always was. In control of the situation. Of every situation. But not here. And he didn't know why.

As they approached Big Bay, Wolfe finally spoke.

"Or something," he finally said.

"What?" she asked.

"You asked me if I was a spy or something, and I just said, 'or something.'"

Terri looked at him, incredulous at his response. "That's no answer," she said. "That's no help at all! I was being facetious. Are you serious?"

"Afraid so," he said stoically. "Best I can do right now, Terri. I'm sorry."

Terri sat in silence as they slowly drove through Big Bay.

"*Anatomy of a Murder* was filmed here," Wolfe said, trying to change the subject. "It was a real hit at the box office. Lee Remick,

James Stewart, Ben Gazzara. Nineteen-fifty-nine, in black and white. A great murder mystery."

Terri looked at him, and slowly nodded. What had she gotten herself into? Was this man crazy? Was he threatening her?

"One more stretch to go, then we have to turn around," said Wolfe.

This next part was the worst for him. As they left Big Bay they entered into a primeval forest that looked as if it hadn't changed in a thousand years. The feelings of uncertainty and illusion were stronger now. He wanted to go as fast as his Jeep would take him, but he knew he had to remain in control. So he drove slowly.

The trees remained untouched, as they had for centuries—or longer. They formed a canopy over the road that completely covered it, blocking out the noonday sun. The forest on either side was almost dark—like twilight—for the same reason. Dead trees lay scattered everywhere, as there was no forestry done here. Some had fallen to the ground and were in various states of decay. Some were newly fallen, while others had been down a long time. Fungus and moss grew on those.

Other trees fell partially over, their descent halted only by the trunk of a living tree next to them. So they just leaned there, waiting patiently until the other tree died too, then eventually they both would fall, reaching their ultimate resting place. The whole place looked eerie. Wolfe had come to refer to it as 'the Haunted Forest.' But it wasn't just the place that bothered him. There was something else.

"This place is strange," Terri finally said. "Do you feel it?

"Yes," Wolfe said. "I do. I always feel this way when I come up here. I'm glad you felt it too. Sometimes I think I'm going crazy."

"Why are we going here? This place creeps me out."

"You need to see something," he said. "You need to see all the things that exist here, that somehow define it."

Suddenly they came to the end of the road. Terri saw a circular turnaround where the pavement ended, with nothing else but trees, and a small guard shack with a traffic arm blocking...what? A road of some kind? No, not a road, she thought. More like a paved path. Or packed dirt?

"End of the road," Wolfe said.

"I see that," Terri said. "So what are we seeing? You said we had to see something?"

"See and feel," Wolfe said. "I wanted to see if you felt what I felt in the woods, and see where this all leads to."

"Well, I felt what you did, at least I felt weird, if that's the way you felt. But what are we seeing, exactly? All I see is trees and a guard shack and the end of the road."

"What you're seeing is a guarded entrance to another world. At least, a world different from the rest of the county. I'll explain later. Right now I want to get out of here, and I want to warn you that we will be traveling considerably faster than when we came."

Wolfe then turned the Wrangler around and gave Terri a demonstration of just how modified his Jeep was.

Wolfe drove at speeds that precluded conversation, which was what he intended. Terri spent the trip gripping the door handle and yelling at Wolfe to slow down. When they got back to Marquette, Wolfe took her back to her motel. They sat in silence as the Jeep cooled down, the metal crackling as the vehicle cooled off.

Finally they got out and went to her door, still without speaking. "Don't ever do that again," she said angrily. "You could've killed us a hundred times over."

Wolfe stood facing her outside her door. "That feeling we had in the Haunted Forest?"

"What about it?" she snapped.

"That may have had something to do with your brother's death," Wolfe said.

"What do you mean?"

"I'm not sure, but I felt disoriented, confused, and maybe a little hallucinogenic," he continued. "Maybe something like that happened to him."

"What makes you think that?" asked Terri.

"I don't know for sure. It just feels that way. But I know one thing for sure," he said.

"What?" she asked.

Wolfe looked at Terri. "I know I'm going to help you find out how he died, and I have a strong feeling he was murdered."

They stood facing each other. As she looked at him, Terri found only genuine warmth in his eyes. "Thank you for believing," she said. "See you tomorrow."

chapter 5

Deep within the trenches of Wolfe's mind it probed. Its intermittent nature was vaguely familiar to him, but he couldn't quite remember where he had heard it before. It seemed to get louder and louder until he could hardly stand it.

Suddenly his hand reached out and he grabbed the white menace by its thin, scrawny neck.

"Hello," he heard a scratchy, almost incoherent voice say. It was an awful voice. It was *his* voice.

"Wolfe? That you?" the voice at the other end was thick with the local Finnish accent. "You sound like shit." It was Eino Loukkala.

"Thank you, Eino," Wolfe mumbled, recognizing the coroner's voice. He tried to look at his watch, but couldn't bring his eyes to focus. "Since I feel the same way I sound, maybe you'd like to tell me why you called me at whatever this unholy hour must be."

"Unholy, is it?" Eino shouted, "I'll have you know that while you've been sleeping, I've been here at the morgue trying to solve your damned case for you."

"How'd you . . ." Wolfe started.

"Stopped in late for a friendly chat with my customers," Eino cut in sarcastically, "if it's any of your business. Saw your note and it piqued my interest. Thought I'd get started since I wasn't sleepy."

"What'd you find?" Wolfe said, almost awake.

"Rather not say over the phone. You'd better get down here, though. I don't think you're going to like this."

"Hang on, Eino. I'll be there in a few minutes."

Wolfe thought about Eino as he was driving to the morgue. Eino Loukkala was one of the best forensic pathologists in the country, and could have easily commanded a salary several times what he was making—except for one thing. He would have had to leave the Upper Peninsula, and that he would not do. He was born and raised in Marquette, the only son of immigrant parents who had moved from Finland the year he was born. After seeing what the world was like during a brief stint in the military, he decided he would die here.

But Wolfe knew one thing for sure. When Eino said he was not going to like something, it was not good news, for Eino was the master of understatement.

Wolfe arrived and let himself in the back door of the morgue, the key a token of his long friendship with the coroner.

"Finally made it, eh?" Eino said, seeing Wolfe's shape loom in the doorway. "Step into my humble office," he continued, his Finnish accent stronger than normal.

"Office, my ass," said Wolfe. "This is more like the library of an English estate than the office of a broken-down civil servant Finlander."

"Ah, Wolfe. Envy doesn't become you."

Wolfe watched as Eino sat in his over-stuffed brown leather chair, smoke from his pipe swirling around furnishings of polished wood and leather. A detailed globe of the world stood next to his desk. Eino stared at Wolfe, a smirk on his face.

"So why are you working so hard on this case, Eino?" Wolfe

said finally as he sat in another over-stuffed chair opposite the coroner. "You usually take forever."

"Your cases are always interesting, Wolfe," he said, ignoring the jab. "Once I got started, I just couldn't quit."

"So what have you got?" Wolfe said impatiently, hoping to hear what the coroner had discovered without his usual, infinitely detailed explanations. The smile on Eino's face as he slowly got out of his chair, clenching his pipe in his teeth, told him he would not be so lucky.

Eino walked over to an oak writing table and picked up his handwritten notes. "I ran the standard tests on the victim as you asked," he began deliberately, "looking for anything that might indicate why the boy died. I tested for drugs, particularly mind-altering ones commonly available from the drug culture. Nothing. I looked for common and exotic poisons which might, under certain circumstances, cause instant death in a healthy male. Again, nothing. I . . .,'

"Look, Eino," Wolfe interrupted in frustration. "I'm sure you ran every test imaginable. I know you worked hard. You always do. So please spare me the gory details and get to the bottom line."

"Oh, but I am getting to the bottom line, Wolfe. You see, it's important you understand all the processes I went through. And how quickly, too. So you'll know no stone was left unturned to ferret out the truth."

"Never mind," Wolfe again cut in. "I'm sorry I interrupted."

"Mmmm. Let's see. Where was I? Oh yes. I tested for drugs . . ."

"You said that already," Wolfe snapped, rising to the bait all too easily.

"Of course. Ah, I also tested for environmental pollutants, thinking that emissions from manufacturing or perhaps from secret landfills may have contributed. Again, nothing."

Wolfe was seething by now, but all he could do was glare at the man who held him captive, watching the thin, six-foot-two-inch, fifty-year-old man pace around the room, lecturing him. His long nose, drooping head and bulging Adams apple gave a striking resemblance to a vulture. Appropriate, thought Wolfe, considering his line of work.

"The bottom line," Eino said, pausing for effect, knowing his audience would return with the uttering of the magical words, "is that none of these tests produced any explanation as to why the boy died."

"Then what's the information you said I wouldn't like?" Wolfe said, waiting for the bombshell. "How did he die?"

"Can't say for sure," Eino replied, "but I think we can rule out natural causes."

"And why's that?"

"Because the boy didn't die where he was found. He was moved there."

"How do you know?"

"Because his clothes were clean."

"What?"

"His clothes," continued Eino, "had no traces of the dirt, sweat or stains he would have undoubtedly accumulated walking in the woods for two days. In fact, his hiking boots were so clean, he could have been dropped from the sky."

"So he died somewhere else and was moved to the location where he was found?"

"That's correct," Eino said. "The question is, why would someone go to all that trouble?"

chapter 6

Wolfe decided not to wake Terri to give her the news until morning. He broke the news when they met in a Huddle House for breakfast. When he did, she was not pleased.

"But why?" she asked as their food was arriving. Terri had already had a cup of coffee, Wolfe had two.

"That *is* the question," Wolfe answered, letting the effects of the coffee come to full strength.

"Shouldn't we notify the police about this?" Terri asked, eager to do something.

"It's not necessary. Eino will have already done that by now. In fact, I imagine it will be in tonight's paper if the reporters from the *Marquette Journal* have anything on the ball."

"Of course. Mysterious homicide—unexplained death. Makes for a great headline all right," she said angrily. "Why did this have to happen?" she said, her eyes moist. "He was all I had. Why would someone want to kill him?"

"That's what we're going to find out," Wolfe said as he paid the check.

When they had finished breakfast, they picked up a copy of the *Journal* at Terri's motel. The article about Kevin's death appeared on the front page. Below the fold was the title: "University Student Dies Mysteriously." Although the article said the police were investigating it as a possible homicide, it gave no information about the body being moved or other particulars.

What did stand out, however, was a quote from Terri saying she had evidence her brother was murdered and she was not going to rest until the killer was found.

"That's not exactly what I said," Terri complained. "I said there was evidence—I didn't say I had it."

"Now you get a taste of your own medicine," Wolfe said with a slight smile.

Terri ignored him. "That's funny," Terri said, picking up an older copy of the *Journal* lying on the coffee table. "What time did Eino say Kevin died?"

"It was about noon on the twenty-fifth," Wolfe said. "Why?"

"Well, it says here that a car went out of control near there and crashed at about that same time. The driver was injured, but not seriously, it says. And here. In another article, a small plane crashed while attempting a landing on a small, private runway near K.I. Sawyer Air Force Base. It says that the pilot suddenly became dizzy and lost his orientation. He's being treated for minor injuries."

"So? What's unusual about that?" Wolfe said.

"The crash took place about 11:00 AM on the twenty-fifth. Also, the driver of the car complained of dizziness just before the crash. Coincidence?"

"Maybe, maybe not," Wolfe said, reaching for the paper. "Let me see that." Wolfe read the articles without saying a word. Finally, he put the paper down. "Let's go talk to the accident victims. Maybe they can tell us something."

As they drove out to see the pilot of the airplane, Terri turned to Wolfe. "Why are you doing this?" she asked, watching his expression intently.

"Why am I driving the car?" he said smoothly enough, a slight smile showing at the corners of his mouth.

"Why are you going to all this trouble for me? I mean, even a person with only part-time jobs has things to do."

Wolfe kept driving, his eyes fixed on the road ahead. His face revealed no trace of his thoughts. "I'm helping you because I like you," he said finally. "You're in a tough situation in a strange town, and I have a flexible schedule. Isn't that enough?"

Now it was her turn to sit quietly. It all seemed so disjointed, yet it made sense. "It's enough," she said finally. "For now."

"Dennis Holben?" Wolfe inquired as the tall, balding man stood in the doorway of his semi-modern brick ranch house.

"Who's askin'?" the man replied, suspicious hostility in his voice.

"Clayton Wolfe. And this is Terri Sommers. We'd like to ask you a few questions about your plane crash, if you don't mind."

"What's your business?" the man said, no more congenial than at first.

"We're from the EPA," Wolfe lied. "Conducting a study on environmental hazards. When we read in the paper about your dizziness before the crash, we decided to check it out."

"Now that's real funny, folks," the man said sarcastically, "cause them EPA fellas already been here. In fact, they questioned the daylights outta me. Told me not to talk about it after they was done. Some kinda confidential study. Now you two show up here askin' the same questions. Ain't that peculiar?"

"I . . ." Wolfe started to say.

"Unless you got some cold hard green like them other fellas," the man cut in, "this conversation's over."

As he started to close the door, Wolfe put his hand out and stopped it from closing. "Wait," he said. "Those men paid you to be quiet?"

"They paid me for my time's what they did. And they gonna pay all my medical bills. And fix my plane, too. So unless you got a condo in Florida you wanna unload for pennies on the dollar, you'd better move your friggin' hand 'fore it gets blowed off."

Wolfe slowly released the door and backed away, keeping his body between Holben and Terri.

When they got safely back in the car, Terri said, "What do you make of that?"

"Looks like we've got some competition," Wolfe said, pensively. "I think we'd better get back to your place."

"Why? What's the matter?" Terri said, the concern in her voice evident.

"Unless I miss my guess," he continued, "there are bigger fish in this pond than I suspected, and I'm feeling a bit undersized at the moment."

"What does that mean?" she said, exasperated. "Why do you talk in riddles?"

"Habit," he answered, absentmindedly. "But it looks like your hunch was right. It all seems related. Your brother's working on a project dealing with environmental hazards. He calls you with a startling discovery that he won't talk about on the phone. When you arrive, he has disappeared. Later he's found dead in a place he couldn't have gotten to on his own.

"About the same time, two people have accidents in the same general area, both having symptoms of dizziness. Now we find out that the EPA has been investigating environmental hazards, and paid a victim not to say anything about it."

"Doesn't look good, does it?" she said.

"Not particularly."

"And don't forget the way we felt in and around the Haunted Forest," Wolfe said. "Maybe that's part of it too."

"I think we'd better talk to the driver of the car," she said nervously.

"I think we'd better," he said as he put his car in gear.

Wolfe found a nearby phone booth and stopped to look up the address.

"What was that name again?" Wolfe yelled from the phone booth.

"John Erickson," Terri shouted as he rifled the pages of the small phone book.

"Do you know what street?"

"No, but it's in Harvey. That's a town, I guess," she finished.

"No, it's a large imaginary rabbit," he shouted back, making her laugh for the first time. She watched him put change in the phone, talk for a few minutes, then return to the car.

"Well?" she asked, apprehensively.

"I got his mother. Seems he's nineteen and lived at home," he said.

"*Lived*?" she said.

"Yea. Some officials from the EPA visited their home, and offered them a paid vacation in exchange for information on the accident."

"She said all that?"

"Not in exactly those words, but that's the gist of it. They're flying out of town tonight and won't be back for at least a month. What do you think?"

"I think the stinking EPA is up to its armpits in a cover-up, and I think by the time I get done writing about this, the only thing EPA is going to stand for is Enough Pushing Around."

"You're going to write a story about this?" Wolfe said with some surprise.

"No," Terri said sharply, "I'm going to write an article about this."

"Who would you write it for?"

"Newspapers," she said calmly.

"Well, I know you're a writer, but I didn't know you worked for a paper," he said, somewhat taken aback.

"Not paper. Papers," she said, savoring the moment.

"You work for more than one paper?" Wolfe said incredulously.

"AP," she said, watching his expression as the full weight of what she was saying sank in. "I write for the Associated Press."

Wolfe stared at her for several seconds, not sure whether or not to believe her. Her smug look answered his question. "Well then," he began finally. "I guess I'd better be more careful what I say around you from now on."

"I'd be more concerned about what you've already said," Terri said with a raised eyebrow. Wolfe looked at her, wondering if she was kidding—and tried to recall everything he'd said to her since they met.

chapter 7

Wolfe decided to head back to Terri's motel room. Things seemed to be getting more dangerous and he was thinking about moving her to a safer location. When they got there, Terri opened the door and gasped.

"What the . . . !" she started to say.

Wolfe pulled her back from the entrance and stepped into the room, prepared for violence if it came. But no one was there. The room was a mess. Drawers were pulled out, contents strewn everywhere. Even the mattress and pillowcases were ripped apart.

"Oh no," she said as it sunk in what had happened. "My clothes . . . my . . ." She started to mist up. "What's going on Wolfe?" she shouted through the tears. "What the *hell's* going on?"

"Quick," Wolfe said. "Grab your things. We've gotta get out of here. I'll take you somewhere safe—someplace where you can get some rest while we sort things out."

"But what about all this? Who's going to pay for it? We'll have to make out a report and . . ."

"Forget that. Just do as I say," Wolfe said, taking charge in a way she hadn't seen before. "I'll take care of this later. C'mon."

He grabbed her suitcase from the closet and opened it on the floor. "Fill it with what you need and leave the rest. We'll come back for it later or buy new. You're in danger."

Terri came to life, grabbing the things that weren't ruined and jamming them into the suitcase. They left by the front entrance, where Wolfe threw the manager his card saying, "Send the bill to that post office box. I'll see to it you're reimbursed." The manager's puzzled look quickly turned to panic as he ran outside and wrote down the license number of Wolfe's car.

"Won't do him any good," Wolfe said to her unasked question as they pulled away from the motel. Immediately he regretted it. By the look she gave him, he knew there would have to be another explanation. But not now, he thought. One crisis at a time.

His place was ten miles north of Marquette, east off the highway a quarter-mile down a two-rut dirt road. At the end of the road, the car headlights painted across a large, log house with a circular drive in front of it. Terri was impressed. As she got out of the car she heard the sound of waves washing up on shore behind the house.

"Lake Superior," he said.

"You're on the Lake?"

"A place I picked up years ago," Wolfe said, trying to make light of it. "Got an offer I couldn't refuse."

"I'll bet," she said, adding another mental question to be asked later. The inside of the house was surprisingly well-furnished and decorated. Although typically male in orientation with lots of brown leather, wooden beams and bookshelves, there were decidedly feminine touches as well. Bright colored throw pillows, wall hangings, and interesting prints added warmth and variety that seemed to complement the rest of the interior. Terri wondered if the female responsible for them complemented Wolfe as well.

Wolfe, she thought. What a name. Could be a first or last name. Or maybe just descriptive. "Mind if I call you Clay?" she said as Wolfe was putting some hot water on the stove.

He hesitated for a moment. "That's fine," he said finally. "Been a long time since I was called that. Nice to hear it again."

"Good," she said, walking into the kitchen that opened into the great room.

Wolfe put out some cheese and crackers. "Coffee, tea, or wine?" he asked, as the kettle began to whistle.

"I think it had better be coffee," she said, wishing she hadn't. "The shape I'm in, I'd end up on the floor after one drink."

Wolfe tried to wipe that image from his mind as he poured coffee and made a fire in the massive, stone fireplace. They sat on the soft couch facing the fire. "In late summer the night air takes on a chill," Wolfe said finally, placing the last piece of dry wood on the crackling fire.

"It's beautiful," she said. The strain of the week had taken its toll. Despite the coffee, she found herself slipping slowly into a trance as the flames flickered and danced, warming her through. "I'm afraid I'm not going to be much company tonight," she said with great effort. "Can you tell me what arrangements . . .?"

"You're sleeping up, and I'm down," Wolfe cut in. "There's a lock on your door, and a bathroom off your room, so you can rest easy. Sleep 'til you wake up."

Terri was so tired she didn't even catch the illogic of his last line. "Thanks," she said as she climbed the open staircase to the second floor. "Good night, Clay."

Affected by the way she said his first name, he quickly recovered. "Good night," he said, suddenly deluged with memories that threatened to engulf him. His eyes glistening, he sat back and watched the fire and listened to the waves gently rolling up on the beach. "Good night, Terri" he said again softly, long after she had gone.

chapter 8

The sound of the waves lapping up on shore gently awakened her. She lay in bed, her eyes closed, aware of the morning light filtering through the trees into her room. The rustling leaves of the poplars outside her window caught the occasional gust of wind, shaking like soft maracas to an unknown beat. It was like living in dreamland, she thought, and she didn't want to wake up.

But the sound of Wolfe downstairs on the phone brought her back to reality. Terri showered and dressed quickly, then came downstairs just in time to see Wolfe putting two plates of omelets on the table. "How'd you know I'd be down just now?" she asked, taking in the fresh oranges, coffee, and sweet rolls he'd set out.

"Just lucky, I guess," he said as they sat down. She looked at him for a moment, contemplating the enigma. Who was this man? His strong frame, muscular body and handsome appearance with sandy brown hair—he seemed confident but not arrogant. His past was mysterious, and he clearly had had training in handling himself, but his touch was gentle and his eyes . . . his eyes seemed to swallow her up. She could swim in those . . .

"You're staring," he said, as he began to eat his food with appetite. "I couldn't wait. Sorry, but I'm starving."

The suddenness of his words shook her out of her reverie.

"Oh. Sorry," Terri said. "I guess I was just daydreaming." She tried to regain her composure. She came down and sat at the table.

"Who were you talking to on the phone?" she asked, as she helped herself to an orange.

"Senator Tom Phillips," he said between bites.

"In Washington?" she asked, surprised.

"Yea," he said facetiously. "I know it's amazing, but that phone line actually stretches all the way to Washington D.C."

"You know what I mean," she said, giving him a playful look of disdain. "You were actually talking to him?"

"Of course. He's our senator. Well, I guess he's not *your* senator. But anyway, when I need some help in Washington, I call him. It's amazing how much assistance they're willing to give if you just ask."

"Sounds to me like you call quite a bit," she said, in her investigative reporter tone of voice.

"Not really," he said, avoiding her eyes.

"And this time?" she probed.

"EPA," he said. "They're not likely to turn over their secret investigation to me, even if I talk dirty to them. Tom—Senator Phillips—agreed to check into it for me. He said he wouldn't be able to tell me the focus of the study if it was really secret, but he could confirm whether or not they are doing one here."

"And?"

"And he's going to call me as soon as he finds out what's going on—if anything. In the meantime," he said as he finished devouring his food, "we have lots to do and not much time to do it in."

"Such as . . ."

"Such as getting your car . . ."

"My car!" she exclaimed. "It's still in the motel parking lot!

Oh my god, I bet it's been towed. They're probably looking for me right now."

"Don't worry," Wolfe said calmly. "I took care of it last night. It's in safe hands. We'll pick it up later."

"Whose safe hands is it in?" she demanded. "I love that car. I inherited it from my father and he kept it in perfect condition. It's a classic now, and worth a lot of money, not to mention the sentimental value."

"Sixty-six Mustang convertible-289 V8," he said wistfully. "I know it well. Trust me. It's perfectly safe."

"Did you have one?"

"Once," he said slowly, "a long time ago. I had just gotten back from a tour of duty in Europe, and I had a wad of pay burning a hole in my pocket."

"You were in the military?" she said with sudden interest, hoping to continue this foray into Wolfe's past.

"Army," he said after a pause. "Four years."

"Where were you stationed?" Terri said, trying to keep the conversation going.

"Mostly Europe and the Middle East," Wolfe said.

"What were your duties there?" she continued, trying and failing to sound casual.

Wolfe was getting uncomfortable with the line of questioning and tried to extricate himself. "Oh, general stuff. Collecting background information on various countries. Research, demographics, that sort of thing."

Terri wasn't buying it. "Pretty expensive to live over there, wasn't it?" she questioned. "I mean, for a low-level military researcher. What were you—a sergeant or something?"

Wolfe was squirming. It was time to end this. "It was a long time ago, Terri," he said, trying to shut down the conversation.

Terri was not to be so easily dissuaded. "So how'd you end up after four years in Europe with a wad of money burning a hole in your pocket? Enough to pay cash for a vintage Mustang convertible?"

"I didn't say it was a convertible, and I didn't say I paid cash for the whole thing," he said defensively.

"I know," she said, traces of an impish smile at the corners of her mouth.

"The police chief," he said suddenly, taking her by surprise.

"What?"

"He has your car in his impound lot—for safekeeping."

Terri realized the trip down memory lane was over. "How did you arrange to have it towed there?"

"The police chief of Marquette is an acquaintance of mine," he said, relieved to be back in the present. "I called him last night and he agreed to take care of it until you needed it."

"Is there anybody you don't know?" she said as they got in his car.

"Sure," he said, as they headed down the dirt drive toward the highway. "Lots of people. At least a dozen—maybe more," he laughed. Terri just shook her head, took a deep breath of the pine-scented fresh air, and settled back in the seat. Maybe things would be looking up from now on.

Then she caught a glimpse of him out of the corner of her eye; a glimpse that showed a sudden change of demeanor, and a dark glance back at the cabin. When she turned to look at him, it was gone, replaced by a genial smile that told her both nothing, and everything.

chapter 9

"We've got to see if we can find Kevin's notes," Wolfe said as they approached Marquette. "Let's start by going to the morgue and picking up his personal effects." Wolfe carefully watched Terri's reaction. "You up to it?"

"I'll be OK," she said, determined to control her emotions this time.

"All right. But if you have a problem, you can wait in the car. I'll understand."

"No, I'm fine," she insisted. "Besides, I'd like to meet one of these *acquaintances* of yours, even if he is a coroner. See if they're real. You know?"

Eino was perkier than usual, owing, no doubt, to the fact that a pretty woman now adorned his office. "Pleasure to meet you," he said, offering his hand. "I wish it were under happier circumstances."

"So do I," Terri said, with a forced smile.

"Here's everything that was turned in when he was found,"

Eino said, handing Terri a brown envelope. "If you would please examine the contents, I'll fill out a receipt for you."

Terri opened the metal clasp and slid the contents out onto a wooden table. Eino described the items. "Wallet, comb, three dollars and seventy-two cents in cash, pocket knife and room key. Like I said. Not much."

"You don't have any idea what killed my brother?" Terri suddenly blurted out.

"Not really," he said apologetically. "I've run every test I know how to run. There was just no cause that I can determine. If you can give me some specific direction to go in, I'd be glad to examine him further, but right now I'm at a standstill."

"Thank you, Eino," she said, standing to leave. "I'm sure you've done all you can. I appreciate your efforts."

"That's OK. It's my job. Unless you're in a hurry for the funeral arrangements, I can keep him here 'til you're ready."

"There won't be any funeral," Terri said stiffly. "Kevin didn't believe in funerals. He'll be cremated and his ashes scattered over the lake without ceremony when the time comes. In the meantime, I'll take you up on your kind offer. Good day," she said, offering her hand to Eino.

It was a side of Terri that Wolfe hadn't seen before. For a moment, she seemed as cold and hard as steel. It gave him an odd feeling—one he filed away.

Kevin's apartment was the upstairs flat of an old frame house two blocks from the University. The stairs were inside the front door, the downstairs apartment having a separate door into what once was the living room. The old wood creaked as they climbed the steps, Wolfe in the lead. Halfway up, there was a landing where the steps turned left, then continued on to the top.

There wasn't much room to stand, so Terri stood down a step

while Wolfe unlocked the door. As he swung the door open, a huge fist smashed him in the face. The force of the blow knocked him back against Terri, sending both of them tumbling down the steps to the landing. Blood was gushing from Wolfe's nose as Terri screamed.

"What are you doing? Why did you do that?"

The man behind the fist said nothing. He was huge and solid, and obviously used to getting his own way. He calmly walked down the steps toward them, reaching into his jacket as he did so. Terri kept looking at Wolfe's bloody face and yelled again at the man. "Who are you? What were you doing in Kevin's apartment?"

Wolfe watched the man's eyes as the man watched him. His hand stayed in his jacket as he approached them. As he reached the landing, he turned so he could stay facing them and began backing down the stairs slowly. Wolfe turned his head away from the man to cough, then suddenly snapped his leg straight out, striking the man in the chest with tremendous force.

The snap of breaking fingers only fractionally preceded the whoosh of air as lungs which were used to having at least some air in them, now had none. The man fell backwards down the stairs gasping for air, his now useless right hand pulling free of the jacket. A silenced gun clattered down the steps below him.

Wolfe leaped onto the man, grabbing him by the front of his jacket, but the man grabbed him by the throat with his left hand and began squeezing, nearly crushing his windpipe. Wolfe finally wrenched free. Gasping for air, he looked for the loose gun.

As the man got up, they both spotted it near the front door. The man was closer and knew it, smiling as he bent over to pick it up. The smile faded as Wolfe snapped his leg out again, catching the man full face with his hard-soled right shoe. Blood and teeth found the floor, but the man did not go down. The remainder of his teeth clenched, he let loose a blood-curdling growl and lunged at Wolfe.

The man grabbed Wolfe around the neck and shoulders with

his good arm and began smashing his head into the wall. Wolfe thrashed and twisted, trying to break his grip, but he was beginning to lose consciousness.

With his last effort, Wolfe reached between the man's legs, and squeezed his testicles as hard as he could. The man bellowed in pain and released him at the same instant. Then, with unbelievable blind fury, he charged at Wolfe again. With his back to the sidelight, Wolfe waited until the last second before contact, then threw himself at the man's feet, tackling him like a pro football linebacker.

Unable to stop his momentum, the man crashed headfirst through the glass sidelight, his neck impaling itself on the remaining jagged spears.

Wolfe heard sirens wailing as if inside his head, and was vaguely aware of men in blue uniforms trying to pry his arms from around the dead man's legs. Then everything faded as the image of Terri, her tears falling on his bloody face, blurred into darkness.

Wolfe sensed more than felt the presence of someone nearby. He began to notice something squeezing his head, accompanied by a throbbing pain. Slowly he opened his eyes, and beheld a fuzzy apparition. It seemed to be hovering above his face only inches away. He tried to focus, then he yelled. "Aaaaaaaaaa!"

The apparition jumped back. "Shit, Wolfe," Eino exclaimed. "What'd you do that for?"

Wolfe's speech was slurred, but he managed to say, "How would you feel if you woke up from what you thought was your last roundup to stare the coroner in the face?"

"Glad you're back amongst the living," Eino said, regaining his composure. "Though I must admit it was peaceful here for a few hours."

"Where's Terri?" Wolfe asked, suddenly concerned. "She's OK, isn't she?"

"She's fine, Wolfe. Just stepped out for a cup of coffee. Should be back any time. I must say, though. You sure did a number on the John Doe. But I really don't need you to go around drumming up business for me, you know."

"Yea," Wolfe began, wincing in pain. "Well, it was almost me in your freezer, not him."

"Any idea who he was?" Eino asked.

"I was hoping you could tell me," Wolfe said, "but I guess your calling him John Doe says it all."

"Not a speck of ID on him, Wolfe. We sent the prints in. But so far, nothing back from the FBI or state crime lab."

"Anything on the gun?"

"Absolutely zilch. Standard .22 caliber long, hollow point with silencer. Off the rack with serial filed off. We're trying to raise the numbers, but it's not promising."

"Great," said Wolfe. "So where are we?"

"We're in Saint Francis Hospital."

"And that's where you're going to stay," Terri added as she came through the door. "At least for a while. The doctor told me you were coming around. He sent me down here to make sure you stay."

Wolfe reached up with his swollen fingers and gingerly touched his bandaged head. "Seems like I've been pretty well taken care of. How's my nose?" he said, moving down his face.

"It's not broken," said Terri. "Though why not is beyond me. The way he hit you."

"Thank you," Wolfe interrupted, raising his hand. "That'll do. My recollection of the event is still painfully vivid. My nose isn't broken. That's enough for me."

chapter 10

Terri changed the subject. "I've filled Eino in on our hypothesis while you were out. I hope you don't mind. You said he was your friend, and I felt we could trust him," she said, smiling at Eino.

"And what if we couldn't trust him?" Wolfe challenged. "What if he was a crusty old bastard who would stab me in the back any chance he could get? Would it make any difference?"

"Not in the least," Eino said. "Besides. Seems to me you could use all the help you can get."

"You're right, there," Terri interjected. "Things have really gotten out of hand. It's time we turned this whole thing over to the authorities and let them do their job," she said with determination.

"And what have the authorities to say about all this, Eino?" Wolfe asked, anticipating the answer.

"They, ah, they don't have any leads at this time, Wolfe," he said. "Nothing on Kevin's death, nothing on the John Doe. And they think you're nuts about the environmental hazard mumbo-jumbo. They say these kinds of accidents happen all the time."

"And their future plans?" Wolfe asked.

"Oh, the cases are still open. The deaths, I mean," he said.

"They'll continue to investigate if they get any new leads. But for the time being, they're just tying up loose ends. As to the two accidents, they're closed unless you can come up with some concrete proof something caused them. Sorry," Eino finished.

"And you want to leave it up to the authorities?" Wolfe asked Terri.

"It's too dangerous," she exclaimed. "I've already lost my brother and now you almost got killed," she said with emotion. "I know something's going on, but I don't know what—and I don't want anyone else dying on me." Terri fought back tears as she turned away from Wolfe.

Wolfe propped himself up a little with an extra pillow. "Let's take a look at what we have for a minute," Wolfe said, trying to draw her back. "One, we don't have any proof someone intentionally killed Kevin, even though it looks like someone cleaned his clothes and moved him to another location after he died.

"Two, the man in Kevin's apartment didn't appear to want to kill us. He was moving away when I hit him. If he was going to kill us, he could have easily done it from the top of the stairs without risking going by us, although I don't think he would have hesitated had there been the need."

"But what was he doing there, Clay?" she said.

"He may have been a thief ransacking the place. Kevin's address was mentioned in the article about his death. Some burglars watch the papers for death notices, then hit their place while family and friends are at the funeral. It's not uncommon."

"Sensitive people," she said, shaking her head. "But the John Doe wasn't taking anything from the apartment when we surprised him. He tore the hell out of it, but he was leaving empty-handed."

"You went in?" Wolfe asked.

"The police wanted me to check the apartment to see if anything was missing," she said. "It was hard to tell since I'd only been there once before. Everything was in a terrible mess."

"Like the motel?" Wolfe asked.

"Exactly. The drawers were out and overturned, the clothes strewn around, and the pillow . . . ."

"Was the pillow cut?" he asked her pointedly.

"No," she said slowly, "but it was in the middle of the floor, and the mattress was flipped up, just like in the motel." Terri paused, looking at Wolfe intently. "You think it was the same person?"

"That's a pretty standard method of searching for valuables," Eino cut in. "People often hide things in pillows and mattresses, although I'll never know why. Still, it's a lot of work for a quick rip-off artist."

"Do you think it had anything to do with the secret EPA investigation or my brother's work?" Terri asked, her reporter's blood beginning to flow again.

"The EPA doesn't make a practice of breaking into people's homes, and they certainly don't issue their agents .22 caliber pistols with silencers. At least the EPA I know doesn't," Wolfe finished, his attempt at humor lost on Terri.

"But it is odd, isn't it?" she said with deliberation. "The accidents, the burglary, Kevin's death, the mysterious EPA guys. I feel they're tied together somehow." Suddenly, a look of cold determination came over her. She turned to Wolfe and looked him dead in the eye. "Kevin *was* murdered, wasn't he?"

Wolfe held her gaze for several seconds. "It looks that way," he answered softly.

"Then we're going to find out who did it, and why, and how," she said, her jaw set, "no matter what it takes."

"How are you feeling?" Terri asked Wolfe as he sat on his couch in front of the fireplace for the first time in three days.

"Just wonderful," Wolfe said, grateful the bandages were finally off his head. Now if only the headache would go away.

"You look like a raccoon with those two black eyes and that bandage across your nose," she said, laughing.

Wolfe threw her a look, but said nothing. The pain was pretty much just a dull ache, but it was a dull ache that covered most of his body.

"I called Senator Phillips' office while you were in the hospital," Terri said casually as she finished preparing split-pea soup and ham sandwiches. She was wearing tan Chinos, a white blouse, and navy v-neck sweater. Even through the pain Wolfe could see that she filled them out in all the right places. She had her hair pulled back in a ponytail, and her hazel eyes sparkled. Suddenly his face wasn't the only thing that was throbbing.

Wolfe said nothing, contemplating what damage she could have done, not knowing his relationship with the Senator.

She decided not to push it, and waited for Wolfe to respond. She looked around his cabin, really for the first time, and took it all in. Maybe she could learn something more about this enigmatic man, thought Terri.

The rug in front of the fireplace looked authentic Persian with deep rich colors of red and orange. The beamed ceiling in the roof was visible from the great room in which they sat, and the open stairs led to a balcony that overlooked the entire living room and kitchen.

The kitchen had all stainless steel appliances of high quality, two sub-z freezers and all marble countertops. There was also a large island in the center of the kitchen with additional cook tops, electrical outlets, and a hanging rack for pots and pans and other utensils.

A large rustic table and chairs completed the area with plenty of space for entertaining, although Wolfe didn't seem the type to be entertaining large groups—or even small ones. Overall, the whole thing looked professional enough for a French restaurant, thought Terri.

At the back of the great room were two sets of sliding glass doors that led to a large wooden deck that looked out over the lake. Chaise lounges faced the water, and there was a round glass table with four outdoor chairs that stood next to a stainless steel outdoor gas grill.

A few steps down from the deck lay a path of sand, leaves and pine needles that wound down to small sand dunes and sea grasses, and finally to the beautiful clear blue waters of Lake Superior.

Terri was impressed with the way everything came together, and with the quality and beauty of it all. But rather than provide clues about Wolfe, it only raised more questions. Who was the woman in his life who was responsible for these female touches? Was she still around? Do they still have a connection? All questions Terri feared might never be answered. Or worse, they would.

chapter 11

Wolfe had still not responded and seemed to be in a sullen mood, so Terri decided to walk out on the deck. The air was warm and the wind was calm. Surprising, after yesterday's cold storm, she thought. The sun shown strong on the pine trees surrounding the cabin, eliciting a pleasant scent of fall trees, fresh lake air, and sweet pine. What a wonderful place, she mused.

Finally a voice croaked from inside—a voice that didn't sound quite human, but that was decidedly Wolfe's.

"So what'd they say?" he finally asked with discernible impatience.

Ha, she thought. Finally out-waited him.

"*They* said he was in meetings," she continued, "but that the Senator would call as soon as he could. I left my name and this number. I hope you don't mind," she said as she carried the tray of food to the coffee table by the fire. "I couldn't stand waiting, doing nothing." Terri sat beside him.

"I'm sure you've done no permanent damage," he said, grunting. He sampled the soup. "Mmmm. Tastes pretty good," he said. "Beats the heck out of hospital food."

The phone rang, and Terri went over and picked it up. "Hello?" she said. "Yes he is. Just a moment, please." She brought the phone to Wolfe. "It's Senator Phillips," she whispered.

Wolfe took the phone. "Senator, how are you?" he asked.

"What's with the formality, Wolfe?" Tom Phillips said. "Oh, I get it. Your lady friend, right?"

"Yes, Senator, that's correct," Wolfe continued, "we're very interested in what you found out."

"All right," Phillips said. "I get the picture. I'll keep it short. I checked with the EPA through informal channels, and found that they are not conducting any secret study, let alone one in your area."

"Are you sure about that?" Wolfe asked. "You're sure of the source—that it's accurate?"

"Hell, yes I'm sure," Phillips responded. "If the damn director of the EPA doesn't know what the hell's going on, then who does?"

"You talked to him directly?"

"What is this—a damned inquisition?" the Senator shot back. "What do you think took me so long? I asked the director if he knew of any such operation, and he said he didn't. I asked him if he would do some quiet checking to make sure some maverick department head wasn't off on his own hunt for glory. He said he would. It took him a while, but he came up negative. No one in the EPA is doing a secret study of environmental hazards in Marquette County, or anywhere else."

"Thanks, Senator. You've been a big help," Wolfe said.

"You wouldn't, by chance, want to tell me what you've got going up there, would you Wolfe?" Phillips asked.

"Not at the present time, Senator. Thank you very much for your help,"

Wolfe said.

"I thought not," Phillips said. "Be careful."

"I will. Goodbye," Wolfe said, hanging up the phone.

"What'd he say?" Terri asked anxiously.

"He said there is no secret study being conducted by the EPA."

"Was he sure?" she asked.

"He's sure," Wolfe said seriously. "Whoever those men were who contacted the accident victims, they weren't from the EPA."

"Then who were they?" Terri said nervously. "According to the people we interviewed, the "EPA" investigators had very official looking credentials. How would they get those?"

"That's what we have to find out—now," said Wolfe.

"We'd better get back to those accident victims," said Terri.

"My thoughts exactly," Wolfe said, getting up slowly from the couch. "If we can convince them to help us, we might be able to identify those men, and be on the way toward solving this."

"I've got the keys," said Terri. "Let's go. Dennis Holben?" she asked.

"Looks that way," Wolfe remarked. "John Erickson and family are vacationing in the sunny south somewhere for another few weeks. We'll just have to wait until they get back."

As they neared Holben's house on a dirt road outside of town, they saw a plume of black smoke off in the distance. "Looks like something pretty big," Terri said, "judging from the distance and the size of that column of smoke."

"Reporter experience?" Wolfe said, smiling.

Terri ignored him, the wail of several sirens commanding her attention. "I wonder what it is," she said, watching them head toward the fire.

"Whatever it is," he said, "I'm sure they'll handle it. We're almost there." As she pulled up to Holben's house, a police cruiser pulled up behind them. Terri got out and walked back toward the officer.

"Is there a problem, officer?" she said, reaching for her driver's license. "Not with you," the officer said. "But I'm afraid there is for him," the officer nodded his head towards Holben's house.

"Ah, we were just going to talk to Mr. Holben, officer," Terri said.

"That's going to be a little hard to do," the officer responded less than tactfully.

"And why is that?" she said.

"You see that big cloud of smoke over there, Miss?" he continued. She nodded. "*That's* Mr. Holben. His plane crashed fifteen minutes ago and there's nothing left but a charred mess. I'm here to see if there's a Mrs. Holben. Want to join me?" he said sarcastically.

Terri spun around and walked back to the car.

"He's dead," she said tersely, getting in the car.

"I heard," Wolfe responded.

"This looks bad, doesn't it?"

"Let me put it this way," he said. "I don't think I'd want to be vacationing with the Ericksons just now."

"You don't think this was . . ." She stopped, looked at Wolfe, the question in her eyes. He nodded. "And you think they might . . ." She stopped again. He nodded again. "The whole family?" she said incredulously.

"Wouldn't surprise me," he said.

"How can you take this so calmly?" Terri turned to face him. "Another man was murdered, and now a whole family is likely to get wiped out by some mysterious people? We have absolutely no idea who they are, and you just *sit* there?" she said, fuming.

"I'm trying to figure out how they plan to kill their next victim," he said quietly.

"Their next victim?" she said. "And suppose you tell me who that's going to be?"

"You," he said, staring straight ahead out the window.

Terri's key stopped halfway in the ignition. "What? Me?"

"Think about it," he said. "Let's suppose there is some

mysterious hazard these faceless men want to cover up. Who do they have to eliminate?"

"Obviously, people who know about it," she said.

"Like your brother," he began. "Who else?"

"I know what you're getting at," she replied slowly. "People who were affected by it."

"People who could answer questions that might lead investigators to the cause," he finished.

"Right. Holben and Erickson."

"Right," he said. "And finally?"

"The investigators," she said as she began to feel the impact of what he was saying. "Particularly the person quoted in the paper as saying she had evidence regarding her brother's death, and was not going to rest until the killer was found."

"You got it," he said.

"The motel room?"

"Yup."

"Well then, you're marked too," she said.

"The thought had crossed my mind," he said, dryly.

"What are we going to do?" she said, feeling like a trapped animal.

"First let's see if we can find out why that plane crashed. Maybe there's a natural explanation. Second, let's see if we can find out where the Ericksons are vacationing. Maybe we can get to them before it's too late. Or maybe we're all wrong, and they'll come back with nothing worse than a sunburn."

"Let's hope," said Terri.

chapter 12

They tried neighbors, relatives, anybody who might know where the Ericksons went. But the Ericksons earned their money. They told no one.

Back at Wolfe's cabin Terri helped make another fire. "I guess we'll just have to wait until they get back," she said, "and hope for the best."

"Let's forget about them for now," Wolfe said, "and concentrate on staying alive. Even if they find my house—and I have every reason to believe they eventually will—it has a pretty good security system. There are sensors built into the landscape down to the lake and out to the road. If someone tries to get to us, I'll know it well beforehand.

"Besides. So far they've been taking great pains to make things look like an accident—or a random crime. That makes it tougher on them and easier on us. Remember, they don't want to be discovered."

"That's comforting," she said nervously. "So far they're doing a great job."

The phone rang and Wolfe answered it. "Wolfe," he said curtly.

"What the hell you doing up there?" Senator Phillips shouted into the phone.

"Tom? What's the matter?" Wolfe said, surprised at his tone.

"You tell me," he said angrily. "Ever since our phone call, all hell's been breaking loose around here."

"What do you mean?" Wolfe said.

"I mean I've got auditors going through my campaign funds with a fine-tooth comb. I've got the IRS auditing my taxes for the last seven years. I've got the ethics commission looking into my travel practices. Hell—I even have the Selective Service looking into my draft status, and I'm forty-seven years old! Now you tell me—what the hell's going on?"

"Tom, I swear I don't know what you're talking about," Wolfe said, astonished at the implication. "What I'm doing up here should have no connection to you other than your check on the EPA for me."

"Well something sure as hell happened to open this Pandora's Box. What're you into up there, anyway?" he said, calming down only slightly.

"I can't really talk about it on the phone, Tom," Wolfe said. "Maybe I'd better fly down and talk to you in person."

"No!" Phillips said sharply. "I don't want you anywhere near this place. I still think you're responsible for this mess, somehow. Stay the hell away from me until I can get this thing figured out. And so help me, if you're holding out on me . . ."

"I swear, Tom," Wolfe said apologetically. "There's no connection I'm aware of. If I find out there is, I'll let you know right away."

"Sure you will," Phillips said, and slammed the receiver down.

"Damn!" Wolfe said. He related the half of the conversation Terri hadn't heard.

"Do you think there's a connection?" Terri said when he had finished.

"I don't know, but I'd be willing to believe just about anything about now. What have we gotten into?"

"I don't know, Clay, but it's beginning to scare the hell out of me. What could be that big to stir up Washington like that? And why?"

"One thing's for sure," Wolfe said. "Your brother had the key. I'm convinced of it. If 'they' have all his papers, we're in deep trouble. But I don't think they do. If they did, they wouldn't have torn apart your motel room and Kevin's apartment."

"You think they're all related, then?" Terri asked.

"It's beginning to look like it. At least let's assume they are until we get evidence to the contrary," Wolfe said, looking out the window at the restless waves.

"Worst case scenario?" she asked.

"They're after us this very moment."

The next morning after a fitful sleep for both of them, Wolfe said to Terri, "I'm going to Washington." They were having breakfast with scrambled eggs, orange juice, toast and coffee. Terri was wearing blue jeans and an oversized Michigan State sweatshirt. Wolfe was in gray sweats and Pumas after his workout.

"Washington?" Terri exclaimed. "I thought Senator Phillips told you he didn't want you to go there?"

"He did," Wolfe said calmly.

"Do you really think that's such a good idea?" she said. "I mean, with all that turmoil going on—aren't you going into the thick of it?"

"Precisely," he said, sipping his coffee. "Sitting here waiting to be picked off is probably not the most productive thing we can do. Besides. I think we can do a little manipulating ourselves, and see what floats to the top. I've got to find out how bad this thing really is, and the best way for me to do it is to go to Washington."

"What about me? What should I do?" she asked.

"Stay here by the phone and wait for information on the plane crash and the Ericksons. Eino is checking on the cause of the crash, although the FAA is handling it. He's going to call here when he finds anything out. You'll only need to leave once, and only for an hour or so. I'll show you how the alarm system works and who to call for help if you need it. The main thing is to follow my instructions to the letter."

"Won't we be more vulnerable split up like this?" she said with obvious concern.

"I don't think so," he said. "Frankly, I think the only reason we're still alive is because 'they' believe you can lead them to the information they're searching for. That, plus the fact that you're a reporter, and dead reporters, especially from a national wire service, tend to raise a lot of questions. Better they just keep an eye on you until you find Kevin's papers or whatever it is they're looking for."

"And then?" she said, waiting for the obvious answer.

"Then," he said with emphasis, "we become very loose ends."

chapter 13

The flight to Washington was uneventful, though Wolfe took a number of precautionary measures to make sure he wasn't being followed. He went to the Capitol building and found Senator Phillips' office. As chairman of the Senate Armed Services Committee, he was a powerful figure in Washington, a fact borne out by his opulent office and multitude of staff.

"May I help you?" an extremely attractive brunette said to Wolfe as he entered the office. She was tall, slender, and well-dressed with that artificial smile that always accompanies receptionists for the rich and powerful. He wondered what she was doing for dinner.

"Yes. I'm here to see Senator Phillips," he said. "Name's Wolfe."

"Is he expecting you?" she asked, performing her screening function well.

"No," Wolfe said, taking in the solid wood paneled walls and plush carpeting. "Just tell him "the wolf" is here. He'll find a way to see me."

"I, ah, I'm sorry, sir," the brunette said, looking at her schedule for the Senator, "but he's tied up all day in meetings. Perhaps if you called back later I could set up an appointment for you—let's see—how about next . . ."

"Just tell him I can be reached at this number." Wolfe handed her a card. "See that he gets it. *Today*. I'll be waiting for his call."

"He might be back late," she began, properly laying the groundwork for future excuses should the Senator not wish to see this man. But after seeing the look on Wolfe's face, she continued, "but I'll make sure he gets it before he leaves for home."

"You do that," said Wolfe. "I knew I could count on you."

Wolfe stood in the doorway and surveyed the smoky bar in Georgetown that was popular with politicians and people of influence. He eyed each of the patrons carefully, to see if any of them looked or acted suspiciously. He was in his wartime mode, where everyone was a potential enemy.

As he slowly worked his way through the room, he checked out the people at the bar, sitting on leather covered swivel seats so they could see everyone who might be anyone they should make contact with—who might be able to advance their careers.

He checked out the tables, mostly at the back of the long, narrow bar. Conspiracies were formed in these places—dark booths where lights were low and voices even lower. Eyes would dart around to make sure they weren't being watched, as if every word they uttered was a national secret. Wolfe knew most of them were not.

He checked out the waitresses and servers, who were always in a position to overhear golden nuggets of information that could advance their futures—or destroy others.'

He checked out the bartenders for the same reason, and then finally people who were just standing around, particularly fit men who were eyeing the crowd, just as he was. No alarm bells went off, though there were some people he would keep an eye on as he met the Senator.

It wasn't until almost ten o'clock that evening that Senator Tom Phillips made his way into the bar. His thin, five-foot ten-inch frame was topped by jet black hair combed straight back. He was dressed impeccably, as always. Spotting Wolfe in a booth at the back of the room, he made his way over to him.

"Good to see you again, Tom," Wolfe said, as the Senator sat opposite him in the low-lit booth.

"Watching people in mirrors again, Wolfe?" Phillips said dryly.

Wolfe smiled, his eyes still on the move. He was dressed appropriately for the environment, as he always did for these occasions—expensive suit, tie, shoes, watch, jewelry. Just another guy on his way up.

"Now what the hell are you doing here?" Phillips opened angrily. He was leaning over to get as close to Wolfe's face as he could, making a futile effort to keep his voice down. "I thought I told you to stay the hell away from here!"

"When people start dying around me," Wolfe said, leaning in like-fashion toward Phillips, "I kinda get curious as to why."

"What?" Phillips said, showing surprise.

"Let me explain," Wolfe said. For the next half-hour, Wolfe covered the events from the beginning, with no interruptions from Phillips. "So that's why I'm here, Tom," Wolfe said, after he had finished. "I've got to find out what's going on, and I can't afford to wait until you can unscramble your own troubles."

Phillips just sat there when Wolfe finished, his gaze fixed on the wall behind him. Finally, he leaned forward and said softly and with great deliberation, "Wolfe, I want you to listen very carefully to what I have to say. You're not going to like it, but you must listen. What you do when I'm done will have everything to do with whether or not you and the girl survive this crisis."

"I'm listening," Wolfe said, leaning back just a little.

"Wolfe," he began at barely a whisper, "we're involved in something very big right now."

"We?" Wolfe cut in.

"As a member of the Senate Armed Services Committee, I am privy to information regarding the defense of this country which very few other men have." He paused, looked around nervously, cleared his throat and continued even more softly. "I've been told by powerful sources that we've developed a defense system that could bring an end to the threat of thermonuclear war forever," he said, his eyes darting nervously around.

"You mean the strategic defense initiative?" Wolfe said. "That's no big secret. Star Wars has been talked about in public and the scientific community for years."

"I can't say any more," the Senator said, the sweat on his upper lip glistening in the dim light. "Just take it from me—this is big. Bigger than you, bigger than your reporter friend," he paused, nervously looking around again. "Bigger than me," he finished below a whisper. "Hell. I suppose I could be arrested for telling you even this much."

"You haven't told me *anything*, Tom," Wolfe challenged.

"I've told you plenty," he whisper-yelled at Wolfe. "This is national security of the highest order," he said, clenching his teeth. "You and your girl just butt out of it and you might—I stress, might—come out of this with your skin intact."

"And if we don't?" Wolfe said defiantly, his eyes boring into the Senator's.

"Wolfe," Phillips said, breathing more quickly now, "you're the reason I'm in this mess with the auditors."

"Me?"

"Your conversation with me, asking me to check into the EPA was monitored. Don't ask me why, but it was. I didn't make the connection before, but *they* did."

"What connection?" Wolfe interjected. "*Who* did?"

Ignoring him, Phillips went on. "This is pressure, Wolfe. Pure and simple. Someone wants me to know I screwed up by checking on this for you, and that it could cost me my job, or even . . ." he hesitated. "You've got to get out of this now—tonight. Take the next plane out of here, go back to Marquette. Fish. Enjoy the wilderness. Do whatever the hell you want. But drop this whole thing. *Now.*"

"Or it'll drop me," added Wolfe.

Phillips sat up straight and pushed back from the table, deep into the soft cushions of the booth. "A lot's done in the name of national security, Wolfe. You know that. Just take my advice and get out of here," Phillips said as he rose to leave, "and stay the hell away from me. I can't afford the luxury of being associated with you anymore." Senator Phillips rose and threw a twenty on the table, then stomped out.

Wolfe sat there in the smoke and the heat, watching all the beautiful, powerful people mingle—impressing each other with their importance, enjoying their status while it lasted. These are our leaders, thought Wolfe contemptuously, looking around the crowded room. The decision-makers. The people who by day, put on the facade of dignity and self-righteousness, making laws, speeches, policy—while by night they made time—squeezing in as much living and intensity as they could. They all know it won't last, he thought, but they all try just the same. To become bigger than life. To become immortal—for a time.

An attractive brunette caught his eye, wondering no doubt, if he was someone important—worth spending some time with. Wolfe solved her problem as he got up and left the bar.

chapter 14

Wolfe stepped out of the bar just in time to see the Senator enter a taxi that quickly drove off. No more cabs were waiting, so Wolfe looked both ways down the Georgetown street, and headed towards the Senator's townhouse, which is where Wolfe was pretty sure the Senator was going. He knew the dangers of walking alone in this area late at night, but he needed to get his thoughts straight. And he *was* armed, though it was illegal in D.C. unless you were a police officer. Which Wolfe was not—he was much, much more.

As he walked, he thought of the events that had transpired. Despite Tom's admonition, Wolfe kept going. There's one more thing I've got to say to Tom before I go, he thought.

He looked for signs he was on the right trail. He had been at the Senator's quaint townhouse only twice before, and then it was years ago. But the streets looked familiar, so he kept walking.

This would be a great time to bump me off, he thought as he carefully scrutinized the couples still out on the town. It could be anyone, male or female; the more innocuous looking the better. Even taxis were not safe; the perfect set-up to lure an unsuspecting victim off the streets and to a remote place for execution, he mused morbidly.

Wolfe thought back as he walked—of the times past when he had come to know Tom Phillips. They had met at Oberlin College in Ohio, when they were both undergraduate students—idealistic, full of enthusiasm, optimistic. Phillips had wanted to go into business, Wolfe into theatre. Neither made it, but then, things change. Idealism becomes pragmatism, optimism is tamed by reality. Still, they had gone through some tough times together, and regardless of what had just happened in that bar, they remained friends. That's why he had to see Phillips before he left. He had to make sure they still were.

Finally, he came to the street where Phillips lived. Rows of immaculate brick townhomes surrounded the tree-lined street, old-style street lamps emitting a soft, inviting glow. Four down from the corner he found it. A walk up the steps and a quick look on the mailbox confirmed it. T. Phillips. The lights were still on, so he rang the bell. Must still be up going over his books, Wolfe thought. He pressed the bell again. No answer.

The upstairs light was on, so Wolfe tried the door. Maybe he's taking a shower and can't hear me, he thought. The door was locked, so he went around to the back. He'd always warned Tom not to hide a key outside the door, but this time he was glad his advice was ignored. Under a clay pot he found the back door key. The lock worked easily, and Wolfe stepped inside the immaculate kitchen.

"Tom?" he said loudly as he closed the door behind him. "It's Wolfe. You here?" There was no answer, so he moved from the kitchen to the living room. "Tom?" he called again. "It's Wolfe. I had to see you one more time before I left. Got a minute?" Again, no answer.

Wolfe began getting a sick feeling in the pit of his stomach. He stood still, listening for any response. Nothing. No shower running, no radio, nothing. A strong feeling of foreboding overcame Wolfe, and his senses became acutely sharp. He slowly crept through the house, careful not to touch anything—afraid of what he might find, sure he would find it. Stealthily he climbed the stairs to the first bedroom.

The light was on, and the door was open. He looked through the crack between the door and the door jamb. He saw that no one was behind it. He walked in. Nothing seemed out of place. The double bed was made. There was an ashtray on the nightstand with an unlit pipe in it, and a book laying face down on the bed.

Next he went to the bathroom. The light was on, and he could see at a glance, no one was in it. The tub was at the end of the room, and the curtain was pulled back. Nothing appeared out of the ordinary.

He made his way to the second bedroom at the end of the hall. The door was closed, and no light shown under the door. This was the room Phillips used as his guest room, Wolfe knew. He had stayed in it twice before. Phillips lived alone, and kept it closed when no one was visiting. Saved on heating and cooling bills, he had said.

Wolfe approached the door slowly, listening for any indication of movement from within. Hearing none, he put his handkerchief on the doorknob and turned it slowly, crouching as he did. With sudden force he threw the door open and hit the light switch at the same instant. No one was there. He checked the closet, under the bed, the dresser. No sign of a disturbance.

Something was very wrong, he thought. There was one room Wolfe had not checked and it was downstairs—the study. He drew his semiautomatic, a .45 caliber Smith & Wesson M&P from under his jacket, and made his way carefully down the stairs. At the bottom of the stairs, he stopped and listened again, his senses fully engaged.

Finally he turned right, and deftly moved down the hall to the door of the study. This door too, was closed. Again he crouched outside the door, listening for any sign of movement within. Satisfied, he slowly turned the door handle and silently pushed the door open.

Immediately in front of him he saw why the Senator had not responded to his calls. Seated in his leather chair at his desk, in front of his computer as if he were studiously at work, sat Senator Tom Phillips, with a bullet hole through his right temple. Blood and brains were spattered on the carpet to his left. His head was tilted back against his leather chair, his eyes stared at a place that was not on this earth.

Wolfe took in the scene without moving. His close friend had been brutally murdered. Of that he was certain. He felt sick the Senator had left the world in this manner. But he had no time to mourn. The person who did this might still be in the house. He had to be certain it was safe before he did anything else. First he checked behind the door he had just swung open. No one there. Next he went to the far wall on the right where the bathroom was located. While keeping watch behind him, he pushed the partially open door open further until it hit the bath tub. No one. The curtain was open, but he checked behind it anyway.

The bathroom was clear, so he carefully walked behind the Senator's chair between the chair and the curtained windows. The curtains were closed, so Wolfe carefully checked behind them, and checked the window to see that it was locked. It was.

Wolfe then proceeded to the remaining side of the room where there was a louvered closet and bookshelves filled with books. He checked the closet first. Keeping his back flat against the wall, he reached for the knob on the door with his right hand, grasped it firmly, and yanked it open quickly.

Simultaneously he crouched down, whipped around in front of the open door, and with the gun in his left hand, pointed directly into the closet. It was clear.

Seeing nothing there but clothes, he popped the other closet door open and pointed his gun at the other side. After moving the clothes inside the closet to make sure no one was hiding there, he moved through the rest of the townhouse, room by room, until he was sure the killer was not hiding somewhere, to take him out when his guard was down.

Satisfied it was all clear, he holstered his weapon and began sanitizing the crime scene. First, he put on latex gloves that he always carried with him, and went through the townhouse again, wiping away his fingerprints from everything he touched.

Next he went back to the Senator's office and began examining it more minutely. He didn't know when someone might show up—someone who might want to ask questions he didn't want to answer, or someone who might want to arrest him, or someone who might want to skip the questions and just kill him. None of these were good options, so he moved quickly.

Finally, he went to the Senator's body. Sadness enveloped him as he thought about the years they had been good friends. He was sorry their last words had been angry ones, but it was too late to do anything about that. His training kept him alert and aware, and he began to examine the crime scene.

A .38 caliber revolver was in his right hand, and a quick sniff told that it had been recently fired. Since it was a revolver, there were no shell casings lying around, and the one fired—if it was only one—would still be in the cylinder.

On top of his printer, behind Tom's chair was a suicide note. Wolfe read the note.

"I can no longer tolerate the mounting pressures of the audits and the slandering of my good name. The funds I embezzled went to pay Clayton Wolfe and Terri Sommers, who are blackmailing me. As far as I know, they presently are living in Marquette, Michigan. They have been extorting money from me for past indiscretions which they uncovered some time ago, and which I deeply regret.

"The file on my desk contains a list of payments I've made

to them over the years, with dates and amounts paid. You should check their bank accounts to see if they had any corresponding entries for those amounts. This has been a very painful experience for me, and I hope you can find them and put an end to their illegal activities."

"Although I have made a few mistakes over the years, I believe I have served my constituents well, and hope they do not think less of me for this. Sincerely, Senator Thomas Phillips." The signature was typed.

Wolfe looked at the letter in disbelief. They were being set up, and set up good. He had to get out of there fast. He picked up the bogus file, grabbed the suicide note, and jammed them both in his pocket. Making sure no one could see him, he went out the back door and slipped safely into the shadows just as police sirens began to wail.

chapter 15

At precisely two o'clock A.M., the phone rang. Wolfe stepped into the booth in downtown Washington D.C. and lifted the receiver.

"Clay? Is that you?" the voice at the other end of the line said. It was Terri.

"Yes," he said softly.

"Look," she said nervously, "I did like you asked. I'm calling from a phone booth and I presume you're in one, too."

"That's right," he said confidently. "They won't be able to tap our conversation this way. We can speak in confidence."

"Yes. Well, you're not going to like my news," she said ominously. "Word just came that the Ericksons had an unfortunate boating accident. It seems their charter boat just disappeared off the coast of Bimini. No wreckage, no visible survivors. They just never showed up on the island. Two days of searching by the Coast Guard produced nothing, and they have given up efforts to locate them. They are presumed drowned," she finished.

"So our theory seems to be holding up on your end," Wolfe said.

"It's doing more than that. Eino just informed me the FAA

found some kind of unusual device in Holben's plane wreckage. They're not sure what its purpose is, but they say it looks like it might be part of some sort of remote control system. He also says they're acting mighty funny about it. They started out being very cooperative, but now they won't talk to him. They won't even answer his phone calls. Fortunately, he found out that much before they put the clamps on. What's happening on your end?"

"Phillips is dead," he said quietly, "and we're being set up to take a rap for blackmailing him."

"What?" she exclaimed, disbelief in her voice. "Senator Phillips is dead?"

"That's right, Terri," he said. "I'll explain more later. I'm taking the redeye out of Washington National in about half an hour. It's Global Air, flight number 731. I won't be in Marquette until late, with all the connections and all, so you may as well get some sleep. At least try. We're going to need our wits about us."

"I don't believe this is happening, Clay," Terri said through tears. "I'm not sure I can . . ."

"Yes you can," he cut in. "Just do as I say, and I'll see you later this morning. Hang in there," he said kindly.

"I will," she said, more under control. "You be careful."

It happened on the leg from Iron Mountain to Escanaba, just north of the Potawatomi Indian Reservation. In level flight at about ten thousand feet the twin-engine turboprop caught fire. There was tremendous confusion, and a great deal of screaming in the roughly thirty-five seconds it took to crash. By the time rescuers got to the site, it had burned with a fire so hot, it incinerated everyone and everything.

Perhaps something being carried in the cargo bay ignited causing the intense fire, some later speculated. Regardless, it was impossible to identify the twenty-two passengers and crew listed on the flight manifest. All that could be said was that one name on that list was that of Clayton Wolfe.

The shadowy figure dressed in black from head to foot crept slowly through the underbrush surrounding Wolfe's home. Terri Sommers was in front of the fire, watching the eleven o'clock news, her eyes red and puffy from crying.

All afternoon she had watched news of the crash. Now, tonight they had pictures. She wasn't sure she could watch. There was no mention of Wolfe by name, but she was sure it was the flight he was on. That much she was able to check. Terri had stayed at his house throughout the day, watching, listening, not wanting to believe the news.

The shadowy figure moved silently closer to the house, a cloud-covered sky blocking any light which might have provided illumination. At each alarmed location the figure paused, deftly defeated each alarm activator, then proceeded to the next.

Terri got up from the couch and went into the kitchen to fix another drink. As she did, she thought she heard something. Standing perfectly still, she listened for a few seconds, then turned down the TV and listened again. Still, she heard nothing. Shrugging her shoulders she turned up the TV and sat down on the couch.

Suddenly something caught her eye. On the carpet toward the kitchen lay a leaf. She was sure it had not been there a minute ago when she went into the kitchen. Panic began to well up in her as she began to realize someone was in the house. Just as she decided to make a dash for the phone, a gloved hand reached over the back of the couch and clamped tightly over her mouth.

She tried to scream, but no sound could come out. Then a voice whispered, "Are you alone?" Terri, eyes wide in horror, nodded that she was. "Good," said Wolfe as he unclamped her mouth, stood up and faced her. "Welcome me back from the dead."

"Clay!" she cried out. "You're alive! How . . ."

He shushed her. "I booked my regular flight, and then I had second thoughts. At the last minute I decided to charter a private plane. I never imagined they would take out an entire planeload of people -- it was just an extra precaution."

She threw her arms around him and squeezed him tight. "Why did you do this to me? I could have had a heart attack!"

"I had to make sure you were alone," he said, returning her hug. "It wouldn't do for others to see that I'm still alive, now would it?"

Terri reached up cupped his face in her hands and looked at him through moist, searching eyes. Quickly their lips came together, full of relief and passion.

"I didn't realize how much I'd miss you," she whispered in his ear as they embraced.

"Me neither," he said.

"To hear the accounts of your death . . . all those people . . ." she began.

"After what I saw, I knew that we were in a great deal of danger. To kill a U.S. Senator, then try to set me up . . . trying to find out what killed your brother, and possibly all these other victims, is something that people very high up do not want us to accomplish."

Terri nodded her understanding.

"But I'm here now," he said, kissing each tear as it made tracks down her cheek, "and we're going to solve this together."

"What about the alarm," she said, regaining some composure. "How did you get in without setting it off?"

"I'm the one who designed and installed it. Remember?" he said matter-of-factly. "If I can't get by it, who can?"

Terri just looked at him as he smiled.

"Don't worry," he said, kissing her on the lips. "It's working just fine. Good as new." Then, releasing her, he said, "We'd better get some sleep. There's lots to do tomorrow, and not much time to do it in."

"Am I still up?" she said, looking at Wolfe through different eyes.

"Huh?" Wolfe looked at her standing at the bottom of the stairs. "Oh. Sure," he said, hesitantly. "If you want. Or you can sleep down. I don't mind switching."

Terri walked over to him, taking both his hands in hers and looked into his eyes.

"Or," she said softly, "I could sleep down, and you could sleep down. Less travel time that way."

Wolfe smiled. Terri's finger traced his lips. Suddenly he pulled her to him powerfully and they kissed again. More passionately. And then they walked eagerly to his bedroom. The fire in the fireplace remained untended for the rest of the evening.

chapter 16

"Fill me in on what happened in Washington," Terri said the next morning.

Wolfe looked up at her sudden appearance. She was wearing a long white tee-shirt that came to almost mid-thigh, and not much else. Her hair was a riot of tangles and she had a smile that beguiled him.

Wolfe took in her grand entrance as she slowly walked down the stairs. He tried to casually take a swallow of his coffee, and nearly drooled it all over himself before he realized that his mouth was hanging open.

"Damn," he said as he tried to wipe the hot coffee from his burned lips.

Terry laughed, obviously flattered.

Wolfe set his cup down, wiped his mouth, and tried to compose himself. He shook his head, took a deep breath, and began.

"It went about as badly as one could expect," he said. He started at the point when he went in the bar, and finished with his exit from the Senator's Townhouse.

"So we're being royally set up by these people, whoever they are," Terri said.

"Looks that way," he said. "I knew they weren't pulling any punches. Even with unlimited power and resources, it takes either guts or insanity to murder a prominent U.S. Senator in the heart of the nation's capitol, fake his suicide, and implicate us through complex bank account manipulation. Whoever they are," he finished, "they're used to getting their own way, and they have a lot of power."

"And now we know to what lengths they'll go to stop us," Terri said soberly.

"Not us. You. I'm dead. Remember? You're the one they're after now."

"Thanks for reminding me," she said. "You're all heart."

"It's something you should be constantly aware of from now on," he added. "And that's why you're going to hire a bodyguard."

"A bodyguard?" she exclaimed. "Where am I going to get a bodyguard? And how am I going to pay him?" she said.

"You're not," he said mischievously. "I'll pay for myself."

"You?" she said, half laughing. "You're going to be my bodyguard? You're dead. You told me so yourself. I can't have a dead man guarding me."

"You can if he's an alive dead man," he countered.

"What are you talking about? Are you a zombie, the undead?" she said, laughing.

"Meet your new bodyguard, Terri," Wolfe said, his back to her. "Say hello to Drake Winslow." He turned around, sporting a brown mustache and full, close-cropped beard. With a strong English accent, he said, "Drake Winslow at your service, Miss Sommers."

Terri stared at Wolfe. "That's the most ridiculous thing I've ever heard of," she said. "You're not serious."

"Most assuredly I am, Miss," he said with the accent. "I must acquire a new identity—one substantially different than my former one. I also must be able to be seen with you, and to stay here. A bodyguard accomplishes both very nicely. I'll be able to change my appearance even more by adding lifts to my shoes, and changing my hair color, style of clothing and mannerisms. Believe me," he finished, "no one will recognize me."

"Which brings up another point," she said. "How is it that I'm still living here after your death? With another man, no less?"

"Quite simple, actually," he said. "That nice chap, Mr. Wolfe, willed it to you. It seems he was quite taken with you and, having no other family, left his entire estate to you upon his demise. Jolly nice of him, wouldn't you say?"

"It would be if he left me the will," she said dryly.

"'Tis no concern of yours," he continued. "Mr. Wolfe is—was—a very resourceful fellow. In fact, I think you'll find this very day that such a document will be forthcoming."

"With the ink still wet, no doubt," she said.

"It wouldn't surprise me a bit, Miss," he said.

"I get the picture, Clay," she said, resigned to the facade. "You can drop the phony accent now. You're hired. Now what?"

"Now," he said, using his normal voice, "we have one hell of a lot of work to do. First, we need to check our bank accounts to see if the bogus payoff deposits have really been made."

"You think they would have put the money in anyway, even without the note?" she said, surprised.

"They may not know that I took the note," he said. "At least not yet. But if they do, then we've got to act fast to clear you."

"And how do you intend to do that?" she said.

"Quite simple, really," he said, unconsciously slipping into the English accent. Seeing the look on her face he realized what he was doing and reverted back. "Sorry," he said. "I tend to get into my parts. Frustrated actor, you know."

"I don't, but I'm beginning to," she said.

"Anyway," he continued, "to answer your question, as Wolfe,

I've mailed a confession to my attorney that is not to be opened or forwarded to the police until he hears from you. In it, I confess to the blackmail, but clear you of any knowledge of the affair. I've already stated in my confession that I made the deposits into your account as well as mine without your knowledge, and that I took care of all the funds and both accounts, personally."

"But we need to know whether or not those deposits were actually made," Terri added. "Because if they weren't, then we probably aren't going to be implicated in his death."

"Exactly," Wolfe said.

"What happens if the money in both accounts is seized as evidence?" she said. "What do I live on?"

"If they freeze the accounts, then there's a sizable sum of cash here in the house that will keep us comfortable for some time," he said. "But that's the least of our problems. The first thing we have to do is check out those accounts."

"Mine will take a little longer, being out of state," she said. "I'll drive into town and start now." She hesitated a moment, then said, "Clay, do you really think I'll be safe?"

He looked at her for a moment. "I don't think they'll touch you," he said finally. "They can't afford to until you find Kevin's papers. That's still the wild card. If they kill you," he continued, watching her reaction—there was none—"they take a chance that the papers will fall into someone else's hands if found. But with you hot on the trail, all they have to do is wait until you find them, then they tie up the last loose end."

"Maybe I ought not to look so hard," she said cynically.

Wolfe smiled.

"How did I meet you, by the way?" she asked.

"What?" Wolfe said.

"How did I come to have a bodyguard? Where did I meet you? Pick you up?"

"Oh," he said, finally understanding what she meant. "I was

recommended to you by your attorney. You're picking me up from the bus terminal in Marquette at three o'clock this afternoon. After you check out the accounts, you can drop me off near the Escanaba bus depot. You'll take me there in your car, where I'll be hidden from view on the floor of the back seat."

"And what if I get stopped by the police?" Terri asked playfully, putting her arms around Wolfe's neck.

"Don't," he said seriously. Then he kissed her warmly on the mouth.

chapter 17

Terri arrived at the bus depot in Marquette five minutes before the bus from Escanaba was scheduled to arrive. The top on her Mustang was down, and the sun shone brightly on her red hair. She sat in the car, letting the breeze from Lake Superior cleanse her with its fresh, pure air. She took a deep breath, and wondered how anything could be bad on a day like this.

Just then, the bus pulled up. Terri got out of the car, deliberately scrutinizing all the passengers as they left the bus. Finally, towards the end, Wolfe got off, suitcase in hand, and stood by the bus. A remarkable transformation, thought Terri. His glance briefly touched hers, then looked away again, searching the crowd.

He looked much larger than she thought he would. His dark hair and beard combined with his black turtleneck sweater and black pants to give him a powerful and somewhat ominous look. As the crowd thinned, she approached him hesitantly. "Excuse me, but you wouldn't happen to be Mr. Winslow, would you?"

"Miss Sommers, I presume?" he said, suddenly smiling.

"Yes," she said offering her hand. "I'm Terri Sommers."

"Pleased to meet you, Miss Sommers" he said, taking her hand

and bowing slightly. "Drake Winslow at your service." His accent was thick, and the exchange was loud enough to be heard by a number of people around them.

"Let me grab my other bag and I'll be right with you," he said. Drake picked up a huge trunk with his free hand, and brought it over to her car. There he effortlessly lifted it and put it in the back seat of her convertible.

"Hope you don't mind if I put them here, Miss," he said as some passengers watched the way he threw the big trunk into the car. "I don't think it'll fit in the boot."

Terri smiled as she watched his amazing performance. "That's fine, Mr. Winslow. I'll have some errands for you to run a little later, but first let's get you settled."

Wolfe opened the door for her, and made a point of taking her arm as she got in the car. He then got in the driver's side, looking mildly perplexed. "What's the matter?" she said, looking over at him.

"Nothing really, Miss," he said as he touched the controls and looked down at the foot pedals as if he'd never seen them before. "It's just a little different where I come from, you know," he said, gesturing with his head toward her side of the car. "Right hand drive, and all that."

"Of course," she said, laughing. "You'll get used to it quickly enough. Pull out in that direction, Mr. Winslow," she said. "I'll direct you to your new quarters."

Wolfe threw her a look for the quarters remark, then started the car and pulled out onto the street.

"Watch it!" Terri yelled, as they narrowly missed an oncoming car. "You're in the wrong lane! Drive to the *right*!"

"Right, Miss," he said apologetically. "Terribly sorry, Miss." Wolfe steered the car into the proper lane and headed towards the house. When they were out of earshot, Terri turned to him.

"That was a nice maneuver back there," she said. "You might have gotten us killed. Did you do that on purpose?"

"Just playing the role of an English bodyguard," he said, dropping the accent. "By the way—just when did my role slip to that of an indentured servant?" he said testily.

"I thought that was a nice touch," she said, pleased with herself. "It just seemed more natural for me to take the commanding role for a change. After all—you *are* working for me."

"Let's not forget whose money you're paying me with," he said caustically.

"A minor point," she said, smiling just slightly.

Wolfe looked at her. She had suddenly seemed to take on the air of an English aristocrat. He even thought he heard traces of an English accent in her voice. "Don't get too taken with the part, *Princess*," he said, all traces of his accent gone. "It's only temporary."

Terri only smiled as she looked straight ahead down the road, her head tilted up ever so slightly.

Instead of going to the cabin as she had stated publicly, Wolfe headed in that direction until they were out of sight of the bus station, and then turned the Mustang down a side road. After making a few more turns, he headed back into town towards the bank.

Pulling up across the street from the bank, he parked the car. Terri hopped out and headed across the street. The bank was substantial, as banks were supposed to be—or appear to be. Solid architecture of stone and marble complemented the thick, wooden door that was heavy to open, giving the whole place a look of stability, wealth, and above all, security.

Terri was a little nervous, and looked around at the people on the street before she went in. There was an elderly couple coming towards her, walking hand in hand, probably more for support than romance. They appeared to be interested only in their conversation.

Across the street near where Wolfe parked the car, a man in his thirties was window shopping at a jewelry store. He appeared to be looking attentively at the display, but she could also see his face and eyes reflected in the glass. If she could see him, he could see her, she thought. He might be watching her. But then he turned and walked further down the street and was no longer looking in the glass. So she entered the bank.

Inside everything seemed normal. There was a uniformed security guard just inside the door who nodded and said, "Good morning," as she walked in. She responded in kind and went towards an open teller's window. Nearby a young mother had a two-year-old boy in tow, who had his own idea of bank decorum. He was yanking on her arm and making quite a fuss as she tried to make a deposit at the teller window. It was hard to tell who was going to win.

At another window was a man who looked like a construction worker. He appeared to be cashing his check. His outfit seemed to match his appearance of rough hands and leathery skin. A yellow hardhat, dirty jeans, red plaid flannel shirt and tan work boots completed his ensemble. Everything appeared to be normal, and nobody seemed to be out of place, so Terri walked up to the open teller.

"How may I help you," the teller asked. She was young, thought Terri, probably no more than nineteen or twenty, with long dark hair, and a pleasant smile.

"I'd like to check any recent transactions in these two accounts, please," Terri said. She gave the teller her account number, and Wolfe's account number, along with Wolfe's fake death certificate and a copy of the fake will, both notarized by a fake notary.

The teller seemed a bit flustered, probably having never seen such documents at the bank before. "Uh, ok," she said. "I'll have to check on this. Just a minute, please," she said as she headed over to her supervisor.

The supervisor looked at the documents, then came around to the teller's window. "Miss Sommers?" he asked, already knowing the answer.

"Yes," Terri said.

He was a tall, trim man with dark, manicured hair. He wore a perfectly pressed dark suit with shiny black shoes and a conservative dark tie. He was the consummate image of a professional and *careful* banker.

"I see you want to check on two accounts for recent transactions," he said, stating the obvious."

"That's correct," said Terri, trying to maintain her composure. "I have provided all the documents, I believe," she said.

"Yes, I see," he said, appearing to examine the documents, which he had obviously had already done. "But there is one thing missing," he said, dramatically.

Terri's heart jumped up in her throat, and her heart started pounding. Trying to stay calm, she said, "And what's that?"

There was a pause, and he said, "Your driver's license."

Terri took a small breath and said, "Oh. Of course. Sorry about that." She dug her license out of her purse and handed it to the supervisor. He took a long look at it, then at Terri, then back at the license.

"It all looks in order," he said finally. Terri put her license back into her purse.

"You're not making a withdrawal or anything like that," he said, "you just want to check the latest transactions and the balance in each account, is that correct?"

"That's right," she said.

Looking relieved, the supervisor said, "Fine. No problem." Then to the teller he said, "Go ahead."

The teller seemed relieved as well, and provided the information Terri requested.

"Thank you," said Terri. "Now I'd like to close my account and open a new account in my full name of Teresa A. Sommers. Please transfer all the funds from my old account to the new one."

The teller had a look of despair that this customer was still at her window, but the request was a reasonable one, and she was reluctant to call her supervisor over again, so she did as requested.

"There," said the teller. "I've closed your present account, opened your new account, and transferred the balance to your new one. Here are the balance transfer and deposit slips. Would you like to order new checks now?" she finished.

"No," replied Terri. "Just some starter checks for now."

"No problem," said the teller. She went away for a few minutes and returned. "Here are your checks with your new account number." The look on her face pleaded for no more transactions from this person.

Terri took the checks. "Thank you," she said.

"You're very welcome," the relieved teller said. "Have a nice day."

Terri nodded and smiled, and quickly left the bank.

chapter 18

"What did you find out at the bank?" Wolfe asked over the wind noise as the convertible picked up speed.

"It looks like we're in luck, so far," Terri answered. "No deposits have been made in either account."

"Good," he said. "Since mine is now frozen and soon to be turned over to my estate for distribution . . ."

"To me," Terri interjected, smiling.

"To you," he repeated reluctantly. "That only leaves your account. Did you close it out today and open a new one like I told you?"

"I did," she said. "I opened it under Teresa A. Sommers instead of my old account name of Terri Ann Sommers."

"Great," he said. "Now they can no longer add the money to our old accounts. And since your new account was opened after Phillips' death, and under a different name, adding money to your new one won't prove a thing. In fact," he continued, "it would draw more attention."

"People would want to know how the money got there," she stated.

"Right," said Wolfe.

"I guess that supports the theory that they're going to wait it out," said Terri.

"Looks that way."

"I'd like to know something," Terri asked, after pausing a minute.

"What's that?" said Wolfe.

"How would they have been able to manipulate our accounts that way? I mean, adding money in after the fact, with past dates and all?"

"That really depends on who they are," he began. "Normally it couldn't be done without some inside help from bank personnel. But if these people are who I think they are, they could easily crack the security code of the bank and manipulate any account they wanted to."

"Then I suppose they could take money out, too—couldn't they?"

"Yes. Or transfer it to another account, or send it to another bank, or even another country."

"That's illegal!"

"So's murder," he said, watching the rearview mirror.

"I see your point. So, who's powerful enough to do this?"

"Not very many people," he said. "It would take a very sophisticated and expensive computer found only in a few locations around the country—mostly research centers like MIT, Stanford, and so on."

Terri turned to look at Wolfe. "You think they'd be involved in this?"

"Not likely," he answered, again eyeing the rearview mirror. "There's one other place, though, with equipment powerful enough to do it easily."

"And where's that?"

"The NSA."

"The National Security Agency?" she said, surprised. "You think they're responsible for this?"

"Maybe not the agency itself," he said, "although that's not out of the realm of possibility. But there might be individuals inside that agency who have different motivations than national security."

"So you think that because they have the capability to do this, that they are the most likely candidate?" she pursued.

"No," he said hesitantly. "There's something else. Remember that phone call you made to me at two AM while I was in D.C.?"

"Yes," she said. "How could I forget? I had to call you from a phone booth. You wouldn't let me call from the nice, comfortable house."

"And I was in another phone booth in Washington."

"Right. So?"

"So there was no way to trace that call, Terri," he said with gravity. "Nobody knew we were going to be in those particular booths until we walked in them. Yet they knew all the necessary information about my flight before I even got to the airport. I didn't make a reservation in advance, so there's no way they could have broken into the airline computer and gotten my flight information. I believe the NSA can, and has been, monitoring all our phone conversations without wiretapping, for some time now."

"How could they do that?" she asked. "Anyway—couldn't they have followed you and found out after you left?"

"They could have—but they didn't. When I got to my gate, there was already a man there—watching me—making sure I got on my flight."

"Are you sure?" Terri asked.

"I'm sure. Unfortunately for him, he didn't see the man in the ubiquitous blue jumpsuit come off the plane just prior to take-off."

"And that was you, I presume."

"It was. It's amazing how one becomes invisible when donning the garb of the working world."

"But why get off the plane? Did you also know they were going to blow it up?"

"Of course not, Terri." Wolfe shot her a look. "I was just shaking a tail—routine in my line of work. Had I known that they planned something that heinous, I would've phoned in a bomb threat. They would have had to search the plane, and would undoubtedly have found the bomb."

"But wait a minute," Terri continued. "There were twenty-two people on that flight manifest—you were supposed to be one of them, yet you got off. Who was the other person on the plane?"

Wolfe grimaced. "A poor standby passenger who was thrilled at having an empty seat suddenly become available."

"That's horrible," Terri said, turning away. "Those poor people! It's all too awful to think about. But I still don't understand how you know the other man was following you."

"I'll tell you why," Wolfe said. "Because the man I saw at the airport is in the car behind us, and has been since we left the bus depot."

chapter 19

"**D**on't turn around," Wolfe said firmly, just as Terri started to look.

"I wasn't going to," she answered calmly. "I can see him in my side view mirror."

"Which you conveniently just adjusted so I can't use it," he said.

Terri just smiled. "How do you know it's the same man? He's too far back to recognize."

"I recognized him at the bus depot. He really gave me the once-over, but there was no startled look of recognition. He mostly kept an eye on you. When we left, he had a difficult time being nonchalant about following us—if you recall my little maneuver," he said, looking over at her.

"I remember *someone* driving like a maniac," she said, looking straight ahead.

"Well if you think we looked bad, you should have seen him," Wolfe said, laughing. "He almost ended up as a hood ornament on a Bunny Bread truck."

"Bunny Bread?"

"Never mind," he said. "You have to live here."

"Back to the problem at hand," she said, shaking her head. "What're you going to do about him? We're almost to your driveway."

"It's a nice day," Wolfe said. "How about another drive to Big Bay?"

Terri thought about the weird feelings she got as they moved through the last miles of the trip. "Those woods really creeped me out."

"No problem," he said, smiling. "I'll protect you."

Terri studied Wolfe's face, then replied, "You'd better."

The ride to Big Bay took less than fifteen minutes. Wolfe slowed as he entered the small town which had seen its heyday years ago. When it looked as though they had just about come to the end, they broke away from the houses and onto a straight, well-maintained two-lane road directly into the Haunted Forest.

Terri refused to look at Wolfe as he drove through the eerie forest again. Finally Wolfe brought the Mustang to a stop at the end of the road as before.

"So, what?" she asked, puzzled. "We're back *here* again."

"Yes, we are," Wolfe said patiently.

"You said you were going to tell me more about something here."

"And I am," said Wolfe, checking his rearview mirror. "But right now we have a car tailing us. So let's sit back and watch a first-class bungled surveillance."

Terri adjusted her mirror as well, and watched as a large, black sedan slowly rolled to a stop a hundred feet behind them.

"Sorry, pal," Wolfe said sadistically, as he narrated the man's plight. "There's nowhere to go but right here. What to do. What to do," he continued, enjoying himself. The car started slowly forward.

"That's it," Wolfe started again. "Let's try the direct approach," he mocked. "May as well make the best of a bad situation." The car pulled up about twenty feet behind them and slightly off to the right, then stopped. The driver then leaned over to the glove box and took out a map.

"Nice touch," said Wolfe, quietly. "The lost tourist approach. I like it. Shall we see what happens next?"

"Let's just get out of here, Clay," Terri pleaded. "He might decide to tie up loose ends right here and now. Besides—there's no way I want to be in these woods when the sun goes down."

"Hold on," said Wolfe. "We can outwait him. If he stays much longer his surveillance will surely be blown. If he wants to keep up any pretense, he'll have to head back up the road. My guess is he'll find a place where he can pull off the road and hide until we drive back past him, then he'll pull in behind us to resume his surveillance, a little further back, I'd imagine."

Just as Wolfe finished, the man did exactly that, putting on a show of frustration with his map. He shook his head in disgust, wheeled the big sedan around and tore off down the road, back toward Big Bay.

"Wow," said Terri. "You must be a mind reader."

"No," said Wolfe. "Just did a million of them myself."

Terri looked quizzically at him, again wondering about his past, and whether she would ever hear the whole story.

Wolfe sensed her thoughts and decided to push past them. "Now," he said as he turned to Terri with an enigmatic smile on his face, "let's take a magical mystery tour." He put the car in gear and slowly drove over to the guard shack. A guard in cammo clothes, forest pattern, came over to the car as Wolfe pulled out some kind of official-looking ID in a thin black wallet, and pushed it out the window for the guard to easily see. The guard looked at the credentials, then at Wolfe and Terri. Then he gave one nod, walked back to the gate, and raised it, eyeballing them the whole time.

"What the heck kind of exchange was that?" exclaimed Terri.

Wolfe said, "Pay attention. I'm going to describe things to you as we go through here.

"OK," said Terri.

As they pulled slowly forward, Wolfe said, "Take a close look at the road. What does it look like?"

Terri had already seen it partially from the dead end outside the gate, and gave her thoughts again. "It looks like a dirt road, though paved in some way. It's brown. I've never seen a brown paved road. But it also seems to have the texture of wood."

"Very good," said Wolfe as they kept moving forward. "Actually, it is a composite wood and other materials designed to look primitive. In reality, it covers a steel structure that is capable of handling ten-ton loads. In fact, most of what you see here is not what it looks like at all."

"What?" Terri asked. "Well what is it then?"

"It consists of the most sophisticated security devices, motion sensors, infrared monitors, pressure plates, and night vision cameras, to name a few. They are expertly hidden in the flora, underground, in the trees. In fact," he continued as they drove slowly into the dense forest, "many of the trees are not trees at all but towers of electronics the likes of which you've never seen."

Terri looked intently as they drove by, examining each 'tree' carefully. "They look like trees to me," she said finally giving up.

"They're supposed to," Wolfe said.

Terri shook her head. "Why all the security? What in heaven's name is *up* here?"

Wolfe paused for a moment. "I can't tell you much about who's here or what the purpose is, but I can tell you that only the very rich and the very elite can be here. Suffice it to say there is a whole community of people living and working here of which most of the outside world has no knowledge.

"So," began Terri, "if this place is so exclusive, how is it that *you* can get in? Or *me* for that matter?"

"You're here because *I'm* here," Wolfe said. "I'm here because someone *wants* me here. That's all I can say."

Terri shook her head. "One day I'll find out, Wolfe. I surely will."

Wolfe just smiled and continued the tour. "On your right you will see some very nice homes on relatively small lots."

Terri noticed they were all made of wood and were of the same hues as the surrounding woods. They blended in, she thought, almost like they *grew* there.

"The residents here don't own these homes," Wolfe began. "They have use of them by virtue of their positions in the world. And they all have to conform to a very strict code of operation and maintenance," Wolfe continued.

Terri looked on in amazement.

"On your left," Wolfe pressed on, "you will see a medical facility of the highest caliber, police, fire and emergency responders, grocery stores, recreational facilities including indoor pools, tennis, aerobic equipment and extensive strength-training equipment, offices and other buildings for various unnamed purposes."

Terri saw a man approach the car and Wolfe slowed to meet him. "Stay here," Wolfe said. "I'll be back in a minute."

Terri watched as Wolfe began talking with the man. He appeared to be in his mid-forties, tall, with dark medium-length hair. He was trim and well built. He had on a black long sleeved t-shirt, black cargo pants, a black belt and black hiking boots. He stood with easy grace, but was ramrod straight. It looked like it a natural position for him, not posed—like it was the way he came out of the womb, thought Terri. Then she shook her head. Why did she think *that*?

Wolfe finally finished talking. He nodded to the man who

nodded back. They shook hands, then Wolfe came back to the car. "End of the mystery tour," he said as he climbed back in.

"What . . . who . . ." Terri began.

Wolfe just shook his head and drove back down the faux drive with the faux trees and probably the faux animals, as far as Terri knew. He didn't solve any of *her* mysteries. In fact, this trip made them *worse*.

It was a quiet trip back to the house. Terri's mind was spinning with questions and overwhelmed by what she saw.

Wolfe studiously avoided looking at her and concentrated on getting away from the area and back to his cabin as soon as he could. The speed he drove precluded much thought. It also made it difficult for their surveillance tail to pick them up or to keep up with them. Neither Terri nor Wolfe saw any sign of him, so they assumed they lost him. Unfortunately, it was a bad assumption.

chapter 20

It was nearly five when they arrived at the house, having stopped in Big Bay to pick up a few groceries on the way back. They hadn't seen the black sedan anymore, the driver obviously realizing his assignment was blown and heading back to his masters to lick his wounds.

After unpacking Wolfe's things, they walked down the twenty-or-so wooden steps behind the house to the soft, sand beach, and frigid, crystal clear waters of Lake Superior.

"Do you think he'll follow us here?" Terri asked, as they walked barefoot along the shore, cold waves washing over their feet.

"I think he knows where we are," Wolfe said, taking her hand as they walked. "But I seriously doubt he, or they, will try to come to the house. We're obviously not going to find Kevin's papers here, and they can monitor every phone conversation we make, so what's the point?" he shrugged. "They'll just follow us until we find what they're after."

"Explain that," Terri said. "How they can monitor every phone conversation we make. How do they do that?"

"First," he began, "I'm not positive they're the ones doing it.

It's just that they're about the only agency with equipment sophisticated enough to do it with the speed, and in the *way* it appears it's being done."

"OK," she said, "You're not positive. I'll keep that in mind. Now—how do they do it?"

"Basically, the NSA is a huge, electronic intelligence gathering machine," Wolfe said, looking out over the water to the horizon. "It has large, state-of-the-art antenna dishes, or receivers, strategically placed all over the world which act as giant vacuum cleaners, so to speak, sucking all wavelengths of the electromagnetic spectrum out of the skies.

"Since virtually all communications are transmitted electronically, and since most of those are broadcast through the atmosphere or to the communication satellites at one point or another in the transmission process, even if you're just calling next door, then they have access to everyone's conversation, from a plumber to the president."

"But isn't a lot of that coded?" she asked. "I mean, governments and businesses don't just send critical information straight out over the air."

"And that brings us to part two of the NSA," Wolfe continued. "Coding and decoding information. That's where the NSA has no equal. They have the most advanced computers in the world," he said, skipping a stone into the water. "In fact, I'm told they are twenty years ahead of anything currently available.

"Which brings me to point three," he said, sounding, to Terri, like a college professor lecturing his students on fundamental spying, 101. "The processing of data. All the information in the world is useless unless you have some way of handling it—sorting, analyzing, classifying, decoding, filing, retrieving—all necessary functions, and all requiring unbelievable technology when you're talking on this scale.

"But the NSA has it," he continued. "They can crunch

astonishing amounts of data in microseconds—and that's what would be necessary to be able to listen to all our phone conversations, no matter where they originate or terminate," he finished.

"Clay," she interrupted finally. "I know about the NSA. I'm a reporter for an international wire service. I know it has amazing electronic eavesdropping capability on virtually every electronic conversation. I just don't know exactly how all of the processes work. So let me give you a hypothetical situation and you tell me how it works."

"OK," Wolfe said.

"I pick up the phone and call you. You pick up the phone and answer it. We talk, we hang up," she said. "You're telling me that no matter where I was making the call from, or where I was calling, that my words got blown, decoded, into space where these giant vacuum cleaners sucked them up?"

"That's about the size of it," Wolfe said matter-of-factly.

"But how do they know what they're looking for?" she continued. "There must be billions of conversations going on all the time. And if they don't know who, or when, or where . . .," she stopped. "How do they do it?"

"That's where the tremendous sorting power of these computers comes in," he said, lecturing again. "Let's suppose we are the NSA and we want to monitor a conversation between a suspected traitor and a foreign spy."

"All right," she said, listening.

"If we knew a phone number the traitor or spy might be calling from, we simply plug that number into the computer, and every call that goes to or from that phone is sorted, recorded, and decoded, if necessary. Now," he continued, "suppose we don't have a phone number, but we know what they might be talking about—take biological warfare for example—we could then have the computer look for a particular word or words, such as 'germ,' 'toxic,' or any other word we want. It would search every conversation uttered anywhere, over whatever time period you specify, until it found them all."

"And then," she challenged, "when you've narrowed it from a billion to a million, what do you do?"

"The computers keep whittling down the pile through the process of elimination, until the right conversation is found. Needless to say," he added, "they frequently come upon some pretty interesting conversations quite by accident."

"I imagine they do," Terri said, thinking back over some of her own past conversations. "And just when you thought it was safe to go back in the phone booth . . ." she quipped. "So how do you think they plucked our conversation out of the sky?" she asked.

"That was easy. We gave it to them," he said. "They knew it would be a call to or from Marquette, and to or from D.C., so that narrowed the chore by a huge factor. They knew it was within a specific span of twenty-four hours, so that cut it down even further. But the coup de grace was the specific subject of the call," he said, watching her eyes move as she figured it out.

"Our names," she said. "We called each other by name."

"What better way to hone in on the right conversation than to have not one, but two names to narrow the search. I'm sure it didn't take them long. In fact, they probably found it fast enough to listen to it live," he said, throwing another stone in the water.

"Doesn't all this scare you?" she said, turning to look directly into his eyes.

"Only when you stop to think about it," he said, turning back down the beach toward the house.

"Clay," she called after him. "Who are you—who are you really?" Wolfe stopped, but did not turn around.

"I mean, you know all this stuff about computers and spies and security systems, you speak with an English accent better than I speak American, yet you're up here in this wilderness with part-time jobs, willing to risk your life for a person you hardly know, against seemingly impossible odds." She stood in the sand, ten feet from his back, staring at him, the breeze whipping her shirt in the beginnings of dusk.

"Why?" Her voice followed him as he slowly walked back toward the house. "Who *are* you?"

chapter 21

Terri looked out the window down into the blackness toward the beach, which she knew was there but could not see. The storm had moved in quickly and without warning, bringing with it sheets of rain and howling winds that seemed to threaten their very existence. Terri shuddered as she returned to the living room. She threw another log on the fire. It didn't really need it, she thought, but it helped her ward off the demons screaming outside, clamoring to get in.

She could hear the roar of the waves above the wind. She recalled the serene, picture postcard of a few hours ago and knew it was now a mad, pounding cauldron. She had heard about the fury of the lake during storms—of how it could tear trees out by their roots, carve huge chunks of real estate away from the landscape, and snap massive freighters in half like they were tinker toys—but this was her first experience in the center of a Lake Superior storm. She was not sure she liked it all that well.

The phone rang. Wolfe looked up at Terri, his half-trimmed beard spread on the table in front of him. Terri looked at him, the unasked question hanging in the air between them. It rang again.

Finally, on the third ring, Wolfe got up and answered the phone, eyes on her the whole time. "Sommers residence, Drake speaking," he said with a flawless English accent.

"What? Who?" shouted the voice at the other end.

"This is Drake Winslow," he said with the appropriate measure of frost. "To whom am I speaking?"

"Oh. Ah, this is Eino Loukkala—coroner," he added as an afterthought. "Terri Sommers there?"

"Miss Sommers is occupied at the moment," Wolfe said, trying to maintain the facade. "Perhaps you could call back in the morning." Terri was waving at him, trying to find out who it was.

"I don't think this'll wait," Eino said. "Can ya get a message to her? Tell her it's about her brother. Something's happened."

Wolfe almost dropped the accent, then caught himself. "Just a moment, please. I'll see if she wishes to be disturbed," he said, holding the receiver at arm's length away from his mouth. She started to say something, but Wolfe shook his head, and pointed at the receiver. "There's a Mr. Loukkala on the phone for you, Miss Sommers," Wolfe said loud enough to be heard. "Something about your brother. Something's happened, he says. Do you wish to speak to him?"

"Yes," she said quickly. "Yes, I'll speak to him."

"Eino," she said, taking the receiver. "This is Terri. What's this about my brother? Drake said something's happened," she said, a look of worry on her face.

"You're not going to like this," he said, "but your brother's body is gone."

"What?" Terri said, stunned.

"I don't quite know how it happened," he said, trying to talk over the storm, "but the best I can piece together, two men came to my office from the Stoddemeyer funeral home about ten this morning, while I was in a meeting away from my office, and said they were here to pick up Kevin Sommers and John Doe.

"According to my assistant who talked to them, they had the proper papers, and a hearse with two caskets. Not knowing any better, she released the bodies to them and they took them to the funeral home."

"How could they do that?" she said in disbelief.

"I know it's a shock, Terri," Eino said apologetically. "I'm sorry. I called the funeral home, and they confirmed the two were brought there and prepared for burial. It seems everything was completely paid for—plots, caskets, burial, everything—fella by the name of John Smythe paid the tab on the John Doe, according to the voucher," Eino said.

"And who paid for Kevin?" Terri asked, anger welling up inside her.

"Why, you did, Terri," Eino said. "Your signature's on the voucher, and on all the necessary papers. Had to be," he continued, "or we couldn't have released him."

"Where is he now?"

"That's the problem, Terri," Eino said, not wanting to tell her. "That's what alerted me that something was wrong. I knew how strongly you felt about cremation, and I couldn't believe . . ."

"Where is he?" she cut in, her voice rising.

"They were both buried at North Lawn Cemetery about four o'clock this afternoon," he said. The storm nearly drowned out his words.

The storm seemed to intensify, if that was possible. Terri and Wolfe met Eino and the caretaker, Eddie Smeele at the mortuary. Eddie was tall and thin, with dark eyes, matted black hair. He wore dark blue work clothes that may have been light blue at one time. Eddie did not appear to have any affinity for soap and water. Needless to say, Eddie was not pleased about the prospect of going back to the cemetery to check their records in this weather—or any weather, for that matter.

"I don't see what all the hurry is," he grumbled, throwing on a rain slicker. "They'll still be here tomorrow when the sun's up and it's nice and dry—and the next day, and the day after, and the day after that . . ." he mumbled on. He unlocked the office finally, the rain from his slicker leaving puddles every place he stood for more than a second.

The wind was whipping fiercely now, driving raindrops into them like tiny bullets.

"I'm really sorry to bother you on a night like this," Terri apologized, "but . . ."

"Yea, yea," he said rudely. "Let's just get this thing over with so I can get home before my house blows down."

Wolfe leaned over and whispered to Terri, "I'd say that'd be good timing. Wouldn't you?"

Terri smiled, but she was still too upset to laugh. "Here they are. Just as I said. Both interred this afternoon about four o'clock—*when it wasn't raining*," he finished gruffly.

"I say, old man," Wolfe began in full British dialect, "are you quite sure the two chaps were interred, and not just the coffins?"

The caretaker just looked at Wolfe like he was from Mars. "Who's he?" he said to Terri, jerking his head roughly in Wolfe's direction.

"Just answer the question, Eddie," Eino said. "Did you actually see the two bodies in the coffins just before they were lowered into the ground?"

"Well, not actually," he started to say, "but I know they was in there . . ."

"We're gonna have to dig 'em up," said Eino, cutting him off mid-sentence.

"What?" Eddie said, not believing his ears. "We're gonna have to what? I ain't gettin' paid enough to . . ."

Eino slapped a court order in Eddie's face, cutting him off again. "Dig 'em up or go to jail," Eino said, his eyes boring into Eddie's, his beak-like nose two inches from Eddie's face. Eddie thought about that for a minute, a *short* minute, obviously giving the latter choice serious consideration.

"All right," he said angrily. "But this is gonna cost you double-time," he said, heading to the garage where the heavy equipment was kept.

"I feel sick," Terri said, taking Wolfe's arm.

"Don't worry, Miss," Wolfe said. "It'll be over soon. Then I'll fix you a spot o' tea to warm you up."

Eino look at the two of them standing there together. "Don't I know you from somewhere, Mister . . .?"

"Winslow. Drake Winslow," Wolfe said as British as he could. Here it comes, he thought.

"Mmmmm," Eino said, his eye cocked at Wolfe. "I dunno. Somethin' about you . . ."

"We all look like someone, I s'pose," said Wolfe, as he turned to look out the window at the progress of the caretaker. "Looks like he's almost got 'em," Wolfe said, trying to change the subject.

Suddenly Enio's eyes lit up. He leaned over to Wolfe, close enough to whisper in his ear. "Wolfe you old son-of-a-bitch, you had me going for a while. What . . . ?"

Wolfe raised his hand, and shook his head. Then he leaned over and whispered to Eino. "I'll explain later."

chapter 22

E ino looked at Wolfe carefully, then nodded. He turned his head and focused back on Eddie. He had known Wolfe for a long time, and if Wolfe was trying to hide his identity, Eino knew it was for a good reason.

They all watched as the caretaker dragged the caskets up out of the graves with a backhoe and chains, bringing them to rest in the mud next to the graves. The wind had relented somewhat, though the rain continued undiminished.

"He's waving for us to come out," Eino said to the others. He pulled his collar up in a futile attempt to shield his neck and stepped out into the driving rain.

Wolfe tried to protect Terri with his umbrella, but the wind had picked up again. The rain was driving so hard, it was coming at an angle nearly parallel with the ground. By the time they got to the grave sites, they were soaking, and their shoes were covered with the newly excavated mud.

"I hope you're enjoyin' this," Eddie yelled as he started unlocking the first casket.

Terri watched as Eddie worked the latches around its top.

Smelling something unpleasant, she looked at the newly excavated soil that seemed to be the source of the odor. The soil was soaking wet, and she watched as little rivulets of muddy water snaked their way down the pile next to the grave site. The soil smelled of decay and death, she thought.

Finally Eddie finished. He looked around hoping to see some form of approval for the proper completion of his odious task, but there was none. Shaking his head and giving a heavy sigh, he began to open the casket. As he did so, the remaining earth slid off the top.

"This one's your broth . . ." Eddie started to say, but he didn't finish the word.

"What the hell," he said, looking in the casket. They all leaned forward to take a look. It was empty. Terri looked at Wolfe. Wolfe stared into the casket, but showed no expression.

"I, I . . ." Eddie shook his head. "Where's the body?" he asked, as if someone else would have that information that he surely should have known.

"That's a good question," Eino said, glaring at Eddie. "You buried him. Did you check the casket first?"

Eddie looked chagrined. "Not exactly," he said, looking around as if he were searching for an exit door from this horrible scene. The wind and rain had abated a little by now, making it almost bearable. "I mean, the caskets came directly from the funeral home, and I just assumed . . ."

"*Assumed*?" shot back Eino. "Aren't you supposed to know who you are burying before you bury them?"

Eddie was now beginning to panic as he saw his job vanishing before his eyes. He wanted to be somewhere else right now. *Anywhere* else. "I, uh . . ." he started. Then Eddie shook his head and shrugged his shoulders, as if that was a sufficient response. It wasn't.

"Well," said Eino, "let's get to the other casket."

Eddie blanched. The other casket. He had forgotten there was more to go. He dreaded opening it because he knew it was going to be empty too. His day was going from bad to worse. The men who had paid him so much money to bury the empty caskets and make no record of it had threatened him that if he told anyone, he should dig a hole for himself, for he would surely die, and not in a pleasant way, if indeed there was a pleasant way. Eddie highly doubted it with those men.

Eddie proceeded to open the second casket, which was in the hole next to the one for Terri's brother. They all peered in. The second casket was also empty. Everyone turned to look at Eddie. He looked at each one in turn, looking for any sign of understanding or mercy. He saw none.

"I guess I'd better go check this out," he said lamely, and turned to go.

"Better not go too far, Eddie," Eino said with menace in his voice. "The authorities will want to have a word with you 'bout this after I call 'em," he shot a look at Eddie. "Which I'm going to do right now." The remaining color in Eddie's face drained completely, making him look as if *he* was just exhumed from the grave.

They followed Eddie back to the mortuary, then went to their respective cars.

"You know Eddie's gonna take off, don't you Wolfe?" Eino said as he was getting into the old black hearse that he used as his personal runabout.

"I know," said Wolfe. "That's what I'm hoping for. Maybe he will lead us to his co-conspirators."

"Co-conspirators?" Eino and Terri both said simultaneously.

Wolfe smiled. "He was sure scared shitless about something," he said, "and I don't think it was us."

"But how're you going to follow him?" asked Terri. "If he takes off, he'll probably never come back. Heck. He could be out of the state in a matter of hours, if he heads toward Wisconsin . . .

"Or out of the country in a few hours, if he heads to the Soo," said Eino.

"The Soo?" asked Terri.

"Sault Saint Marie," answered Wolfe. "Either way, you're both right."

"So . . ." started Terri. "How're you going to . . .?"

Wolfe cut her off. "I bugged his car," he finished. "It's a satellite transmitter that'll track his car anywhere in the world."

That got Eino's attention. He stayed outside his car to hear the rest of the story.

"What . . . how . . ." started Terri again, seemingly never being able to finish a sentence.

But Wolfe gave her a glance, and she decided to let that one go unanswered—for now.

As they stood by their cars, Eino said he would inform the authorities of the two missing corpses. Terri and Wolfe climbed into her Mustang and Wolfe drove her home.

"What're we going to do now?" she said, her tears mingling imperceptibly with the rain drops on her face. The wipers on the car tried, but failed to clear the windscreen long enough for Wolfe to catch more than a glimpse of the road.

"They can't keep on killing people, breaking into their homes—stealing their bodies," she cried. "What's so damned important that it has to be protected like this, Clay? When's it going to end?"

Wolfe drove silently for a minute. Then he put his arm around her, and pulled her as close as he could, considering the bucket seats. "I can't answer that, Terri," he said, trying to comfort her. "But I will say this. We're not going to just sit around and be targets anymore."

"We're not?" she said looking over at him.

"No we're not," he continued. "There are a lot of things a dead man can do that a live one can't, and I intend to start doing them."

"Meaning?" she said, hope returning to her eyes.

"We're going on the offensive," Wolfe said, with a look on his face Terri had never before seen.

chapter 23

"**D**id you check out the license number of the car that followed us yesterday?" Terri asked Wolfe the next morning after breakfast.

She looked rested and fresh, as if she had just walked out of a Cover Girl ad, thought Wolfe. An impossible task after their previous wretched day. Yet, there she stood, white sun top, baby blue jeans, and white Keds sneakers. She looked for all the world like she was going on a picnic—in the 1950s.

Wolfe cleaned up as well, but did not look nearly as fresh as she did. He had on tan Dockers, a forest green shirt, and cordovan loafers. Hmmm, he thought. Maybe they *both* were going on a picnic. The thought made him smile.

His fantasy was short-lived as he realized that this was probably not the right attire for what they were planning to do. But this morning, with the clear blue sky and bright sun wiping away all traces of yesterday's gloom, he was going to relish the thought anyway. Plenty of time for gloom and doom later.

"I did," Wolfe said, responding to Terri's question. He suddenly noticed that she was giving him an odd look. "It was a rental, as expected. Taken out by a Mr. Tom Jones," he continued. "Can you believe that? First John Smythe, now Tom Jones."

"What they lack in originality," she said, "they make up for in brutality."

"Well," he said, deliberately quoting Sir Arthur Conan Doyle, "the game's afoot." Wolfe opened a black leather satchel and placed it on the kitchen table.

"What's that?" asked Terri, as she watched him remove several odd-looking pieces of equipment.

"My game bag," he replied, smiling mysteriously.

"What're all those things?" Terri said as she walked over for a closer look.

"Toys for my game," he said, carefully examining each piece.

"Everything's black. What's the name of your game?" she asked suspiciously.

"Hide-and-seek. Only it's a little different kind of hide-and-seek than you're used to."

"Oh?" she said. She watched him clean, and in some cases, make adjustments to the pieces with what looked like jewelers tools.

"Yes," he said matter-of-factly, examining something Terri thought looked like a primitive blow gun. "You see, in this game, I'm always 'it.' Only my opponents don't know I'm 'it', and they keep hiding, watching someone else who they think is *it*."

"Me," said Terri dryly.

"Exactly. Now the object of the game," he continued, "is to find and tag all my opponents without them discovering that I'm really *it*. When I've done that, I take my information to the game official, and he disqualifies all the other players and declares me the winner."

"And what happens if, while you're tagging all your opponents, one of them catches you and finds out you're really *it*?" Terri asked.

"Ahh. There's the rub," he said, slipping in a different dialect.

"When that happens, I'm afraid the game is over," he said, carefully replacing the items back in the satchel.

"And what about the other *it*?" Terri said testily. "The one all your opponents were watching while you were slithering around trying to tag them?"

"She gets to start a new game," he said soberly.

"And what's that one called?" she asked.

"Survival." Wolfe snapped the bag closed and lifted it off the table.

"Are you going to tell me what those things are in your black bag?" she asked.

"Nope," he said, walking away from the table.

"I didn't think so," Terri said. "You're going to play this game alone, aren't you?"

"That's right," he said, as he walked down the steps into the basement. "C'mon down. I've got something to show you I think you'll find very interesting."

Terri followed him downstairs. It was a walk-out, with a door facing the lake. It contained a furnace, hot water heater, and shelves filled with snow shoes, skis, and parkas. It was nicely paneled with real knotty pine. On the wall opposite the door was a large, Finnish sauna.

"This is my pride and joy," Wolfe said, opening the door to the beautiful, redwood sauna.

"Wow," she said, looking inside. "It's beautiful."

"Go on in," he said, holding the door for her. She looked at him for a second, then stepped up onto the wood floor and walked to the back of the sauna. Wolfe turned the light on and closed the door behind them. It shut with a heavy, metallic click that surprised her.

"Sit down," he said. She sat on the lowest bench on one side of the sauna while he sat on the other side, facing her. There was a second, higher bench on both sides further back, so that if she sat on it, her head would have been about a foot from the ceiling and her back against the wall.

Next to the door, she saw the traditional metal heater with smooth stones piled on top. The stones were about the size of a flattened lemon. Next to the stones and heater was a bucket of water with a ladle, for pouring water on the heated rocks. This created a dry steam that caused the sweating that the Finnish in the area loved so much.

The floor was about six feet wide between the benches. Wider than usual, she thought, but it gave the sauna a comfortable, spacious feeling.

"So what do you think?" he asked, watching her reaction.

"What's going on?" she said like a school teacher who had just discovered an errant pupil about to blow a spitball across the room. "You didn't bring me down here just to show me your fancy sauna. What else've you got up your sleeve?"

"It's not so much up my sleeve," he said smiling, "as in my hand. Watch," he said pointing toward the back of the sauna. Wolfe pressed a button on a small, rectangular device in his hand that looked like a TV remote control. As she watched, the center portion of the back wall slowly swung away with a quiet hum. When it had fully opened, a light came on revealing a small adjacent room.

"What . . ." Terri said in amazement as she stood to look through the doorway. "What is this?" she said.

"C'mon. I'll show you," he said, taking her hand.

Terri stepped into the room. It was roughly twenty feet square, eight feet high, and appeared to be made entirely of concrete. At the back of the room was a tunnel opening, approximately six feet square, also made of concrete. Around the room there were wooden cabinets of various sizes and shapes, and in the center of the room was a black motorcycle.

"Where did you get that?" she exclaimed, walking over to get a better look at it.

"That's one of my special toys," he said.

Terri looked at the bike. It was a medium-sized motorcycle, with saddlebags on either side of the rear wheel, and a black fairing that swept sleekly back from just behind the front wheel. Everything was flat black, including the engine and exhaust pipes. There wasn't a speck of chrome anywhere. Turning her attention from the bike to the tunnel, she said, "Where does that go?"

"The tunnel leads to another piece of property I own on the other side of the road. It comes up inside an old hunting camp that has been abandoned for years. I use it when I want to leave here unnoticed. Works real well."

"I imagine it does," Terri said, eyeing him suspiciously. Then, after a pause, "Are you a spy?" Wolfe said nothing and she continued. "What about the Mafia? Drug runner? White slaver? I mean," she went on, "what need does a part-time professor have for all this?"

"You forget," he responded. "I assist local police departments with criminal investigations."

"Right," she said. "So you built a quarter-mile long tunnel so that neighbors, who don't even live within two miles of here, can't spy on you coming or going from your home. That makes sense."

"It might make a little more sense," he said patiently, "if you consider the type of life an undercover drug investigator has to live. Believe it or not," he continued, "this part of the state has a number of isolated drug factories which supply a good portion of Michigan and surrounding states with millions of dollars of contraband drugs. With stakes that large," he paused, climbing on the bike, "I think you can understand why I wouldn't want drug dealers or their enforcers following me home for a friendly game of Parcheesi."

"And you do those types of investigations?" she said, still suspicious.

"Of course," he said. "The local police don't have the resources to do what I can do."

"Aren't you a little old to be playing the part of a drug dealer?" she asked, not convinced.

"Not really," he said, flipping the kick-start out to its ready position. "The big dealers are the ones who survived over the years. They wear business suits," he said. "Expensive ones. And they run a little longer in the tooth," he said, giving the pedal a kick. "Like me."

chapter 24

The engine did not roar to life. In fact, it didn't seem to start at all. Then Terri noticed a soft, purring sound. Suddenly she smelled the exhaust, and Wolfe twisted the grip giving it some throttle. The engine revved. Still, there was no roar—just a higher pitched purr. "It's so quiet," she exclaimed. "Aren't these things supposed to make a lot of noise?"

"Normally, yes," he said, turning the engine off. "But this one has a computer that takes the sound of the engine, digitizes it, and then makes a sound that is exactly opposite in frequency and amplitude, through those speakers." Wolfe indicated two louvered boxes above the engine.

Terri examined the speakers. "I don't understand. It makes more sound, and that makes it quiet?"

"The waves cancel each other out," Wolfe explained. "Kind of like math, you know? Five plus negative five equals zero. Same principle."

Terri nodded. "I guess it makes sense. That is, as much as any of this makes sense."

Wolfe smiled. "Stick with me. It'll all work out."

"I hope you're right," she said, shaking her head.

"They're going to follow you when you leave," Wolfe said after he had pulled Terri's convertible into the garage and shut the door. "I've got to make sure there's no Birddog on you so they'll have to stay relatively close to the car or risk losing you."

"Birddog?" Terri said.

"Oh," he said apologetically. "It's an electronic transmitter that can be magnetically attached to your car. It constantly sends out a signal which can be picked up by a receiver on the same frequency—usually within a mile or so of where you are."

"And you think there might be one of those things on my car?" she said, walking over to the Mustang. She bent down and began inspecting the rear wheel well.

"I aim to find out," he said, taking a black box out of his satchel. The device was about as big as a paperback novel and had a telescoping antenna on top which Wolfe extended. The flat surface of the instrument had a toggle switch, a dial, and a window through which a needle and numbered scale could be seen.

Wolfe flipped the toggle switch and a small red light came on. The window lit up, and the needle came to life as Wolfe pointed the antenna at the car and began twisting the dial. "This frequency analyzer," Wolfe said, indicating the device he held in his hand, "will not only tell me whether or not there's a transmitter on your car, but also what frequency it's transmitting on."

Terri watched as he slowly walked around the car, twisting the dial, watching the needle. "What then?" she said, walking behind him.

"If we find one," he said, reaching underneath the gas tank at the rear of the car, "we disable it in such a way that they'll think it malfunctioned rather than that we found it."

"Why do that?" she said. "Why not let them know we're onto them?"

"Because then they'll just use a more sophisticated device the next time—one we may not be able to find so easily," he said. "Or," he continued seriously, "they might figure the jig's up and decide to cut their losses."

"Meaning?" she said.

"Meaning the game's over and we lose," he said, turning off the device and collapsing the antenna.

Terri watched as he put the analyzer back in the satchel. "Well?" she said impatiently. "Did you find anything?"

"No," he said slowly, "and that bothers me."

"Why?" she said, puzzled.

"Because if our theory's correct," he said, "they've got to be following us at all times. And to follow us at all times, they've either got to have a Birddog or something similar on the car, or they have to keep us in sight when we're moving all the time."

"So what's the problem with that?" she said. "If they're closer, we can keep an eye on them easier. We'll know where they are."

"But they'll have to know that's the case," he said. "They'll know that it's only a matter of time before we discover they're following us. It's just too hard to surveil for very long in a small town like this without sticking out. If they're not using electronics," he continued, "then they have to know they're gonna be discovered."

"And that means," she interjected, "that they either want us to know we're being followed—to put pressure on us—or . . ."

"Or they don't care," he finished.

After dark, they went into the secret basement room where Wolfe changed clothes and prepared to leave. Terri looked at him as he mounted the motorcycle and cranked it to life. He was dressed in black from head to foot, including black gloves, helmet, and smoked face shield. Not an inch of skin was visible.

"You look ominous enough," she said.

"Just make sure you give me five minutes to get into position," he said. "Then drive into town as we discussed. I'll be out of sight the whole time, so don't look for me. When you're done, return as usual. I'll be back sometime later. If all goes well, I'll be able to pick up your tail and then follow him back to his boss. So don't wait up. It might take some time."

"You *will* be careful," she said, more as an order than a request.

"Don't worry about me," he said, pulling the bike off its stand. "Remember—twenty minutes," he said as he switched on his headlamp and pulled into the tunnel.

"Ten minutes," she said, as she watched him disappear into the blackness.

Wolfe drove quickly through the tunnel, the damp mustiness of the concrete filling his nostrils. Near the end, the grade inclined, forcing the engine to work harder as it pulled him underneath the highway and up to the abandoned camp five hundred yards on the other side.

Near the end of the tunnel he pressed a button hidden on the lower side of the fairing. A steel covered wall swung slowly toward him. The other side of the wall, covered with logs and cement, was the back of a small cabin which had been built into the side of the hill.

Wolfe pulled the bike into the cabin, and reactivated the wall mechanism that closed the door. He flipped up his face shield and surveyed the seams, making sure it was still undetectable. He looked slowly around the camp for signs it had been disturbed. Although he had it securely locked, he always checked on the off-chance someone was able to break in. He checked the kitchen windows, to see if they had been jimmied or tampered with in any way. He checked the glass to see if it was new, in case someone had broken a pane, unlocked the window, gained entry, rummaged around, stolen items, planted bugs or bombs, and then replaced the glass. He checked for disturbed dust on the window sills, or for any fingerprints that shouldn't be there.

He checked the other windows in the same manner, as well as the front door. There was no back door. He went outside and looked for any signs of disturbances, such as footprints, disturbed soil, scratches or tool-marks on the doors or windows. Then he climbed a few extended logs that provided means to climb to the roof and check for any signs of holes being cut, antennas being erected or wires strung across as alarm systems. Everything seemed in order.

So he climbed back down and did an electronic scan for listening devices. Checking all the rooms, he found none. Then he did a physical search for listening bugs, because sometimes new frequencies are used that scanners haven't been programmed to detect. He looked in and under all the lamps, furniture, drawers and cabinets, heating vents, the toilet and fixtures in the bathroom, behind pictures and curtains, beneath rugs. Nothing was found.

Seeing no signs of tampering, and satisfied that no one had been in or around his cabin, he unlocked the door, pulled his bike outside, then relocked the cabin door. There was no road to the camp, so Wolfe took his normal route through the trees toward the highway. Quietly the bike slipped over the leaves and pine needles, roots and rocks, until he came within a hundred feet of the highway. There was no entrance or drive or road or path or marker to be seen from the road to indicate there was anything living in those woods other than the flora and fauna whose home it was.

chapter 25

Even though his bike was virtually silent, he switched off the engine anyway, and listened intently for several minutes. Soon the wildlife noises returned, indicating that there was no threat in the woods this evening.

Wolfe removed his helmet and pulled a set of night vision goggles from his satchel.

Although the starlight was dimmed by the trees, the goggles were able to amplify it thousands of times to make the surrounding forest look nearly like daytime. Wolfe figured that if his opponents had similar devices, they would not be looking in his direction, and therefore he was relatively safe from detection as long as he was quiet and still.

His breath became visible in the cool night air as it often did, even during summer. He scanned the forest around him, then scanned again—nothing. They've got to be here, Wolfe thought. If his theory was right, they had to be following them to find Kevin's material. Yet, there seemed to be no one watching. Maybe when Terri's car pulls out, they'll come out of hiding, he thought, focusing on the drive to his beach cabin.

A few minutes later, her headlights began to appear, winding up the drive toward the road. Wolfe watched as she pulled onto the highway, looking for any signs of a tail car.   As her car accelerated slowly out of view, he watched in vain. No other car appeared. *Damn*, he thought. How are they doing this? Frustrated, he started the bike, put it in gear, and slid silently over the leaves and sand onto the highway, accelerating rapidly in Terri's direction. Within minutes she was in view, but nobody was behind her.

Wolfe reached down and flipped a switch cutting off the sound-canceling system, allowing the engine to sound like an ordinary motorcycle. The noise seemed to come out of nowhere, but there was no one around to notice.

A few miles down the road, Wolfe noticed a telephone truck in front of Terri slowing down. The passenger was shining a spotlight on the phone lines that paralleled the right side of the road. The driver slowed even more, then put his arm out the window motioning Terri to pass. Terri slowed, then as they half-pulled off the road, she drove around.

Wolfe was still a quarter mile back when the phone man switched the spotlight off and pulled back onto the road behind Terri. Interesting, thought Wolfe as he cranked the throttle, closing the distance between them. That could have been a front-surveillance.

It appeared to be a normal telephone truck from the back, but he made a mental note of the license number anyway. The truck was several car-lengths behind Terri, but they were obviously no longer interested in the phone lines. Let's see if we can get a look at these guys, Wolfe said to himself as he down-shifted, and began pulling around the truck.

The driver's window had been raised, but Wolfe glanced quickly in as he passed to see if he could identify the occupants. A baby-faced giant stared back at him, with a look that told him this was definitely not customer service.

The truck maintained its distance behind him for several miles, until Wolfe began slowing down on a curvy stretch of the road. The double yellow line and the lack of visibility ahead forced the truck to slow down as well, and they began losing sight of the car. Now we'll see what you're made of, thought Wolfe as he kept careful watch on his rearview mirror.

The answer wasn't long in coming. The driver of the telephone truck first began flicking his bright lights on and off. When that didn't work, he pulled the truck closer to Wolfe, and began honking his horn. Wolfe continued to slow, until Terri was out of sight.

That brought an end to civility as the truck down-shifted and gunned the engine. Wolfe watched his mirror intently. The road was still winding, and there was no place to pass. He's going to ram me, thought Wolfe. Sure enough, the truck gained speed and made no attempt to pull around him. Just as it appeared there would be an imminent collision, Wolfe down-shifted, gave it full throttle, and screamed away from the truck at the last second.

The truck kept accelerating, but the motorcycle pulled away with ease, and Terri's car came quickly into view. Wolfe slowed for the car, but the truck kept coming. Let's see how mad you are, thought Wolfe, as he raised the middle finger of his left hand in the air so the driver could clearly see it. The road had straightened out and Wolfe pulled around Terri just as the truck came within ramming distance of him.

In his mirror Wolfe could see the truck slam on the brakes. It seemed to weave slightly from left to right and back again as it came upon Terri's car. Wolfe was about a hundred yards in front of her when all of a sudden he looked up to see three deer standing in the middle of the road.

Frozen by the headlights, they stood staring, blocking both lanes, oblivious to the fate about to come upon them. Wolfe leaned hard to the left, almost laying the bike down, and drove through the three-foot gap between the first and second deer. Terri slammed on the brakes, spinning the rear end of her car around to the front, which then slammed into the center deer knocking it to the ground.

The truck fared worse. With Terri and the one deer in the center of the road, and the other deer now scattering in opposite directions across the road, there was nowhere to go. The driver made a futile attempt to swerve to the right, but the high center of gravity of the truck did not lend itself well to emergency maneuvers.

As the rear slid to the left, the truck seemed to hang in suspended animation, sideways to the road, as if awaiting further instructions. Then it suddenly flipped, rolling over before it came to rest on its top. The driver's side door was mashed up against a massive white pine next to the road.

Wolfe spun around, bringing his bike quickly back to Terri. "You OK?" he asked, flipping up the face shield.

"Yes, I guess," she said, obviously shaken up. "Aren't you going to see if they're hurt?" she asked, pointing to the smashed truck.

"In a minute," he said. "Right now, you get outta here. Go back into town as we planned."

"What about that deer?" she said, pointing to the back of her car. "Is it dead?"

"Probably just bruised," he said. Just then the deer got to its feet, looked around for a second, then limped off into the woods. "Now go, before someone else comes along. I'll meet you at the house later."

"All right," she said, getting back in to her car. "But those men . . ."

"Don't worry," he cut in. "There may be more to this than meets the eye. Just go. I'll take care of it."

Wolfe watched as Terri turned the car around and headed back down the road toward town. Then he walked over to the truck, surveying the trail of debris it had left on the highway. Probably not the way they envisioned the break-up of AT&T, he mused as he bent over to see if they were alive.

chapter 26

"I don't understand," Terri said, the heat from the fireplace warming her through. "The truck was smashed and both men were unconscious. You saw it, I saw it. It was there."

"Not when the rescue squad and police got there it wasn't," Wolfe said, sitting on the couch next to her. "I went back to check."

"You sure they were in the right location?" she said.

"I'm sure," he said, kicking off his shoes. "I went back myself and looked. Not so much as a dial tone to be found."

"What about the tracks in the shoulder of the road?" she asked. "I mean, there had to be some trace of the accident."

"I'm telling you, Terri, there was nothing. No tire tracks, no bits of yellow plastic from their rotating beacon—nothing. Whoever cleaned up that mess did one hell of a job."

"In one hell of a hurry," she added. "Somebody must have come by when they were cleaning up—they must have seen who was doing it."

"Not many people come down this stretch of road late at night," he said. A half-burnt log rolled off the fire onto the hearth. "And even if they did, it's not unusual to see wreckers towing smashed vehicles. Happens all the time here—especially in winter."

"What about the men?" she said. "Wouldn't people be curious to see an ambulance loading two bodies and carting them away?"

"Maybe," he said reflectively, putting the errant log back on the fire. "If there *was* an ambulance."

"What do you mean by that?" she said.

"Whoever they were," he continued, "they only had about twenty minutes to clean up the whole mess before the authorities arrived. I figure they just hooked a wrecker up to the truck, and hauled it away—bodies and all."

"But you said they weren't dead when you checked on them," she said, not believing.

"They weren't."

"Then, wouldn't they give them first aid before moving them?"

"Not if they were in a big hurry," he said, turning to look at her. "Not if they didn't want to be discovered."

"Not if they weren't really phone company employees," she added.

"I think that's a safe bet at this point," he said, putting his arm around her.

"You think it's them?" she said, looking at his profile—afraid of his answer.

"Looks that way," he said as he turned to face her.

Wolfe looked at her, suddenly mindful of emotions he hadn't felt in a long time. There was something about her eyes—how they darted around his face, taking in every feature—cautious, yet hopeful. It reminded him of memories long since buried—memories too painful to recall. Yet they persisted, swelling to the surface, mingling with new feelings he could no longer contain.

They took in each other's features, as if examining them for the first time. Their lips touched, almost imperceptibly at first. Slowly, carefully, they found each other, pushing out the past, denying the future.

chapter 27

"I guess you're right," Terri said the next morning as she pulled back the curtains, letting streams of golden sunlight into the bedroom. She opened the window and a breeze of fresh, lake air blew the cobwebs from Wolfe's mind.

"About what?" he said, trying to focus his eyes. The teddy she was wearing was doing more to make him 'rise and shine' than the sunlight.

"The truck," she said. "I called the phone company this morning to inquire about the accident, and they said there was no accident that they knew of. I gave them the license plate number and location, but they said they have no such plate registered to them."

"When'd you do this?" he said, squinting at the sun.

"About an hour ago," she said, hopping off the bed.

"What time is it, anyway?"

"Eleven-fifteen."

"What?" Wolfe exclaimed. "I've slept half the day!"

"You needed it," she said. "Besides. I have a feeling things are going to break today."

"And what makes you think that?"

"Women's intuition."

"I never thought I'd hear you make a sexist statement like that," Wolfe responded playfully.

Terri smiled as she watched him walk to the bathroom. He was wearing Jockey shorts, and nothing else. She watched him move—so lithe, powerful, graceful, confident—and oh, so sexy, she thought. Who is this enigma of a man, she asked herself, and why is he in her life?

They both showered and put on robes for breakfast. Wolfe made them a cheese omelet, wheat toast, and coffee. They ate with zeal, Wolfe gobbling down his portion as if he hadn't eaten in a week.

They were both deep in thought when the phone rang. Terri answered.

"Miss Sommers?" the timid voice at the other end of the line said.

"This is Terri Sommers," she responded, cautiously.

"I'm Professor Frankel—Leo Frankel," the voice said, thick with a Hungarian accent. "I am—was—Kevin's major advisor."

Terri listened to his labored breathing. "What can I do for you?" she said, suddenly attentive.

"I had a very difficult time finding you," he continued, as if she hadn't said anything. "The police finally gave me this number."

"Excuse me, professor," she said, "but what can I help you with? Is it something about Kevin?"

The breathing continued, getting worse. "Yes—No! I mean, it's about his work—his thesis." The tremor in his voice was more than noticeable.

"What about it?" she said, her voice rising.

"I . . . I need it—his notes, I mean," he said. "The research he was doing for me was very important, and I'm afraid he did not see fit to leave me copies of it. I was hoping maybe you would know where he kept it," he said, his voice cracking. "I know this must be a bad time for you but . . ."

"What is it he was working on, professor?" she said carefully. "What is it I should be looking for?"

Wolfe looked over at Terri, hearing her half of the conversation.

Another long pause with heavy breathing. Then, "Ah, it really wasn't anything. Just notes on environmental factors mostly," he said, hesitantly. "Should be in a notebook or binder of some kind. I'm not sure what he kept them in. Perhaps he gave it to you before he . . ." Frankel trailed off, the sentence choked off in his throat.

"Why is this so important to you, professor?" she said, her reporter's instincts bringing a sharper edge to her voice. "First you said it was very important, then you said it really wasn't anything. Which is it?"

"I shouldn't have called," he croaked. "This is a bad time for you. Please call me if you find anything. Thank you. Goodbye." The last was rushed, almost inaudible.

Terri slowly hung up the phone. Professor Frankel hadn't left a phone number or address. "I think we'd better make a trip to the University," she said to Wolfe. "We just may have our first lead."

chapter 28

Terri told Wolfe the other half of the conversation with Frankel. They decided to go to the campus, so they cleaned up and got ready to go. Terri changed out of her shorts into blue jeans, an NMU sweatshirt and white sneakers. Wolfe changed into his black on black attire in the persona of Drake Winslow, then they headed off to campus.

Fifteen minutes later, they arrived in town at the campus of Northern Michigan University. They checked the campus map on the sign at the visitor's entrance, and found Kevin's building. It was a fairly large, two-story building dedicated to earth sciences. Terri and Wolfe parked in the visitor's space and entered the brick building's front double doors.

They opened a door marked 'Environmental Science' and found a middle-aged woman with grey hair, and wire-rimmed glasses, sitting behind a desk full of papers, with which she was intently occupied.

"Professor Frankel, please," Wolfe said in his best English accent. "Tell him Miss Sommers is here to see him."

"And you are . . . ?" the woman said, looking at Wolfe with an air of intimidation only professor's secretaries seemed to perfect.

"Winslow, Madame," he said stiffly. "Drake Winslow. If you please, the professor? We're in a bit of a rush."

"Not as much as he was," she said, going back to her papers. "Left here a few minutes after he arrived this morning. Haven't heard from him since."

"Did he say anything before he left?" Terri asked. "Where he was going?"

"No he did not," she said, not looking up. "Just said he was leaving for a while. Can't say when he'll be back."

"Well, when you see him," said Terri, "please tell him I was here and would like to talk to him about my brother's papers. He'll know what I'm talking about."

"Say," the woman said, looking up again at Terri, the light finally coming on. "You're Kevin's sister, aren't you?"

"That's right," Terri said, waiting for the obligatory condolences. They never came.

"This just came in the mail this morning," the woman said, looking under the various piles of papers. "It's here somewhere." She kept pawing through stack after stack, moving first one pile, then another. "Ahh," she said finally. "Here it is." She slid an envelope out from under one of the piles. "Can I see some ID please," she asked before she handed it to Terri.

"Of course," said Terri, and showed her her driver's license.

"OK," said the secretary after giving it a good look, and handed it back to Terri along with the letter. "I don't know why the bank sent it here, but you may as well have it. Don't know who else to give it to," she finished, going back to her papers. Terri looked at the envelope. It appeared to be a bank statement, with Kevin's apartment address crossed out and, "forward to Northern Michigan University" written next to it.

Terri stuck the envelope in her purse. "I don't suppose you could tell me where the professor lives, could you?" she asked.

"Not my place to give out private addresses," she said perfunctorily, her head still buried in the papers. "It's in the book, though," she said, looking up over her glasses. "In the hall."

"Thank you," said Terri sarcastically as they walked out the door. "You've been a *great* help." The phone book yielded his address, and they headed over to the professor's, hoping he was there and that he could tell them more about Kevin and his project.

The old house on Ridge Street was large, as houses at the turn of the century often were in this lumber-rich part of the county. Three stone fireplaces graced the seven-bedroom mansion which stood near the crest of the hill overlooking the blue-green waters of the harbor. Tall hardwood trees, majestic and stately, lined the streets and filled the yards of the houses up and down the street.

"I wonder if he lives alone in this big house," said Terri as they stopped in front.

"I guess we'll find out," Wolfe said, opening the car door. He rang the bell, but there was no answer.

"Try the knocker," Terri said, indicating the big brass knocker on the solid oak door. Wolfe tried the knocker, but there was still no response. "Maybe we should check the back," she said, walking around to the side of the house.

"I'm not sure that's such a good idea," he said, again in his English role. "There is such a thing as breaking and entering, you know—even up here."

"We're not breaking and entering," she said stubbornly. "We're just trespassing a little."

"We're trespassing a lot," he mumbled as he followed her around to the back of the house.

"Look. It's open," she said, pushing gently on the back door. It swung open, revealing a large, all-white kitchen.

"This isn't a good idea," Wolfe said, but Terri ignored him, pressing on into the house.

"Hello?" she said loudly. "Professor Frankel? Anybody home?" Hearing no answer, she walked through the dining room into the living room, then into the library. Books and papers were stacked everywhere, and old, overstuffed furniture graced the library in a somewhat haphazard fashion. A large work table stood by the window on the side of the house next to the driveway, upon which were more papers and books. The room had a faint musty smell, owing no doubt to the aging documents and old volumes strewn around.

"What a mess," Terri said, looking around the room. "We're going to have a heck of a time finding Kevin's papers here," she said, "if they even *are* here."

Wolfe shook his head in dismay. "Well, Terri, I think we can safely say we have crossed the threshold of breaking and entering. Good thing the state prison is so close by."

"I'm just looking for the professor—that's all," she insisted. "There's no harm in that."

"You're snooping," he said.

Terri picked up a book from his desk, then quickly set it back down.

"I am not," she said defensively, turning to look at him. "Just curious."

"And what, pray tell, happened to the cat?"

"It croaked," said a raspy voice behind them. Terri jumped as Wolfe spun around to confront an apparition standing in the doorway. Facing them was a large, puffy specter in the form of a man who'd seen better days. His large, hairy arms hung from short sleeves clearly not designed for such bulk.

What was showing of his face was bruised and swollen, his bandages mercifully covering the more damaged portions. Wolfe stared at the man and the man stared back. He'd seen that look before. Intractable, defiant, inescapable. It was the driver of the telephone truck—it was not-so-attractive Babyface.

"Who are you?" Terri said, finally getting her wits about her.

"Who are *you*?" the man rasped, not moving an inch.

"I'm Terri Sommers, she said. "I'm . . . we're looking for Professor Frankel."

"He's not here," Babyface said, moving a few inches closer.

"Do you know where he is?" she said, regaining some of her composure. "It's important we see him."

"He's dead," the specter said, matter-of-factly. "Boating accident."

Terri looked shocked, the color draining from her face. "He can't be," she started. "We just talked to him a short while ago. He said . . ." Terri stopped mid-sentence. Looking down she saw, for the first time, his hands and pants stained with blood.

Babyface followed her eyes down to his hands, then slowly looked up, an obscene smile on his face. "Happened kinda sudden," he said menacingly as he began to walk toward them. "Slipped on the deck and broke his neck. Real tragedy."

"I say, old chap," Wolfe began, trying to divert the hulk's attention. "That's a bloody shame. What say we get some flowers, Miss, for the family?"

"Flowers," she said hesitantly, watching Babyface move slowly closer and closer. "Yes. Flowers. We'll order some now—across town—for the funeral," she said. They were being backed into a corner, and there was no other exit from the room.

"Jolly good to have met you, mister . . ." Wolfe said, extending his hand toward Babyface, who was almost within reach. Terri saw what Wolfe was planning and prepared herself.

"Death," the specter said as he grabbed Wolfe's hand in a vice-like grip. "Call me Mister Death, *Mister* Wolfe."

Wolfe froze for a micro-second as he realized that the hulk knew his name. Looks like I'm busted, he thought. Wolfe stared into the menacing grin. Then he suddenly jerked back, pretending to pull away. Babyface tightened his grip, and yanked Wolfe toward him, an evil look of anticipation on his face. But as he did so, Wolfe extended the knuckles of his left hand and drove them deep into the specter's throat.

Babyface released Wolfe's hand, his unbandaged eye bulging as he began clawing at his crushed windpipe, futilely trying to get air to his lungs. Flailing his arms in panic, he tried to run outside, as if the open air could somehow magically enter his lungs. Babyface ran to the curb, crashing his formidable body against the side of Terri's car, then slowly slumped to the ground.

Wolfe walked over to where he lay, and stared down at his now blue face. *Baby blue*, Wolfe thought with no feeling. His gaping mouth and unseeing eye were grotesque, frozen in a sculpture of terror.

Terri rushed to his side, not wanting to look—unable to stop herself. "Is he . . ."

"He is," Wolfe said as he took her arm and started back toward the house.

Terri stopped him. "He called you Wolfe."

"Yes, he did."

"Then they know you're still alive."

"I would presume so," he said as he began walking again. "I guess the charade is over."

"This is not good."

"No it's not," he said as he picked up the pace. "C'mon. Let's finish checking the house before the police arrive. I have a feeling we're going to find Professor Frankel somewhere in there."

"I hope he's in better shape than Babyface."

"Judging from those bloodstains on his clothes, I'd say the prognosis is less than favorable."

chapter 29

Wolfe was the first to find Professor Leo Frankel.

"In here," he shouted to Terri.

"Where are you?" she called from another room upstairs.

"In the master bedroom—at the end of the hall," he said. "Better brace yourself though. It's not pretty."

Terri walked to the other end of the hall and into the master bedroom. Professor Frankel was lying on the floor, his face bleeding and swollen. His hair was matted on the right side of his head where the blood was attempting to clot over a huge gash. Blood was seeping from both ears.

"Is he still alive?" she asked, almost not wanting to know.

"Yes," Wolfe said as he knelt over the professor, "but not for long." Terri turned away, nauseous.

Wolfe knelt over the professor. "He's regaining consciousness." Terri watched as Wolfe leaned closer. "Can you hear me?" he asked.

Frankel's eyes opened briefly, then closed, then opened again. He seemed to be trying to say something, his mouth working at the words. But nothing came out.

"Professor Frankel," Wolfe said softly. "I'm Clayton Wolfe.

I'm here with Terri Sommers, Kevin's sister. We know Kevin was working on something for you—something very important. We think the person who did this to you is somehow connected with Kevin's work."

Wolfe stopped, watched the professor as he struggled to speak—but again nothing came. "Professor," Wolfe continued, "a lot of people have already died because of Kevin's work. We need to find out what he was working on. Did you find his papers after you called Terri this morning?"

Terri, agitated, said, "I'm calling 911," and turned away to make the call.

The professor became agitated, shook his head no. "Do you have any idea where he kept his papers—his research?" Wolfe continued. Professor Frankel shook his head again. He seemed more upset. He was trying to say something but the words wouldn't come out.

"Leave him alone," Terri said, after making the call. She could no longer watch. "Can't you see you're just tormenting him? He can't talk yet you keep asking him questions. Wait 'til the ambulance arrives."

"Do you have pen and paper in your purse?" Wolfe asked, ignoring her statement.

Terri looked at him for a moment, then realized what he wanted to do. "Here's a pencil and my steno notebook," she said, handing the items to him.

Wolfe held up the notebook in front of the professor's face and said, "Can you write down anything that might help us, professor?" Tears began welling up in Leo Frankel's eyes as he raised his forearms. Wolfe thought he was reaching for the pencil and began to hand it to him when he suddenly looked in shock at the professor's hands. All of his fingers had been broken.

"Damn it!" Wolfe said in frustration. He turned toward Professor

Frankel as he tried to raise his head. "What is it, professor?" Wolfe said, listening intently. "What can you tell us?"

Guttural sounds emanated from professor Frankel's throat, his eyes wide with effort. Suddenly the guttural sounds took shape, and his mouth began to form a word. "Rmmmmm," he said through thick, swollen lips. He was obviously in great pain. Again he tried. "Rmmmmm."

Now both Wolfe and Terri were leaning over the professor, trying to figure out what he was saying. "Try again professor," Terri said intently. *"Please."*

Professor Frankel again lifted his head slightly and with great effort said, "Rmmmm . . . ooo . . . lt."

"Rmmmm . . . ooo . . . lt," Terri repeated. "I don't know what it means."

"Me either," said Wolfe.

Terri was saying it over and over again to herself, when suddenly she said, "remület."

Professor Frankel's eyes widened, and he nodded. "Rmmmoolet." Suddenly his eyes rolled back in his head. Wolfe felt for a pulse, but in vain. "I'm afraid he's dead, Terri."

Terri turned away. "I can't believe this is happening," she said to Wolfe. "Everywhere we go people die. This is awful," she sobbed. "Just awful."

"I'm sorry Terri," Wolfe said. "Maybe we should turn this over to the authorities and pull you out of it. I can handle it from here."

Terri looked at him for a moment. "Clay, I know you're trying to protect me, but I'm capable of taking care of myself. I'll be OK, just give me a minute. I'm just not used to this stuff like you are."

Wolfe held her until she regained her composure. Then he said in a soft voice, "I understand."

Terri wiped her eyes and took a deep breath, then let it out. "I know it's dangerous, but I'm committed to this, even if it means I die trying. There is something evil here and it has to be stopped."

Wolfe looked at her intently. Terri's strength reminded him of someone in his past, long ago buried. Someone whose memory was too painful to recall. He quickly shook off the feeling and snapped back to reality. "If that's what you want," he said. "There's more work than one person can do, anyway."

"Then that's settled," she said, pleased she had made her point.

"And now maybe you can tell me what this word is you recognized from Professor Frankel's last gasp," Wolfe challenged. "It was gibberish to me."

Terri smiled. "I didn't actually recognize it," she began. "I just tried to parrot back what he was attempting to say."

"Then you don't know what it means."

"I didn't say that, either," she said, enjoying her momentary advantage. "I was stationed for a short while in Budapest, Hungary, on assignment. While there, I picked up a few words and phrases. One of them sounded like the word the professor was trying to say."

"And?"

"Loosely translated," she continued, "remület means terror."

"Terror?" he said, surprised.

"As best as I can figure, that's correct."

"You think he meant it was terrorists?"

"I don't think so," Terri said, running her fingers through her hair. "I think he was trying to say the name of something. A group, or a person—maybe a thing. I don't know. I told you I just picked up a little while I was there."

"Well we can check it out easily enough," Wolfe said. "In the meantime, we'd better keep digging. I've got a real bad feeling about this Hungarian word for terror."

chapter 30

"And what is the Hungarian word for murder?" came a voice from behind them. They both spun around to find Sheriff Ed Josephs standing in the doorway. Wolfe recovered almost immediately.

"Good of you to show up, constable," Wolfe said, still clinging to the facade. "At just the right time too, I might add. Bloke seems to 'ave met the Grim Reaper."

"I'd say he had someone introduce him," the sheriff said as he looked at the body. "And now it seems appropriate to ask who you are and what circumstances brought you to the dead professor's house, or more to the point, to the dead professor."

"Ah yes," began Wolfe. "Well you see . . ."

"Thank you, Winslow," Terri cut in, joining him in the subterfuge, "but I can answer for myself." Wolfe looked startled at her interruption, then settled into uncomfortable silence as she continued. "We came over to Professor Frankel's house to retrieve some papers he had—papers belonging to my brother who died recently."

"Ahh. You're the one," Sheriff Josephs said.

"I'm not quite sure what you mean by *the one*, sheriff," she responded, "but the professor did have a project my brother was working on, and I simply came over to retrieve it."

"And did you find what you were looking for?"

"What we found," she replied, "was that hulk outside who tried to kill us, and the professor here, as you see him."

"Except that when you found him he was alive," Josephs said, looking at her intently.

"Barely," she responded.

"And of course you immediately called for an ambulance and notified the authorities when you found him," the sheriff pursued.

"Well, not immediately," Terri said.

"No, I guess you wouldn't have had time for that," he continued. "Not with having to kill that fellow out on the front lawn, then come in here and pump the dying professor for information about your brother's college project."

"Look, sheriff," Terri began, "I know this doesn't look great on the surface

But . . ."

"Miss, it doesn't look great on the surface, underneath or on the sides. You'll pardon me if I don't jump for joy at your answers, but ever since you've come here I've had a rash of dead bodies that you seem to be involved with one way or another, and that's just not healthy. People here frown on that sort of thing. People who elected me. They kinda wish I'd do something about all this. Think I'm out of line so far?"

"Of course not," she began. "It's just that . . ."

"I'm afraid you and your limey lackey are going to have to come in for questioning," Josephs cut in, motioning them toward the door. "I hope you have some good answers."

Wolfe bristled at the last, but said nothing as they left the room.

Sheriff Edward Josephs sat behind a large, mahogany desk in his spacious office. Wolfe watched as he leaned back in his worn, leather swivel chair, steepling his fingers as he did so. His hands rested on his belly which was uncharacteristically flat for a sheriff in his forties, though his trimmed moustache was now salt and pepper, as was his short-cropped hair. He wore a brown suit with an appropriate tie, and Wolfe could see his sidearm peeking out behind the right side of his coat. The office looked clean and modern, with freshly painted walls, a couple of tasteful paintings, beige carpet, and two leather chairs, in which sat Terri and Wolfe.

Suddenly, the office door opened and in stepped the gangly coroner. "Mind if I join you, Sheriff?" he asked, still not quite in the room.

Josephs appraised Eino for a moment, then decided. "C'mon," he said, waving Eino in. "Sorry there's no more chairs, but . . ."

"No problem, Sheriff," Eino cut in. "I'll just stand here and listen. Most of my work's done standing up anyway," he said, smiling.

Sheriff Josephs just shook his head. "That's fine." The room was silent. Josephs seemed to be gazing off in the distance, focused on something light years away. Finally he leaned forward, and began spinning the blade of a pewter helicopter that sat on his desk. He spun it several times, each time seemingly surprised that it didn't lift off and buzz around the room.

"Any reason why I shouldn't charge you both with two counts of homicide?" he said finally. He stopped spinning the blade and sat up, looking at both of them in turn, ignoring Eino.

"Yes, there is," Terri said.

"And what pray tell might that be?" Josephs said.

"Because we didn't do it," she said, leaning forward in her chair. "Haven't you been listening to a word I've been saying?"

"I have. But why should I believe you?"

"Because it's the truth," she said.

"And how do I know that?"

"Because they're lying," Eino said.

"Lying?" said Josephs. "Who's lying?"

"This man isn't Drake Winslow," Eino continued, pointing toward Wolfe. "Don't you recognize him?"

Josephs leaned forward a little more and focused on Wolfe. His vision had gotten worse over the years, but he refused to wear glasses, so he began squinting. "Then who are you?" he said, looking at Wolfe.

Wolfe smiled and dropped the accent. "Your old fishin' buddy, Sheriff. I guess my disguise worked."

"Wolfe?" he started. "Is it really you? Why are you trying to fool me?"

"He's not trying to fool you, Sheriff," said Terri. "People have been trying to kill him, and me too, and he thought that if the killer or killers thought him to be dead, he would be free to investigate without having to watch over his shoulder all the time."

"And this woman has also been perpetrating a lie," Eino said turning to Terri.

"That so?" said Josephs.

"Yup," Eino said. "They've been living together in sin, too, I might add."

Josephs relaxed a bit, the trace of a smile gracing his countenance for the first time. "In sin? In *sin*?" he repeated with mock gravity. "Well, that tears it. Looks like hard time to me—don't you think, Eino?"

"The hardest," Eino said, now smiling.

"Welcome back from the dead, Wolfe," Sheriff Josephs said, rising from his chair. "You shoulda told me though, Wolfe. I could have been helping you."

"I know," said Wolfe. "It all happened so fast. I was running for my life, but I didn't know who was chasing me."

The Sheriff didn't seem too worried, saying, "O.K. Then why

don't you fill me in on everything, so we can pool resources and find out what the hell's going on?"

"Sounds good," Wolfe said. "I don't think we know how bad this all is, but you're in."

"Me too," Eino chimed in, looking for all the world like a puppy eager to go for a ride in the car. "I'm *already* involved."

"Fine," said Josephs. "You too."

chapter 31

S everal hours and countless cups of coffee later, everything had
been laid out in detail from beginning to end. They had moved
to the Sheriff's lounge where a cloud of smoke now hung, half-ob-
scuring its occupants. Less sumptuous than his office, the place
still was professional, though the leather chairs were replaced with
vinyl and the table tops with Formica.

"So where do we go from here?" Terri asked.

"Wherever we go, we go carefully," said Josephs. "We've got
to act together and keep each other informed."

"And we've got to keep our electronic communications to a
minimum," Wolfe added. "We'll need to develop a code for when
we do have to use the phone and stick to it."

"Agreed," said Eino.

"I'll work on the code," said Wolfe. "In the meantime, we've
got to track down Kevin's body. Assuming it hasn't been destroyed,
we still may be able to learn something from it—sorry Terri, but it
has to be done," he said turning to her.

"I understand," she said stoically.

"I'll try to track down the body," Eino said."

"You do that," Josephs said. "In the meantime, I'll keep tabs on all the deaths in the area and investigate the circumstances surrounding each. The bodies themselves you'll have to deal with, Eino."

"No problem. I'll run additional tests on each one that comes into the morgue," Eino said. "In the meantime, when you folks get a better idea of what I should be looking for, let me know."

"We will," said Terri. "And I'll see what I can come up with through my channels on any government cover-ups. The ruckus in Washington—the EPA connection—NSA—anything that might be remotely connected. I'll tell my editor I'm onto the story of the century."

"You may be," Eino said.

Terri took a notepad out of her purse and flipped it open. As she did so, the envelope the professor's secretary had given her fell onto the floor. Reaching down, she picked it up and stared at it. "I'd totally forgotten about this," she said as she opened it.

"What's that?" Sheriff Josephs asked.

"It's a statement or something from Kevin's bank," Wolfe said. "It was forwarded to the University after he died."

"That's right," said Terri. "It's a bank service fee. It seems it was set up to be an automatic withdrawal every six months but his account didn't have enough funds to cover the fee."

"What's the fee for?" Wolfe asked.

Terri looked at Wolfe. "A safety deposit box."

They all stared at her for what seemed like an eternity. "Do you think?" she began.

"Makes perfect sense," said Wolfe. "Did you know he had a safety deposit box?"

"No," she said. "No one did, as far as I know. He never had anything valuable enough to put in it."

"Until now," finished Josephs.

"We'd better find out what's in it," said Eino. "It might be what we're looking for."

"And it might be our death sentence," Wolfe said.

"That's right," said Terri. "The fact that we haven't yet found his papers has been our only insurance policy."

"At least that's the theory," added Wolfe.

"Nonetheless," said Josephs, "if his papers are indeed in the box, and that has been what 'they' have been waiting for, well . . . I think we've already seen what they're capable of. I suggest we approach this very cautiously."

Terri began tapping her pencil on the table. "I think we can get what's in the box and still not put our lives in too much jeopardy—at least for a while." All eyes were on her.

"You have the floor," Josephs offered.

Terri stood and began walking around the table. "First, we write down everything we know or suspect about ELF and the people involved and make multiple copies. Second, if we do find Kevin's papers in the safety deposit box, we add whatever damaging evidence we find, as well as references to other material, and send a copy by certified mail to my editor. And then we call my editor to say the materials will be coming by mail."

Eino scratched his head. "Why do all that?"

"Because," Josephs said as he stood up, "announcing the material is on its way will be transmitted by phone over the airwaves and will be picked up by the NSA or whoever's monitoring us."

"There'll be handy references to the EPA and other red-flagged words, no doubt," added Wolfe.

"That's correct," said Terri. "They're sure to pick up on it and know we found Kevin's papers."

"So what's to keep them from killing us and taking the papers?" Eino asked.

Terri stopped pacing and looked at Eino. "Because along with this information will be a set of instructions detailing what to do with the reports should anything happen to us."

Eino was not convinced. "But what'll stop them from going to your editor and killing him and then taking Kevin's papers? I mean, I know that you think the press is sacred, but these people don't seem to have much regard for the sanctity of human life. I would think that freedom of the press ranks pretty low on their list."

Terri smiled. "I'm sure it does. But I don't think they'll do anything because there will also be references to other, unnamed people who are to be given the information as well. They won't know who else has it. Therefore, their only insurance policy is to keep us alive."

"Impressive," said Wolfe, "but when your editor really gets this information, he's going to go wild. You don't think he's going to just sit on a story like this, do you?"

"*She's* not going to do anything," Terri said looking at Wolfe. Wolfe just smiled. "The mail won't actually go to her. It'll go to my office. No one will look at it 'til I get back."

"What about the evening news?" said Josephs. "If it's on TV, it will be out there for everyone to see."

"I thought of that," said Terri. "But then we've lost all control. And they have no need of us. As soon as it's out, we become completely expendable."

"Right," said Wolfe. "With us gone and nobody with any direct knowledge around to substantiate it, they can wage a smear campaign to discredit us and taint everything that was sent out. We'd look like fanatics, and all of our families would be tainted forever."

"I see your point," said Josephs.

"We want them to think we're scared, said Terri. "We'll say that in the message. Even though we think that what they're doing is horrible, we know our lives are at stake, so we're building an insurance policy. We're trading our lives for their secret."

"Very self-serving," said Josephs.

"Absolutely," said Terri. "Something I'm sure they'll understand."

"What's the real reason?" Wolfe asked Terri.

"The real reason?" she said.

"Why we're not spilling the beans now—taking it public?"

"Because we're scared," said Eino.

"That's right," said Terri. "Plus we don't have all the facts, and we haven't found my brother." Everyone looked at Terri. "If we blow the whistle now, we may never uncover the truth behind this conspiracy."

"The trick is to make this very believable," said Eino.

"That is the trick," Wolfe said. "And it isn't going to be easy. We're dealing with partial facts, suppositions, nameless people from nameless organizations involved in some unheard of project that's scaring the hell out of everyone who thinks it's going to leak out."

"Maybe even the Department of Defense is involved," said Terri.

"The DOD?" Josephs said.

"Yes," said Wolfe. "Didn't I mention that when I was talking about the incident with Senator Phillips?"

"No, you didn't," Josephs responded gruffly. "Perhaps you'd better elaborate." Wolfe filled them in on his conversation in the Georgetown bar.

"Well that puts a whole new light on things," Josephs said when Wolfe finished.

"What do you mean? Terri asked. Everyone's attention was focused on the sheriff.

"I mean, I think I know what the tie-in might be. Let's see what's in that box. If I'm right, we're in deeper shit than you ever imagined."

chapter 32

Terri decided she should go to the bank alone. She had to show the papers to the bank personnel anyway, so that as executor of the estate she could claim Kevin's belongings.

As Terri approached the bank, she was more nervous than before. So much was at stake, including their lives. Terri entered the bank and glanced around. It was similar to her bank in the way it was laid out, but it was a local bank, not national like her own. She was nervous, holding the new briefcase, afraid any minute someone would challenge her and the scheme would be blown. The wait for verification seemed interminable.

Finally, after what seemed like hours, a bank officer came over and handed her the key to the safety deposit box. Terri followed him into the vault to her brother's safety deposit box. The bank officer put his key in and then Terri put her key in, and they both unlocked the deposit box door and opened it. Then the bank official removed his key.

Terri pulled the long black box out of the wall and took it over to the table in the middle of the room. She set it down, then looked over at the bank officer. The bank officer stood there looking at her for several awkward seconds. Terri just looked at him, indicating her need for privacy. She began to wonder why he wasn't leaving. Finally the bank officer gave a feeble smile, then turned and walked out of the room.

Taking a deep breath, Terri flipped the clasp up which held the lid down, and swung it back. Inside there were two hard-covered three-ring notebooks—one red and one blue. Her hands now shaking, she removed the notebooks one at a time and set them on the table. Then she put the empty box back in the slot and shut the door, removing her key as she did.

Since there was nothing on the outside of the notebooks to signify their contents, she picked the blue one up and opened it. The first page was a title page, and read, "AN ANALYSIS OF ELECTROMAGNETIC RADIATION IN THE EXTREMELY LOW FREQUENCY RANGE—ITS USES AND EFFECTS ON ANIMALS AND VEGETATION INDIGENOUS TO THE UPPER PENINSULA OF MICHIGAN". Several lines below the title, she read, "by Kevin Sommers."

Tears began to well in her eyes, and she quickly closed it and went to the red notebook. In there she found nothing of a formal nature. It was filled with notes, mostly handwritten, raw data charts, and clippings from local newspapers. Terri closed the notebook and put them both in the briefcase.

As she left the bank it seemed all eyes were on her, but Terri knew it was probably just her imagination. She got into her car and began driving the pre-determined route. Sheriff Josephs had the bank under surveillance and watched as she left to see if anyone was following her. Not seeing anyone, he pulled in behind her, keeping a discreet distance from her car. At the stoplight at Lincoln and Washington, he disabled his car, blocking traffic behind him.

Popping the hood, Josephs pretended to look at the engine, while actually watching to see if any driver behind him tried any extraordinary maneuvers to catch up to Terri. Noting none, he cleared after a few minutes and returned to the jail.

Wolfe had picked up Terri just past the road block and followed her, completing a similar maneuver. Again, nothing out of the ordinary was observed. Feeling fairly certain she had not been followed, Wolfe met up with her at a third pre-determined location and signaled her to return to the sheriff's department.

Terri drove her car to the entrance of the security garage used by police agencies to bring prisoners to the jail. The external video camera recorded her arrival and Josephs activated the electronic garage door. Once safe inside, the door was secured. Wolfe led her from the garage to the lounge where they had previously met, and which had now been informally dubbed, "the situation room".

Terri walked in and sat down at the table. The smoky haze from their previous session was still lingering, but the faces were different. Instead of confusion there was intensity—an almost tangible excitement as she sat down and opened her briefcase. Without fanfare, she took the two notebooks out and laid them on the table. "Electromagnetic radiation and its effect on living organisms," she said matter-of-factly.

"Let me see those," Josephs said, reaching for the red notebook.

"Take this one," Terri said, shoving the blue one into his reach instead. Sheriff Josephs took the blue notebook, opened it and read the title page. "I knew it!" he exclaimed. "It's that damn ELF project of the Navy's."

"The Navy . . ." Terri repeated. "This is *so* not good. I mean, it's one thing to speculate that the DOD might be involved. To have it confirmed . . ." She shook her head. "We are in deep doo-doo."

"Let's begin by checking out Kevin's papers," said Josephs. "If they are what we think they are, we'll have to begin the next phase of our plan as soon as possible."

"That's right," said Eino. "Let me take a look at Kevin's papers too. Might help me with my analysis of the bodies." But Sheriff Josephs was already deep into the paper.

"Looks like Ed's our man," said Eino, as he watched Josephs tear in to the notebook.

"Fine," said Terri. "Clay and I will go over our plans while you two review the material."

"Let us know when you're done, eh?" Wolfe said, mocking Eino's Finnish accent.

Eino looked up at Wolfe with his vulture's stare. "Just remember—I always get the last laugh. In fact, I'll make sure they put on your tombstone, 'Here lies Clayton Wolfe—he was a dandy, eh?'"

"You do that Eino, and I'll have you stuffed and mounted in the lobby of the Holiday Inn as an ancient relic. You'll go well with the Nordic theme of the bar," Wolfe said, laughing as he left the room. Eino yelled something else after him but he couldn't hear what it was. Probably best that way, thought Wolfe.

chapter 33

Wolfe arrived at the Paquette brothers' cabin shortly after Eino's telephone call. He had been right. The place was a mess. Set back from a long unused logging trail in northwestern Marquette County, the cabin could have easily been mistaken for one built by early French settlers. But the Paquette brothers had built it themselves over twenty years ago, a testimony that the old techniques were as relevant today as they were a century ago.

The quiet peacefulness of the wooded scene stood in stark contrast to the carnage Wolfe now surveyed in the one-room log cabin. What was left of the Paquette brothers was being carefully examined by Eino and Sheriff Josephs as Wolfe entered the cabin. "Glad you could join us," Eino said without looking up. He was bent over the remains of Emil Paquette, the younger of the two brothers.

"The pleasure's all mine," Wolfe responded. "What the hell happened?"

"You tell me," Josephs said. "We got a call from Emil's ex-wife that he hadn't shown up at the grocery store for his daily purchase of beer and pasties in over two days. When you're as regular as clockwork for five years running, a two-day absence is cause for concern."

"She thought there might have been a hunting accident or something," Eino added, "so she asked Ed to check. When he got here he found this."

Wolfe saw Emil lying on the wooden floor of the room, his back propped up against the wall by the stone fireplace. Clutched in his hand was a hatchet covered with blood. Part of the red plaid flannel shirt had been torn from his chest by a shotgun blast, a gaping hole where his heart used to be.

His brother Leo fared no better. He lay on his back in the center of the room, eyes fixed on the timbers above, a neat split opening his forehead vertically. Blood was everywhere.

The contents of the cabin told Wolfe the story. There had been a long, ferocious fight before their deaths. Furniture was overturned, lamps broken, pieces of glass strewn throughout the room.

"Let me guess the scenario," Wolfe said finally. "One of the brothers said or did something to irritate the other. Shouting quickly turned to physical violence, as evidenced by the numerous minor cuts and swelling on their faces." Wolfe paused, then continued. "Finally, Emil grabbed the hatchet and ran to split his brother's head open.

"Leo, in turn, grabbed the always-loaded shotgun from the brackets off the wall and swung it around, aiming it at Emil's chest. How'm I doin' so far?" Wolfe asked, watching the two continuing their examinations, both studiously ignoring him.

"Great," Wolfe said with mock enthusiasm. "Then I'll continue. By this time Leo had gotten his finger on the triggers—there are two on the double-barreled shotgun, aren't there?" Wolfe asked rhetorically. "Well, as I said, Leo had gotten his finger on the triggers, but not before the momentum of the hatchet carried it deep into his face.

"Unfortunately for Emil," he continued, "at the same moment, his chest reached the end of the shotgun barrel and Leo's last reflex jerked both triggers. The resulting force blew Emil back against the wall and Leo onto his back in the middle of the floor. All in all, not the prettiest sight I've ever seen."

"Not bad, for a civilian," Josephs said as he walked over to Wolfe. "I'd say you're pretty much on the money. The big question is, why?"

"Why not?" said Eino. "This stuff happens all the time. Liquor, rivalry, cabin fever—any number of things can set off violent behavior in a confined environment. People do strange things," he finished.

"Nothing to indicate an intruder was involved?" offered Wolfe. "Tried to set this up to look like fratricide?"

"No," said Josephs, "I don't think so. At least there's no evidence we can find—no tire tracks, footprints, fingerprints—nothing to indicate anything else happened other than what you surmised. The only thing that bothers me is, why now?"

"What do you mean?" Wolfe asked.

"These brothers have been living together out here for twenty years—other than the short stint when Emil took an unsuccessful stab at domestic life—and they've never had any problem getting along."

"Maybe it was a woman," suggested Eino.

"I don't think so," Josephs responded. "This is a pretty small town. If there was something going on between one or other of the Paquette brothers and a woman in town, I would have heard about it. Those guys have had a reputation for being oddballs all their lives. It was news when Emil started seeing Jeanie, his ex-wife—and it would be news now. They're well-known and equally well-gossiped about."

"Well," said Wolfe, "if we've ruled out third parties, and cabin fever isn't likely to be a cause in the middle of summer, either they were drunk, or . . ."

"Or some other, unknown factor caused them to kill each other," Eino finished.

"Like, maybe, ELF?" said Wolfe.

"Maybe," Josephs responded pensively.

"But how?" Eino said.

"Eino," Josephs said as he walked to the door, "would you finish up with my deputies when they arrive? I've got some things to follow up on and I need to get started right away."

"Sure," said Eino. "I'll do tests on blood-alcohol-content to check that angle. Don't worry about the rest. I'll see to it."

"Thanks, Eino. See you later," Josephs said as he left.

"What d'ya think?" Eino said after the sheriff had gone.

"I think he may know what caused this," Wolfe said. "I *hope* he does. We sure don't need an epidemic of brutal homicides."

"No," said Eino, the image of bloodied corpses scattered throughout the County welling up in his mind. "We don't."

"Dead end on the bodies," Eino said as the four sat back in the situation room of the sheriff's department.

"Did you have to, Eino?" Terri said of the tasteless pun.

"Sorry," Eino said sincerely. "I forgot. He was your brother."

"Never mind," she said. "You couldn't locate either of them?"

"No leads," said Eino. He adjusted the wire-rimmed glasses further back on the bridge of his nose. "Everything was paid in cash. No signed receipts, no witnesses. I'm afraid wherever they are, they're going to remain until something more turns up."

"Well, I can see we're off to a good start," Terri said unhappily. "My news isn't much better. As far as I'm able to determine there are no experiments being conducted by the EPA in the Upper Peninsula, or anywhere around here, for that matter." Terri flipped a few pages in her notebook, then stopped. "As for the NSA, my sources tell me that finding out about any activity on their part is virtually impossible."

"Not surprising," Sheriff Josephs interjected, shifting around in his chair. "In fact, I'd have been mighty suspicious if you *had* found something. Those people guard information like it was the crown jewels."

"What about you, Wolfe?" Eino asked. "You turn up anything?"

"Not exactly," Wolfe said as he sat up straighter at the table. "I couldn't find out anything about Senator Phillips or the DOD connection. However," he continued before anyone could comment, "I did come up with a code for using electronic communications." Wolfe pulled three copies of several scrawled pages out of a leather valise and handed one to each. "Commit these to memory as soon as you can. They are the only copies in existence. As soon as you have them memorized, return them to me and I'll destroy them. They're relatively simple, but effective. Any questions?"

"Yes," said Terri. "I have one."

"And what's that?" Wolfe responded warily, noting the not-so-innocent look on her face.

"If the NSA is such a great electronic spying machine, aren't they going to crack your code fairly easily?"

"Sometimes the simplest codes are the hardest to break," Wolfe responded. "When there's limited information to communicate, the cracker jack box codes can sometimes be the best."

"Well I have something that doesn't need decoding," Josephs said, twisting the ends of his moustache.

"What is it?" Terri asked.

"There's information here I'm sure the Navy would not want made public."

chapter 34

Josephs opened Kevin's notebook. "First he starts out with a general description of what ELF is. I'll summarize the salient points." Josephs leaned over the notebook, his fingers and eyes scanning the first page in speed reading fashion.

"ELF stands for extremely low frequency electromagnetic radiation," he began.

"We know that," Eino piped in impatiently.

"Let him go on," Terri cut in. "This may be basic to you, but I'm starting from scratch."

"Go ahead, Sheriff," Wolfe agreed. "Start with the basics—just to make sure we're all on the same wavelength." Terri looked at Wolfe with the 'how could you' expression, but Josephs continued on undaunted.

"And speaking of wavelengths," Josephs said, addressing Wolfe as a schoolmaster would an errant pupil, "that's what this is all about. Wavelengths of the electromagnetic spectrum. The electromagnetic spectrum is made up of waves of varying frequencies," he said, reaching into his shirt pocket and pulling out a hitherto unseen pair of glasses.

"I didn't know you wore glasses," said an astonished Eino.

"There's a lot of things you don't know, Eino," Sheriff Josephs said caustically.

"Now if I may be allowed to continue," he said looking around the room for any sign of further interruptions. Seeing none, he looked back down at the notes. "All radiation is in waves. The length of the wave determines what characteristics it exhibits.

"For example," he said leaning back in his chair, "light waves are part of this spectrum. They have a very high frequency compared to ELF waves. So are ultraviolet and x-rays, as well as short-wave radio waves and radar. They are all high frequency waves with extremely short wavelengths."

"What size wavelengths are we talking about?" Terri asked.

"At the high end they are extremely short. For example, an x-ray wave is from .01 to 10 nanometers. A nanometer is one-*billionth* of a meter."

"So," injected Eino, "short then."

Josephs just shook his head. "Right, Eino. Short."

"Just checking," said Eino, his version of a grin appearing on his face.

"So how long are the ELF waves?" Terri said, ignoring them both.

"That depends," continued Josephs. "Under one hundred Hertz, one wave could be hundreds, or thousands of miles long."

"Maybe you should explain what a Hertz is," Wolfe cut in.

"That's another name for frequency," Eino explained. "In the electromagnetic spectrum they call the number of cycles per second, *Hertz*, after the scientist who proved the wave theory of electromagnetism. One Hertz means one cycle per second. In general terms, a cycle is also called, a *sine wave.*"

"Thank you, Eino," Josephs said with mock gratitude.

"Not at all," Eino said. "Just wanted to put in my two cents worth."

"And so you have," said Josephs dryly. "At any rate," he continued, "we know the higher frequencies have their uses as well as their dangers. X-rays can be used for diagnostic purposes in medicine, but they can also cause cancer and kill you. Microwaves can cook your food—or cook *you*, if there aren't proper safeguards."

"Like radar," Wolfe offered.

"Radar's a good example," Josephs said. "Or any broadcast dish used for TV. If the power source is high enough, the waves can literally cook you from the inside out, just like your microwave oven. The waves are so short and the frequencies so high, that they excite the molecules in substances they come in contact with causing great friction and heat.

"On the other hand, the effects of lower frequencies are much less known, partly because there has been no apparent use for them, and partly because the waves are so long, it's hard to get an antenna long enough to receive them, or a power source strong enough to broadcast them."

"Until ELF," Terri said.

"Right," Josephs replied, leaning back in his chair. "One of the advantages of shorter waves is that by modifying the amplitude of the waves . . ."

"Which is your basic AM radio," Wolfe cut in.

"Correct," Josephs said. "Amplitude modulation of radio wave frequencies is how AM radio is broadcast and received. That's what AM stands for—amplitude modulation. And, since we're using this example," he shot a look at Wolfe, "the modulation of the *frequency* of the radio wave is what FM radio does. It modulates or changes the frequency of the wave to transmit sound."

"So what does this have to do with ELF?" Terri asked.

"The purpose of ELF, at least as far as we are lead to believe," Josephs continued, "is to allow land-based naval personnel to communicate with their submarines without the requirement that they surface. High frequency waves can contain greater amounts of information, but they lack the capability of penetration. That is, they bounce off solid surfaces or liquids. In the event of a war or other emergency, the only way to communicate with the subs is to have them come close enough to the surface to raise an antenna, which exposes them to attack."

"But how do you tell them to come to the surface to get a message?" Terri countered.

"Precisely," Josephs acknowledged. "You can't. Therefore, the subs have to surface—or nearly surface—frequently, to see if there is a message being transmitted to them."

"And in the event of a nuclear war," Wolfe added, "it would be too late."

"That's right," Josephs said, taking off his glasses. "A nuclear war could be over in one hour, start to finish. Enemy missiles could be over the continental United States within twenty minutes of launch. Our counter-missiles would have been launched within minutes of confirmation of the launch of enemy missiles. Within thirty to forty minutes of the initiation of the first launch, all missiles would have been launched and reached their target."

"So, unless the submarines were near the surface at the time of the attack . . ." began Eino.

"There might be no one left to send a message," finished Wolfe.

"Even if there were an automatic message sender which was activated at the first moment of launch," continued Josephs, "the atmosphere would be so disrupted by electromagnetic impulses from the nuclear explosions that the message would never get through. It would be like trying to whisper to a friend on the other side of an auditorium during a rock concert."

"So ELF lets the subs stay down where they are protected to receive instructions at any time in the event of an attack?" Terri summarized.

"Pretty much," said Josephs, as he sat back in his chair and again began twisting the ends of his moustache again. "It can't send much information, but a short code for a pre-arranged message would give them enough to launch a counter-strike. After that, it's anybody's guess."

"So what about the effects we've been witnessing?" Terri asked. "How do they tie in with ELF?"

"I think what we're saying," Wolfe said, looking at Josephs, "is that there may be another purpose for ELF, at least for some people, in addition to communicating with submarines."

"He's right," said Josephs, staring at the wall. "It looks like it may have a dual purpose, though it may have been unintentional."

Terri thought for a minute. Then, looking at Josephs, "You mean these effects might be accidental?"

"Could be," said Josephs. "But there could also be a group within the Navy or other parts of the government that has found another use for ELF."

Wolfe jumped in. "It could be that this group, if it exists, has been conducting experiments without the knowledge of the higher echelon."

"I suppose that's possible," Eino added. "But the next question is, why?" Josephs twisted his moustache even tighter. "And who?"

chapter 35

"OK," Wolfe began. "So what else is in Kevin's notebook? Josephs repositioned his glasses atop the bridge of his nose and continued. "He quotes some research from a scientist by the name of Zimmermann. Let's see. Says here, the ELF band below 100 Hertz has the most hazardous frequencies."

"Hazardous to whom?" Terri asked.

"Animal life," Josephs responded, flipping a page. "It seems the low frequency waves affect a lot of things which regulate the biological processes of living things, particularly animals."

"But didn't the Navy conduct a lot of tests on the effects of ELF on plants and animals?" Eino asked. "In fact, they came out and said there were no adverse effects on plant life and negligible effects on animal life, if I recall."

"They did research," Josephs said, his nose buried in Kevin's notebook, "but not directly. They contracted most of it out to the private sector, much the way they do military hardware design and development."

"That way they could distance themselves from the results of the tests if they were challenged," Eino concluded.

Josephs nodded. "Undoubtedly."

Terri stood up and started pacing. "Maybe the results showed something else. Maybe they showed there *were* adverse effects on animals, and they wanted to hide them to avoid a public outcry."

"Or maybe the Navy wasn't told about the adverse effects," Wolfe added. They all looked at Wolfe. "Maybe these private researchers are the 'group' we have been hypothesizing."

There was silence as his words sank in. Then Eino spoke. "But what about the NSA and the EPA and all the other groups we've said are involved?"

Wolfe shrugged. "I don't know. It seems far-fetched that persons from all those agencies would be working together on a conspiracy to subvert ELF without the legitimate authorities knowing about it. But it's a possibility we shouldn't eliminate out of hand."

Josephs returned to the notebook. "Well it appears, at least, that there was some selectivity in reporting test results, if not in conducting them. It says here that there were detailed reports on the effects of ELF waves on the lower forms of animal life, but they did their studies on small animals."

"I remember the press release," Eino said. "I think it was worms, fish, insects—stuff like that."

"Right," Josephs continued. "And according to Kevin, those results were probably pretty accurate." He stood up, stretched his arms, and began pacing.

"So where's the problem?" Terri interjected. "Why hide their research if there's no adverse effects?"

"Because there *are* adverse effects," Josephs said, removing his glasses and rubbing his eyes. "Kevin cites more studies. Here." Josephs again donned his spectacles. "Kevin states that ELF waves have a greater effect on larger animals than smaller ones. The larger the animal, the bigger the antenna and the greater effect. Also, he writes, ELF can interfere with the central nervous system, including development of the brain. It can also cause DNA damage, and have a negative effect on reproduction."

"Damn!" Eino exclaimed. "What the hell are they tryin' to do?"

"Maybe this *group* is working on some kind of brainwashing," Terri said. "Or maybe population control?"

"It doesn't go that far, at least in his notes," Josephs responded.

"What are the frequencies of the human brain?" she asked.

"Ah, let's see." Josephs ran his finger down several pages until he found what he wanted. "OK. The human brain functions on frequencies from zero, which is no wave at all, up to about twenty Hertz."

"Our electrical appliances operate on a frequency of sixty Hertz, to give you a reference point," Eino chimed in. "Maybe that's why there was so much uproar over the problems ELF was causing with the electrical power lines and interference with television, radios, and toasters when it first started."

"What problems?" Terri asked.

"Oh, there were some real problems with appliances at first," he continued, enjoying the temporary limelight. "Still are, for that matter. TV pictures had lines running through them, and you could hardly hear the radio in some areas—AC-powered, that is. Microwave ovens got fried, and toasters would come on all by themselves."

Josephs leaned forward, tapping his pencil on the table. "That would lead me to believe that they're operating in the sixty cycle range."

Wolfe nodded. "Maybe the legitimate operations *are* in the sixty cycle range."

Terri looked at Wolfe. "Are you inferring that this group could be using ELF in the lower range?"

"Maybe. If they had the right positions, they could be changing the frequency for their own purposes."

"I don't know," Terri said. "This seems like a lot to swallow.

There'd have to be a lot of key people involved. I think that'd be pretty hard to pull off."

Josephs leaned back in his chair and steepled his hands under his chin. "You could be right. But then, as Wolfe said, let's keep the option open."

"So what are the effects of these brain-level ELF waves?" Terri said as she left the table and poured the remnants of her coffee into the stainless steel sink. "What do they do?"

"It doesn't say," Josephs said, closing the notebook. "But he does give some references he was planning to check. Doesn't look like we'll know if he ever did, though."

chapter 36

The gray-green swells of Lake Superior bounced Scott Frazier's small boat around like a cork in a bathtub. The sudden wind had raised the gentle two-foot waves to four-foot whitecaps and he was getting a little nervous. He knew about the capricious nature of the lake and how a storm could instantly appear out of a clear blue sky. That's why he had stayed relatively close in toward shore. He knew that if he capsized, he could swim the mile or so to the marina without too much trouble.

Still, the sky was becoming more menacing by the minute. Scott opened the throttle full as the thirty-five horse power outboard struggled to climb, then descend the perilous mountains of water. Suddenly, halfway up a threatening whitecap, it broke over his bow, sending his craft immediately on its final quest to the bottom of the lake.

Scott wasted no time getting out of his clothes. Even though leaving them on would reduce the chances of hypothermia, they could also drag him down, and right now he needed speed more than warmth. Besides, he thought, the workout would be enough to keep him warm.

Taking a bearing on the lighthouse as he had done so often before, he began the long, rhythmic strokes that had won him his nickname on the university swim team—Night Crawler. Scott didn't mind. He had to swim at night so he could work during the day to pay his expenses and still have time to attend classes. Better that, than not swim at all.

As he swam, he thought of all the people afraid of sharks. Of course, there was no fear of Jaws in this freshwater lake, though he had heard the Coho salmon bred for game fishing years ago were getting good sized. He smiled at the thought of himself swimming underwater, his jaws wide, closing in for the kill on a Coho.

His mind drifted back to his high school days when his swim coach had been standing over him at the edge of the pool scream-ing at him to keep up the pace—to push himself past his best time, toward the school record.

He drifted back to the times after his workouts, when he was bone tired and he would come home and flop into bed without eat-ing. The soft mattress would engulf him, and his eyes would close and he would be asleep almost instantly.

And he would dream about swimming. And the more he dreamed, the more he swam. And the more he swam, the more he dreamed. And the pillow was so soft; and the mattress so inviting. And his head hit the pillow; and his eyes closed. And he dreamed about swimming.

The Coho salmon watched curiously as Scott's lifeless body settled slowly down through the cold, clear water, until it rested on the sand, two hundred feet from the surface with the four-foot whitecaps.

And in a windowless room not many miles away, a man reached up and flipped a toggle switch to the off position. ELF had had its test for the day.

chapter 37

"Where do we start?" Terri said as they stood in the reference area of the university library.

"You should know," Wolfe teased. "After all—you're the investigative reporter. How do you normally look up background information about a subject? Oh. I forgot," he said smiling, not waiting for an answer. "You make it up."

Terri refused to take the bait. "Here's half the references," she said, handing Wolfe one of Kevin's handwritten lists. "I'll use this terminal and you can use that one over there," she said, indicating the library computer terminal next to hers. "The reference desk will search the stacks for us if the sources are here."

"O.K.," said Wolfe. "I'll follow your lead." Wolfe watched her as she began typing the appropriate information into the Library Computer System. Suddenly Wolfe put his hands on the keyboard. "Stop."

"What?" she exclaimed, startled by his actions.

"Just . . . stop." Wolfe deleted her entry and reset the screen.

"What are you doing?" Terri exclaimed, looking at the blank screen. "What is the matter with you?"

"Is this library connected with other university or state librar-
ies?" he said softly.

"How would I know?" she said, staring at him. "Yes, I suppose
so," she answered. "Most are these days. What are you getting at?"

"What do you think Kevin did to look up his other sources—the
ones we have notes on?"

"He probably came here and used these terminals just as we . . ."
She stopped, her jaw suddenly slack. "You don't think . . ."

"Why don't we find out?" Wolfe cut in. They walked to the
reference desk and waited until an unenthusiastic student employee
acknowledged their presence at the desk.

"May I help you?" he managed to say, his tone connoting anything but a desire to help.

"Yes," Wolfe began politely. "Do you have a direct computer
link to any other library systems?"

The student looked at Wolfe like he was from Pluto. "Where
you been, man?" he said, chewing something Wolfe hoped was
gum. "Of course we're linked up. You think we got enough volumes
in this dinky library to meet all the bird-brained requests that come
in here each day?"

Ignoring the young man's rudeness, Wolfe continued. "I don't
suppose, in your infinite wisdom, you might happen to know the
names of the systems you're linked with, do you?"

"We got 'em all, man," he said. "Yeah. We're hooked into
the big mama outta Ohio. National Computer Library Network.
They're all hooked into that one. We can get 'bout any volume you
want. Quick, too. All electronic." He smiled as if he had made a
startling revelation. In a way, he had.

"Thanks. You've been a great help," Wolfe said as they left the
desk and walked back to the terminals.

"You think they got onto Kevin because he used the computer
to locate his source material?" Terri asked once they were out of
earshot.

"It's possible," Wolfe said. "If they're tied into NCLN, there's not much doubt that the NSA has the capability to enter and monitor all volumes being queried. Hell," he continued, "they probably even subscribe to the service."

"So what do we do—search the stacks by hand?"

"I'm afraid so," Wolfe said. "Not much different than what we had to do before computers."

"I wouldn't know," Terri said with a smile.

"Don't tell me. Before your time. Right?"

"I didn't say it."

"Hell you didn't," he said, putting his arm around her waist and walking toward the elevator. "Better hold onto the feeble old man. No telling where his feet might wander off to."

"It's not his feet I'm concerned about," she said, removing his hand from the position to which it had slipped.

chapter 38

The fishermen, if you could call them that, had had enough anti-freeze in them to ward off the most severe chill the lake could offer this time of year. The old thirty-foot boat with its spacious cabin and deeply weathered wood deck held four great pretenders plus a fishing guide who had guaranteed them their limit of lake trout for the two-hundred dollar charter fee. But the weather wasn't cooperating, and by late-afternoon they were only half-way to their limit.

"Gimme another line, cap'n," a white-haired man by the name of Harry Meetch slurred as he staggered out of his fishing harness and attempted to move from one stern-facing chair to another.

"What're you doin'?" shouted the leather-faced guide with the very Finnish name of Arno Toyja. He moved quickly over to Meetch who was about to go over the back of the boat. "Stay put!" Arno said, guiding him to the nearest chair. "The fish'll bite just as good over here as there." Arno fastened him safely into the harness.

"Bullshittt," Meetch slurred. "I know my poles, and that one's no damned good. Ain't had a damn bite all day."

Ain't been fishin' all day, moron, Arno said to himself. Guy comes out after drinking all morning, throws his pole in the water for half an hour and expects to get his limit. What a jerk, he thought as he checked first one line then another. There were four lines out now, two from the chairs directly off the stern, and one out each side—all with down-riggers, necessary when fishing at depths of two hundred feet or more.

Arno shuttled back and forth between the wheel and the lines making sure there was nothing on them. Hard to tell whether or not there's a fish on the line, he thought to himself. After all these years it was still hard to tell, even with a big lake trout hooked. Pulls like a log from that depth, he mused.

Just then Meetch's line became taut and the big pole began to bend. Then the ratchet sounded, unable to stop the line from pulling out against the carefully tensioned brake. "Told ya it'd work!" shouted Meetch as he began trying to reel it in.

"Hold it!" Arno shouted as he cut the engines, slowing the boat to a crawl. "Let me check the line." Arno went to Meetch's line and pulled slowly, steadily to see if he could feel the tell-tale tug of a fish fighting on the other end.

"C'mon," Meetch said, trying to jerk the line from Arno's grasp. "Let me reel it in. Gotta be a big one by the feel of it," he said, belching as he reeled up the slack and started to pull back on the pole.

"Damn it, Harry. I said hold it a minute. I don't think this is a fish. Must be hooked on a log," Arno said, pulling slowly up on the line with his hand. "There's no fight to it."

"Could be snagged on the bottom," one of the other great-pretenders said, pulling his orange coat tighter around him.

"Nope," said Arno. "She's comin' up slow but sure." Arno kept tension on the line as Meetch reeled in the slack.

"I think I see something!" shouted Meetch as he let go of the rod and freed himself of the harness to get a better look. Arno was now intently focused on the water as he continued steadily pulling up on the line. "I *see* it! I see it!" shouted Meetch, but Arno was silent. "Over there!" Meetch pointed to where the line disappeared into the water.

"It's huge," the other fisherman said as he watched a large, white form become visible. "What is it?"

But Arno already knew. He had seen it once before. Lake Superior had long been known for its reluctance to give up its dead. Acting as a giant, liquid ice box, it cooled its hapless victims below the point where gases form, sending them permanently to the bottom of the lake—where their lines were.

But Meetch had robbed the grave. They all stood transfixed in horror as the snagged leather watchband brought the blue, lifeless body of Scott Frazier bobbing to the surface.

chapter 39

"What a pain," Terri said as she replaced the last card index drawer. "I think if I had to do this for all my stories, I'd find another profession."

"I doubt it," Wolfe said, smiling slightly.

"I suppose you're right. It's the love of my life."

"I'd gathered."

"You find all yours?" she said, changing the subject.

"Just finishing the last one," Wolfe said, gathering up all his notes. "This is going to take a while without the help of the computer and the library staff."

"Then we'd better get started," she said with determination. "Where first?"

"How about we start with those farthest away and work our way back? That way we carry the heaviest load the least distance."

Terri looked at him quizzically. "What are you—an efficiency consultant or something?"

"Or something," Wolfe said.

The musty odor of aged parchment filled Terri's nostrils as they carefully searched out Kevin's material. It took her back to her college days and the many hours spent researching her favorite subject—American history. 'The past is the key to the future' she was once told by a professor who stole it from someone else. Someday she would have to get back to it. But not now, she thought.

"Here it is," she called to Wolfe, spotting one of the volumes they were looking for.

"Good," said Wolfe. "I've got two. I think that's all for this area."

"Third floor next?" she said, picking up her notebook.

"Third floor it is," Wolfe said as they walked to the elevator.

"How're we going to check these out?" Terri asked as they dumped their load on the reference desk.

"Damn," Wolfe said softly. "I hadn't thought of that. "You're right. As soon as he runs that reader over the computer numbers on each book, it'll be fed into the main system which lets everyone know which volumes are out and for how long."

"Will they be able to trace it to us?" Terri asked quietly.

"Probably," Wolfe said, turning to Terri. "How were you planning to check them out? Do you have a university library card or something?"

"No," she said with deliberation, "I figured you'd have one. After all—you *taught* here, didn't you?"

"Yes," he said, replying to her skeptical tone, "but that was only part-time. The card's good only for that semester."

"I know," she said excitedly.

"What?"

"Maybe I could use Kevin's card. It's still valid for the rest of the semester."

"Don't you think they would have deleted his name by now?" Wolfe asked.

They both looked as the cretin suddenly appeared from a door behind the desk, his forefinger probing deep within the recesses of his right nostril.

"I'm guessing 'No'," she said with disgust.

"Get Kevin's card," Wolfe said. "I'll wait here with the books."

"Back in a flash," she said as she hurried out the door.

"Looks like a normal drowning to me, Ed," Eino said as Sheriff Josephs stood looking down at the corpse. The shiny stainless steel examination table in the morgue stood in stark contrast to the bluish body of Scott Frazier. Debris from the boat and lake still clung to his lifeless body.

"I don't know," said Josephs. "Parents say he was a strong swimmer. They said he never ventured more than a mile from shore in that small boat. Should have been able to make it."

"Maybe it was hypothermia," offered Eino.

"Maybe," said Josephs. "Anyway—that's what you're going to find out. Right, Eino?"

"Do pigeons have lips?" the coroner said, already beginning the examination.

"Mmmmm," said Josephs, unsure just exactly what Eino meant.

"I s'pose it could be a heart attack," Eino said as he began cracking open the chest. "Get 'em younger these days."

"That surprises me," Josephs said, turning away slightly as Eino removed Scott's heart. "I'd think with all the exercise craze that . . ."

"It's not the exercise so much as the food that does 'em in," interrupted Eino as he weighed, then sliced open the heart. "It's the cholesterol. Marbled meat. Cheese on everything. Barbecued. Fried. Whole milk. You know—the health kick?" Eino looked up at Josephs and laughed. "Hah. Health kick my ass. What it really does is clog up the arteries. Then one day, bamm!"

"I see," Josephs said, not watching.

"Not this one though," Eino said after examining the heart. "This one's healthy as a horse."

"Was," Josephs said, taking a few steps back from the table.

"Of course," Eino said, now intent on the liver.

"How about a stroke?" Josephs said, facing the wall as if in contemplation.

"No thanks," Eino said without smiling. "Never touch 'em."

"Very funny," Josephs said dryly.

"Doubt it," Eino said, serious again. "About the stroke, I mean. But I'll find out. Always do. When I'm done, I'll know more about this boy than his own mother."

"Just find out what killed him, will you Eino?"

"I'll sure as hell try, Ed. Just give me some time."

"OK. I'm gonna leave you to your work," said Josephs. "Let me know what you find out. I'll do some more checking on the stats. Maybe there's a pattern here somewhere."

"You do that, sheriff," Eino said, his attention now focused on another organ. "I'll be in touch the minute I find anything."

Eino smiled slightly as Josephs hurried from the room, a sweat-dampened handkerchief clamped tightly over his nose and mouth.

chapter 40

"What're you doing out here?" Terri said as she approached the front doors of the university library. Then she noticed the books piled on the steps.

"How'd you get those out here without the card?"

Wolfe sat on the steps and smiled. "Magic," he said.

"All right. What's going on?"

"I found a back door open so I kinda went for a stroll."

"That's stealing. I got the card. We could have . . ."

"Been caught," he cut in.

"What?"

"Even if they hadn't deleted his name from the computer, Kevin would have shown up as having checked out the books. I'm not sure how things are now, being so old and all," he said with a straight face, "but the last time I saw a dead man check out a book . . ."

"So they know he's dead," she cut in. "We know that, they know that, and they know we know they know."

Wolfe gave her a double-take, then said, "Right. And since dead men don't check out books, who's the most likely person to have his card?"

"They'd know we found his notebook."

"And?"

"And that we were hot on the trail," she finished, shaking her head. "How could I have been so stupid?"

"Don't leave me out of this," he said, putting his arms around her waist. "I was about ready to do the same thing. I just had some time while waiting for you to think through what we were doing. At least we caught it in time."

Terri suddenly turned to face Wolfe and put her arms around his neck. She looked deep into his eyes and held his gaze.

"I guess I've been blinded by my emotions over Kevin's death," she said, her lips inches from his. "We haven't made love since that night at your cabin, and I am missing it."

Wolfe swallowed. "Me too," he said. "In fact, I'd like to do it again—soon."

"Are you sure?" she said, pulling her body tight against his. "How about right now?"

"You pick the strangest times to get . . ."

Terri cut the words off mid-sentence with a sudden, warm kiss. Then she smiled and said, "Later—at the cabin." Then she broke away, grabbed up the pile of books and said, "C'mon Wolfe. Let's do some research first."

Wolfe hesitated, looked down at his growing bulge. "Thanks a lot," he said, as he followed her to her car. "Your timing's *impeccable.*"

They went directly to Wolfe's cabin. Wolfe poured two glasses of Cabernet and started a fire in the fireplace. Terri sat cross-legged on the floor next to the stack of books, which was placed safely away from the fire that was now crackling as the hardwood became fully engaged. They worked in silence, reading all the materials as rapidly as they could, pausing periodically only for refreshments.

It was nearing midnight when Wolfe brought two mugs of hot coffee and sat them on the table. "Time for a break," he said, plopping down on the couch. "Let's review what we've found, if you don't mind. I don't think I can concentrate much longer. How about you?"

Terri finished a paragraph, marked her place, and looked up. "I think I am too, though I could probably go a little longer. But I agree. Let's take a breather and review, then we can decide what to do."

"I agree," he said. "How about you go first?" Wolfe settled back in the couch, and watched her intently.

"O.K.," she said, gathering up her notes and putting them in order. "It looks like most of Kevin's research was on frequencies lower than those the Navy is supposed to be using in ELF," she said, flipping the page of a large blue book. "Most of his was *under* thirty Hertz."

"That's interesting," said Wolfe. "Makes me wonder what they were really working on."

"Me too," said Terri."

"What else did you find?" asked Wolfe.

"More background," she said, pausing to review what she had written. "There is one bit of information that might have some bearing."

"What's that?" he responded.

"One study showed that when human subjects were exposed to a frequency of forty-five Hertz, that there was a decrease in cognition."

"That could explain some of the physiological effects in the victims we've been researching," said Wolfe.

"It sure could, said Terri." Makes me wonder what some of the effects of the other, lower frequencies might be."

"Maybe those will be in his research as well," said Wolfe.

"Let's hope," said Terri. "OK, now it's your turn," she said.

"I'm sorry," said Wolfe stretching. "Can we pick this up tomorrow? I'm kind of tired right now."

Terri smiled. "Sure. I think we both need a good sleep tonight."

chapter 41

The next morning, after showers and a quick breakfast, they started in again reviewing the research materials they got from the library.

"OK, let's hear about your research that you failed to give me last night," Terri said, stretching her arms as she sat up in the straight-backed chair in the kitchen.

Wolfe pulled out his notes and reviewed them for Terri. "Exposure to ELF wave lengths at ten Hertz over a period of time could cause headaches and fatigue; also, a tight feeling in the chest and sweating palms. And worse, sometimes hostility and even paranoia."

"What was the maximum length of time of exposure during the experiment?" Terri asked.

"A little over thirty minutes," Wolfe said.

"Hmm," said Terri. "I'm thinking about the Paquette brothers," she said, her stare fixed a thousand yards away.

"You think there might be a connection?"

"If you look at the evidence. I don't know. It's possible. They lived together all those years and never had that kind of trouble. You tell me."

"After reading that," he said nodding his head slowly, "I think it's possible. Maybe even probable if they were close enough to the antenna. You have any idea where the ELF ground terminals are in relation to the Paquette's camp?"

"You're ahead of me," Terri said. "What do you mean by ground terminals?"

"Sorry," he said. "Every so many feet along the length of the antenna which is buried several feet underground, a thing called a ground terminal penetrates the surface. This terminal contains high voltage, and can be deadly if you come in direct contact with it."

"Is that important to the wave field?" she asked.

"I'm not sure," he said, leafing through his notes. "But I do know that the closer one gets to the antenna, the stronger the field. It's also interesting to note," he continued, "that during the test period at Clam Lake, Wisconsin, most of the animal life left the area of the antenna grid—a fact which I'm sure accounted for the low count of animal hazards in the preliminary tests."

"If the animals aren't there they can't be affected," Wolfe finished.

"Right," said Terri. "The more I read, the more I see anomalies in the Navy's research methodology. At least the methodology we are allowed to review."

"I'd better get this information to Eino," Wolfe said, getting the keys to his car. "There may be some kind of test he can run using that frequency to check for any effect it may have had on the Paquette brothers."

Terri went back to her books. "I'll have some more for you when you get back."

"Right," said Wolfe. "Back soon."

Eino was in his office when Wolfe arrived. "Just caught me," he said, his Finnish accent stronger than usual.

"Been back with the relatives again, eh Eino?"

"And what of it?" Eino said defensively as he looked up at Wolfe.

"Nothing, Eino." Wolfe laughed, holding up his hand. "Nothing. You have a wonderful family. I just noticed the joy on your face you get when the clan gets together, that's all."

"Bullshit," spat Eino. "You're makin' fun of my accent again, aren't you?"

"No, Eino, I swear."

"One of these days," Eino said, "you're gonna be laying in the middle of the woods bleeding, and some old Finlander's gonna come by and you're gonna ask for help, and he's gonna say, 'I don't t'ink I can understant what you're sayin', eh?' And he's gonna walk off and leave you to die. That'll be your punishment and I'll laugh my ass off as I cut you open to see if there's anything inside your head. And there won't be because all your brains are in your smart-ass."

Wolfe grinned, further agitating Eino. "You're just saying that 'cause you love me."

"Loathe is more like it," Eino mumbled as he turned to go into his office. "I'm sure there's a reason you tore yourself away from your hide-away to come and spar with me," Eino said, seating himself comfortably in his brown leather chair. "You gonna tell me what it is, or am I supposed to guess?"

"Right," said Wolfe, still standing. "Let's say a person is exposed to ELF waves of, say, three to ten Hertz over a period of half an hour or so."

"At what level of intensity?" Eino said, focusing on Wolfe.

"I don't know," Wolfe said, looking out the window. "They didn't say. Let's say the equivalent of ten volts per meter."

"Ten volts per meter," Eino scribbled on his pad. "Three to ten Hertz. Go ahead."

"What I want to know," Wolfe said as he turned from the window and began pacing, "is whether such exposure would produce any permanent cellular change which could be detected at a later time."

"Like in a dead person," Eino said rhetorically.

"That's right."

"I don't know. That could be tough." Eino scratched his eight-hour stubble. "Problem is there's no way for me to generate such a field to observe what changes, if any, occur. I suppose I could speculate based on extrapolations of known frequency exposures, but that range is so far from any studies I've ever seen that I doubt it will be very helpful."

"Give it your best shot, will you Eino? It's the only thing we've got so far."

"Do my best," Eino said, pulling a book off his shelf, already deep in thought. Suddenly he stopped and looked at Wolfe. "Oh. By the way. Another DOA came in today. Fella by the name of Scott Frazier."

"Is that supposed to mean something to me?" Wolfe said.

"Not really. Dunno why I mentioned it, really," Eino said hesitantly. "Funny thing is, though, he drowned. Only he shouldn't have."

"What do you mean?"

"The boy was a great swimmer," Eino answered, looking back into the book.

"So?" Wolfe came back. "A lot of great swimmers bite the dust out here. They think they can do anything they could do in their pool back home. They don't take into account the wind, waves, and the cold. They test nature and lose."

"Well this one lost, but it wasn't at the hands of nature. He had plenty of reserves left when he died."

"Meaning?"

"Meaning I don't know why he drowned," Eino said, snapping the book closed. "He could have—should have—kept going. Possibly to safety. But he just quit and started breathing water." Eino began pacing around the office, agitated at the enigma.

"And you don't know why," Wolfe repeated dumbly.

"It's like he just gave up." Eino stopped and faced Wolfe. "Like his brain just shut down."

"Maybe it did," Wolfe said, looking intently at Eino.

"You think this has something to do with ELF?" Eino asked.

"I don't know," Wolfe said. "The stuff Terri and I are finding relates to the central nervous system. Maybe ELF caused it to shut down somehow."

"Just one person?" Eino exclaimed. "Wouldn't there be more people dead now if that was the case?"

"Not if it was stronger in the water," Wolfe responded. "In water where there was only one person swimming," he finished.

Eino stared at him as Wolfe turned around shaking his head. "Hell. I don't know," said Eino. "Maybe I'm seeing things that aren't there. Seems we're ascribing an awful lot of things to ELF. Pretty soon I'll probably be saying it causes bad breath and zits. Right now I think the important thing is to keep an open mind. There'll be time enough later to weed out the ones that don't fit. *Eh?*"

Wolfe smiled. "Thanks, Eino. Let me know if you find anything."

"I will," Eino repeated, no longer listening as he flipped through the pages of his dusty, leather-bound book.

chapter 42

Terri had amassed a considerable pile of notes by the time Wolfe returned to his cabin. Books lay scattered on the kitchen table, propped open to specific pages, while she scribbled furiously, referring first to one, then another.

"Writing a dissertation?" he said. Terri jumped at the unexpected voice.

"Why don't you just scare me to death?" she said as she turned in her chair.

"That wouldn't be any fun," he said playfully. "Then who would I have to torment?"

Terri smiled and shook her head.

Wolfe opened the bar and fixed a stiff gin and tonic. As he poured, he looked up at a painting hanging on the wall next to the bar. It was of a young woman standing on a beach, her hair blowing behind her as she looked out to sea.

Terri walked over and saw him staring at the painting. "She's beautiful," she said, looking at Wolfe. "Anyone you know?"

Wolfe's stare continued for a second. "It's just a painting," he said finally, then walked over to the couch in front of the empty fireplace. "So what d'you have?" he said.

"Just a minute," she said as she gathered up her notes and walked over to him. "Any room for me?" she asked.

"Sure," he said, sliding over. Terri studied his profile as he stared into the empty fireplace. His mood had changed. He seemed cold and distant—like he was existing in another world—a world she was not part of. But worse, he seemed to have erected a wall around himself. Hard as granite, yet translucent. She could see the form but not the substance. Look, but don't touch.

"I suppose I've been a little unfair," she said finally, as nicely as she could. Terri looked for signs the wall was fading. Wolfe stared into the black hole of the fireplace.

"I'm sorry if I've been a little difficult," she said, placing her hand on his forearm. "I've been preoccupied. Thinking only of myself. I know you must be upset too. You've placed your home, your possessions—even your life—at risk to help me. I'm not even sure why. I don't know why you're doing all this for me. I appreciate it, yet it bothers me. I keep waiting for the other shoe to fall. To find the bill collector suddenly at the door demanding payment—payment I can't give.

"Look," she continued. "I'm a reporter. Reporters are skeptical by nature. Trust no one. Be suspicious of everything. Verify and re-verify. Look past the surface. That's normal. Then when my family gets involved—and me—well . . . the danger signals really flash." Terri stopped and looked at him for a moment. His jaw muscles seemed to relax a bit, but there was still no expression.

"Clay," she began softly, her barriers down as far as she dared, "I don't care what you have buried that you can't tell me. Not really. If it's that important to you—or painful—it doesn't matter." Terri turned away to join Wolfe in the black hole, a tear working its way down her cheek. "It doesn't matter."

"It was ten years ago," Wolfe began.

Terri turned her head, looked at Wolfe. "What was?" she said, wiping away the tear.

"I was working for the government on special assignment in a foreign country—which one doesn't matter." Terri started to say something, then thought better of it.

"I was assigned to join the government's space program as an undercover agent. Someone was altering key electrical components of the launch systems, causing disastrous malfunctions and delays." Terri thought she saw his eyes begin to glisten. After a pause he went on.

"I befriended a technician within the division making the components—as part of my job. Her name was Mary. She was beautiful, and innocent. I mean, you know—she had that child-like innocence. She was open and friendly—and vulnerable. I used her to get information—sensitive information that would help me pinpoint who the saboteur was. Unfortunately, in the process, I fell in love with her. She had raven black hair and the darkest brown eyes I've ever seen. I can still feel her lips against my skin as she whispered my name."

Wolfe stopped, the words choked off in his throat. Terri watched his agony, felt his pain. "Go on," she said softly, her hand on his arm.

"I couldn't tell her what I was doing, but she never asked. She just trusted me," he continued, barely regaining his voice. "But I still couldn't get at the saboteur. That was the hell of it. I knew who it was, but I had to catch him at it. And I couldn't do it without her."

"Did she help you?" Terri asked softly, trying to encourage him to get it all out.

"Oh, she helped me," he said, his eyes glistening. "She sure helped me. I caught him with the goods—the evidence I needed. But he took her hostage. She didn't know what was happening when he grabbed her. Her eyes got wide, more with bewilderment than with fear—at least at first.

"Then he started shouting his demands. 'Leave or I'll kill the girl', he'd said. He had a knife at her throat and the evidence I needed in his coat pocket. 'Leave—now,' he'd shouted, pressing the knife tighter against her skin. I couldn't let him walk away. Too many lives were at stake. And he had Mary." Wolfe stopped, got up and walked over to the window.

"I assessed the situation as I had been trained to," he continued, finally. "There was no choice. I had to take a calculated risk. If I was lucky, I'd get them both."

Wolfe paused, still standing at the window, his back to Terri. Though she knew what must come next, she gave the final prompt as gently as she could.

"What happened Clay?" she said.

After several seconds, he answered. "I got the evidence. I even got the spy," he finished.

"And Mary?" Terri had to ask, as if in a play where she didn't write the lines.

"Oh, I got her too," he said as he turned back to Terri, eyes red. "But not before he shoved the knife through her heart," he choked. "I knocked him out. He laid there unconscious while I held Mary in my arms, her big brown eyes not understanding—focused on forever."

Terri wrapped her arms around him as he stood there staring off into oblivion. "Clay, Clay," she said with tears. "I'm so sorry. I had no idea. It must have been awful. The pain all these years. Please hold me. Hold me," she begged. Wolfe raised his arms as if they were lead and put them around Terri. She looked up at him—into his eyes. There was more. "What else happened?" she asked, not wanting to know.

"He got away," Wolfe said flatly. "The bastard escaped while being transported to the penitentiary to await trial. Killed two guards. Now he's free, and has been for all these years, as far as I know. And that's all there is."

"I'm sorry," she said, putting her head against his chest and hugging him as hard as she could. "I had no right."

"Maybe it's better," he said finally, returning her hug. "I've kept it in all these years. Maybe it's better that it's out. Maybe I can let go of her now.

Terri put her arms around Wolfe, and they reclined on the couch. She stroked his head, whispering sweet things to him, to herself. The words, 'I love you,' may have been spoken; or maybe just thought; as they fell asleep in each other's arms on the couch in front of the empty fireplace.

chapter 43

The jarring sound of the phone ringing startled them both. Wolfe fumbled himself awake, then reached over Terri and snatched up the phone. "What?" he barked.

"It's Eino, Wolfe."

"Can't you wait 'til a decent hour, Eino?

"It *is* a decent hour, Wolfe, and no, it can't wait," Eino barked back. "We got a . . ." Eino tried to remember the code. ". . . Situation red. You'd better get your . . ."

Wolfe sat upright on the couch, suddenly alert. "I understand. Should I bring . . ."

"Her too," Eino interrupted impatiently. "All of us. We need to meet."

"On the way," Wolfe said, hanging up the phone before Eino could respond.

"What is it," asked Terri, now alert.

"Eino needs us all. Code red," Wolfe said. "We've got to go *now.*"

"What've you got?" Wolfe asked once they were all seated in the situation room of the sheriff's department.

Josephs pushed his spectacles back up on the bridge of his nose, tweaked his mostly gray moustache, and began.

"First off," he said, steepling his fingers once again, "some person or persons blew up two of the ELF terminals just installed this week."

"Nothing was said on the radio," Terri said, surprised.

"That's right," Josephs continued. "Military's put a lid on it. They're real upset, to say the least."

"I imagine they are," Wolfe said. "Any idea who did it?"

"Nope," Josephs said, tilting his head up at Wolfe. "At least none they're willing to talk about. Hell. They wouldn't have told me except they knew I'd hear about it sooner or later and they're afraid I'd go in and mess things up."

"What'd they tell you?" Terri asked.

"Guy by the name of Wallick—Andrew Wallick—came to my house—woke me up. Said he was going to let me in on a problem, but I had to keep it quiet—national security, you know?" he said sarcastically. "He told me a couple of their ground terminals had 'inadvertently' exploded, and that his people were conducting an investigation. He asked me to let them handle it since it was a Navy project, even though it happened on county property."

"Inadvertently exploded," chimed in Eino. "Now that's an original. Only the military . . ."

"Yea, well that's what they said," continued Josephs. "Asked me to handle any inquiries on the Q.T.—let them know if I come across any information that might help them."

"But *they're* handling the investigation," echoed Terri.

"Yup. And they wouldn't even tell me what they're looking for," Josephs said as he leaned back in his chair. "Now I don't know how I'm supposed to let them know if I come across any information that could help if I don't know what the hell it is I'm looking for—do you?"

"I have a feeling there's more," Wolfe said after no one responded.

"Oh, hell yes, there's more," Josephs said leaning forward again. "Seems one of their top scientists committed suicide—two weeks ago."

"What?" exclaimed Terri and Eino at the same time. Terri leaned toward Josephs. "I didn't see anything about it in the paper."

"Or hear anything on the news," added Eino.

"That's right," said Josephs, "and the reason is that it wasn't reported."

"Where'd it happen?" said Wolfe quietly.

"Presque Isle," Josephs said. "Jumped off the north side head first onto the rocks."

"Jeez," said Terri. "Somebody must have seen that—or at least heard about it. There'd have to be an awful mess." Terri turned her head away as if from viewing the scene on the table.

"Coast Guard handled it," Josephs continued. "Direct orders from Washington. Recover, clean up, hush up."

"Well they must have gotten there quickly," Terri came back, "to get all that done without being seen. Besides—the cutter would have drawn attention to any rescue operation on that part of the Isle."

"They did get there quickly," Josephs went on. "Almost too quickly. Seems this scientist left a note in his office after hours. Wasn't supposed to be found 'til the next day. But his commander needed some papers from his office and went to get them. He found the note."

"Sounds like he wanted to be found publicly—like he wanted passers-by to find him like that, all . . ." Terri began.

"Well they didn't," Josephs said as he removed his glasses and rubbed his eyes. "And they didn't use the cutter. Frog team slipped up quietly, pulled him into the water and out to their skiff. No one saw 'cause it was nearly dark when he jumped. And the team musta got there just after he did it."

"Who was he?" asked Wolfe, taking it all in but saying little.

"Wouldn't tell me," Josephs said replacing his glasses. "Said it wasn't important."

"Then why'd they tell you?" Terri jumped in. "They had it all neatly covered up. Nobody knew about it except military personnel."

"It was a mistake," Josephs said, smiling slightly. "It kinda slipped out."

"How'd that happen?" Wolfe asked.

Josephs folded his hands on the table, looked down at them in mock humility. "He was talking 'bout the explosions. I said there had been a lot of unusual activity lately, trying to prime the pump, you know. He got kind of a funny look on his face and asked, what other unusual activity. I knew I had a reaction, but I didn't know what for. Quickly I said, 'Why, the young man's mysterious death of course.'

"Now I was thinking 'bout Scott Frazier. Wallick's face changed to a greenish hue, and I knew I had something. He apparently thought I knew something about it, and hoped it wasn't too much. Trying to sound natural without giving away the store, he said, 'terrible way for a young man to take his life.' I played along and said it was, then I went fishin' a little. 'I s'pose it coulda been an accident,' I said, watching him intently, still thinking it was Frazier. Startled, he looked at me strangely, then he said, 'yes, I guess he could have slipped.'

"Now he was watching me real intently, and I knew then he wasn't talkin' 'bout Scott Frazier. Playing a hunch, I said, 'but I guess the note points pretty clearly to a suicide.' Suddenly he exclaimed, 'Damn! How'd you find out about that? That's top secret!' I told him I was paid to know what was going on in my county. He said, 'I told them they couldn't keep it quiet. Damn weapons scientist dives of a cliff head first onto some rocks and they think they can cover it up like it never happened.'

"I kept playing along. 'Pretty hard to cover up the results of that act,' I had said, shaking my head.

'I guess someone saw the Coast Guard frogs pull him off the rocks, huh?' he said. I just nodded slightly. 'Damn,' he said again. 'I told them someone would see. Presque Isle's just too damn busy this time of year—even at dusk.' Then he regained his composure and said with some gravity, 'you know you can't reveal any of this? It being national security and all.' I said I understood that and he said, 'good,' then left shaking his head."

Terri looked disturbed about something, and Josephs said, "Something bothering you, Terri?"

"Back there you said he called the dead man a weapons scientist. Is that right?"

"That's what he called him."

"Any idea what weapons system he was working on?" She asked.

"Nope. Never said."

"I'd bet a month's pay it's ELF," Terri said confidently.

"Why's that?" Eino said.

"Because this isn't the only place there have been mysterious deaths of scientists working on defense projects."

"England! Started in sixty-eight, then more in the seventies," exclaimed Eino. "String of eight or nine unusual deaths—suicides, homicides, disappearances—most working on defense systems."

"*Underwater* defense systems," Terri added.

"Right," Eino said. "They say there's no connection between them. Just random coincidences."

"Well, it looks like we've got another damn 'random' coincidence happening right here," Josephs said, pounding his fist on the table. "What the hell's going on?" he shouted.

"It gets worse," Wolfe said softly as everyone turned their attention to him.

Terri looked at him and knew something was wrong. "What, Wolfe?" she asked anxiously. "What could be worse?"

"The local scientist who dove off the cliff," he said, pausing.

"What about him?" she said, her voice rising. "He committed suicide. What could be worse?"

Wolfe stared straight ahead for long seconds, then said, "He wasn't the first."

chapter 44

"What do you mean he wasn't the first?" Terri said.

Everyone's attention was riveted on Wolfe. He said nothing for a moment, then spoke slowly, deliberately. "There have been at least two other suspicious deaths here over the last year. Both were military scientists. One died accidentally, the other was a suicide—so they said."

They all stared at Wolfe in disbelief. Finally Josephs broke the spell. "You been holding out on us, Wolfe?"

Wolfe looked at Terri, her expression less than friendly. "Not really," he said, looking away from her. "I didn't believe there was any relationship between the incidents—until now."

"How could you do this?" she asked. "After all we've been through. You couldn't be honest with us?"

"It didn't seem relevant to . . ."

"Relevant?" Terri left her chair and walked over to Wolfe. "It didn't seem relevant that two ELF scientists died mysteriously while we're fighting for our lives trying to find out what the hell's going? While people are dying all around us? Like my *brother*?" Terri said, her tone biting and accusatory.

"Look, Terri," he tried to explain. "A lot has happened. I came across this information a while back, and it didn't seem to be related to our problem, until now."

"Weak, Wolfe," Eino said with disgust. "Really weak."

"How'd you 'come across' this irrelevant information, anyway?" asked Josephs.

"Let's just say it popped up during one of my confidential investigations long before any of this happened."

"In other words, you're not going to tell us," said Eino.

"It serves no purpose," responded Wolfe. "I found it out, and passed it on to you when it became necessary. That's all you need to know. Anyway," he added, "that's all I can tell you without compromising the confidentiality of my source."

"That's a lot of bull-crap and you know it," complained Eino. "You know as well as I do the importance of this information. It might have changed our whole direction—or at least helped us focus it—if we had known about this earlier."

"I doubt it," Wolfe said, now cold and detached. "Besides. Changing direction may not have been good. This way our approach has been broader. We've discussed possibilities we might not have otherwise discussed. Focusing too early sometimes blots out the larger picture."

"I see," said Terri, fuming.

"Well," Josephs cut in, rearranging the glasses on the bridge of his nose once again. "It appears to be a moot point. Mr. Wolfe, for reasons known only to him, has chosen not to fully confide in us. And that's fine. We'll get along without complete information—we have so far. It has, however, put a dent in the trust factor."

"Dent, my ass," mumbled Eino not quite under his breath. "It's smashed it to hell."

"I guess you're right, Sheriff," Terri said, now more hurt than angry. "I'm sure we can survive without Mr. Wolfe's complete faith in us."

"Good," said Wolfe, seemingly unaffected. "Now we can get back to work."

"I think it's time for a break," said Josephs. "I'll get some coffee and doughnuts and then . . ."

Everyone turned to look at him.

"*What?*" said Josephs. "There's a reason cops love them. Breakfast of champions," he said, the shadow of a smile gracing his appearance as he turned and left the room.

After he returned, they sat in relative silence, giving dirty looks to Wolfe as they ate. Wolfe said nothing, appearing to contemplate weighty matters as he studiously avoided their accusatory glances.

Finally, Wolfe put down his coffee cup. "First," he started, "I think we should clear up inaccuracies," Wolfe now seemed to be assuming the de facto chair of the group. Leaving his chair, he went to the head of the table. He addressed Terri first. "To clear up a point, I did not say that the two scientists killed were ELF scientists. That is a conclusion you jumped to, to castigate me."

Terri's look was not apologetic. "*Castigate*," she said, "is not quite the word I'd have chosen—but it's close."

Ignoring her quip he went on. "All I was able to find out from my source was that they were working on top secret defense research. But there was no indication it was ELF related." He paused, looking at each in turn. Hostility and hurt reflected back. He continued.

"Although there was nothing in the information given to me that directly indicated their deaths were anything other than what they appeared to be, I was somewhat suspicious at the time, and am more so now. There was more to it."

Curiosity began to overtake pride. "What made you suspicious?" Josephs asked.

"My client was the wife of one of the victims," he said. "The one who supposedly committed suicide. According to her, he had no reason to take his own life. They had been married for five years and she felt she knew him pretty well. Although he couldn't tell her what he was working on, she could tell when he had good days and bad days. She said he believed in what he was doing, and was proud to serve his country."

"So what happened?" asked Eino.

"She's not sure. One day, a few days before his suicide, he came home troubled. When she asked what the matter was, he didn't answer. He just kept saying it wasn't right. That something was wrong. She asked if it was his work, but he wouldn't answer.

"Then, the night before he died, he started shouting in his sleep. 'Stop it! Stop it! You'll ruin everything!' His wife woke him and asked what he had been dreaming about. He was sweating profusely, and just stared at her for several seconds. When he realized what had happened, he asked her what he had said. She told him, after which he made her promise to forget it and not to mention it to anyone. The next day he killed himself."

"How?" asked Terri, the last to come around.

"According to the military, he went to work the next morning, and, about an hour after arriving, put his government issue .45 automatic in his mouth and blew his brains all over the lab."

"Did you ask her how he acted that morning?" said Josephs. "Like he was at peace with himself?"

"No," said Wolfe. "I know what you're getting at. The telltale sign of a person about to kill himself. No, according to his wife, he was still troubled. He wouldn't say much, just that he was going to straighten a few things out, one way or another."

"Some could say that was the sign of a suicide," Eino piped in. "He was either going to get his way or end it all."

"Not according to the base psychologist," Wolfe responded. "According to his wife, he was as stable as the rock of Gibraltar. He had to undergo a barrage of psychological tests before getting clearance for this position, and had been told by his commander that he passed with flying colors."

"So you think he didn't commit suicide based on that?" asked Eino.

"No," said Wolfe, "as I said before, on its own merits, there didn't seem to be enough to refute the military's claim—just his wife and her knowledge of him and his behavior patterns. It was the second incident six weeks later that really began to raise my eyebrows."

"Are going to tell us about that one?" Terri asked, "or do you still think we're a security risk?" Wolfe shot her a look, and she suddenly wished she hadn't been so quick to cut.

Wolfe continued. "He was single, and working on top-secret defense systems like the other. When he didn't report for duty one day, his supervisor went to his quarters to find out why, and couldn't raise a response. When they finally gained access, they found him face down in a foot of water in the bathtub—quite dead."

"Any signs of a struggle?" Eino asked.

"None. Looks like he just laid face down in the tub and started breathing water like it was air."

"Was an autopsy done?" Eino fired again, his coroner's nose smelling foul play.

"Don't know. Probably," Wolfe said. "They usually do in those kind of circumstances. But nothing was said to me."

"I don't know about any of the rest of you," Josephs finally said, twisting in his chair, "but isn't anybody the least bit curious how Wolfe came by this information?"

"Yea," said Eino suspiciously. "Who told you all this?"

"Same guy you talked to, Ed."

"Wallick?" Josephs exclaimed.

"He told you all this?" Terri echoed.

"That's right," Wolfe responded matter-of-factly. "Remember, I do investigations for all kinds of clients, both civilian and governmental. I've helped in military investigations before, and they came to me after the second suicide because they were at a loss to explain what was happening. And they were worried."

"What did they expect you to do if they couldn't find anything?" Terri asked.

"I'm not sure," said Wolfe. "I've solved some peculiar cases before, and I guess they were hoping I'd do it again."

"And did you?" Josephs asked.

"Obviously not," Wolfe said. "What bothers me is that they would tell me about the first two but not this one."

"You didn't know about the one off Presque Isle?" Josephs said, surprised.

"Not until you called this meeting," Wolfe said. "In fact, they didn't actually tell me about the first either. It came up in discussing the second suicide when I was asking whether Wallick thought there was a connection between the two. He seemed surprised at first that I knew about it, then made some statement to the effect that, 'yea, I suppose you'd know about that too, wouldn't you?'"

"So he didn't know you had been retained by the wife of the first victim to investigate his death?" Terri asked.

"Apparently not. At least, he put on a good act if he did," Wolfe replied.

chapter 45

"So where does all this leave us?" Josephs asked, more to the group than to Wolfe.

"It leaves us," said Terri with her reporter's summation instincts, "with dead scientists, inconsistent military investigators, and a civilian enigma growing stranger by the minute," the last aimed straight at Wolfe.

"And a blown-up ground terminal," added Josephs, "which is what got us here in the first place."

"Excuse me, sheriff," Sergeant Maki said, poking his head into the room, "but there's a guy by the name of Wallick on the phone for you and he's pretty upset. I told him you were in an important meeting, but he . . ."

"What did he want?" Josephs interrupted impatiently.

"He wants to talk to you about an explosion or something . . ."

"I already know about that," Josephs said angrily. "He was here just a . . ."

"No, I don't think that's what he means," Maki said, his turn to interrupt.

"What the hell are you talking about?" shouted Josephs in exasperation.

"The explosion, sir," Maki said, trying desperately to extract himself from the room. "The one he talked to you about earlier— that's not why he's calling."

"Maki, so help me . . ." Josephs said menacingly.

The Sergeant was now almost fully retracted from the doorway. "Another one, sir. There's been *another* explosion."

"What? Where?" Josephs said, coming out of his chair.

"Dunno," Maki said as Josephs brushed by him in the doorway. "This one'll be easier to solve though," he said as Josephs reached the phone.

"And why's that?" Josephs said, only half listening as he picked up the receiver.

"'Cause the bomber's still there," Maki said, a grin on his face. The Sheriff looked at Maki, not quite comprehending. "At least most of him is."

"Maybe now I'll have a lead," Eino said in response to Maki's revelation.

"You think this is tied in to Kevin's papers?" Terri asked Eino.

"Don't know," he said. "But at least it's something to go on. Hopefully we'll be able to identify the bomber. Then maybe we can trace him from there to other individuals."

Josephs walked back into the situation room. "Wallick's fit to be tied," he said, running his hands through his thick salt and pepper hair. "Seems this one did considerable damage to their system."

"Not to mention the bomber's," Eino said

"Bad taste, Eino," said Terri, shaking her head at his joke.

Changing her focus again, Terri asked, "So what now?"

"I've got some bombings to investigate," Josephs said. "Eino has his own odious task ahead of him . . ."

"Hey—speak for yourself," Eino jumped in. "I love jigsaw puzzles!"

Groans arose from the group.

"What?" Eino said, looking around the room.

"As to what you two are going to do . . ." Josephs started, indicating Wolfe and Terri.

"We'll work on the suicides," Wolfe began, then looked at Terri. "That is, if you agree."

Terri's look softened a little. "Fine," she said. "There's enough work for two, that's for sure."

"Good," Wolfe said, relieved. "Maybe they'll tie in with the people who are after Kevin's papers."

"You think they're related?" Josephs asked.

"Maybe," Wolfe said. "Let us know as soon as either of you find out anything."

Terri took Wolfe by the arm. "And we'll do the same."

"Tell me more about the suicides," Terri said to Wolfe as she drove her convertible toward the air base. She waited for his answer, as she watched the scraggly jack pines flash by. The base was fifteen miles directly south from Marquette on M-553. It was a pretty straight stretch of two lane road, with some areas of thick, short pines, while others were sparsely wooded—mostly desolate and uninhabited.

Wolfe finally spoke. "First one's name was Talbot—Roger Talbot. He's the one who used the gun," Wolfe said.

"You know his name?" Terri said, momentarily looking at him.

"Yup. And also the second," he continued. "Dennis Mercer. Wallick gave me the second when he asked for my help. I wormed the first out of him."

"So you don't know the name of the latest one—off Presque Isle?"

"That's what we're going to find out now."

"Wallick?" she asked.

"That's right. If he wants my help, he'd better give me as much to go on as he can."

"You mentioned before that you had done work for them in the past—tough cases," she said, watching the road.

"I did. Unusual problems that required the perspective and freedom of a civilian."

"What about the local police. Why didn't they call them?"

"Still government employees, albeit at a different level," he said, checking his watch. "They needed someone not saddled with government restrictions."

"But if you're acting as an agent of the government, even if you're a civilian, don't the restrictions apply to you as well?"

"Not bad," Wolfe said, smiling slightly.

"I know my constitutional law, Clay."

Clay. We're back to that again, he thought to himself. Too hard to jump back and forth through those emotional hoops. Yet it still felt good to hear it—particularly the way it was said.

chapter 46

Terri slowed the Mustang as she turned left onto the base. She stopped at security and showed their IDs, stating why they were there and who they wanted. The guard told them where to go, and she headed to the parking lot near Wallick's building.

They entered the typical, drab military building where Wallick's office was. Wolfe knocked on the door.

"Who is it?" barked the voice on the other side of the door.

"Wolfe," he shouted.

"Come in," the voice said.

Wolfe opened the door to see Wallick facing them, sitting in his green chair behind his green desk in the green room. All in a green building. May be the forerunners of the environmental movement, thought Wolfe. Of course they also had the nuclear weapons, the B-52s with their eight engines pouring CO_2 into the atmosphere by the ton around the clock, millions of rounds of ordinance, and mountains of toxins such as nerve gas, chemical agents, and who knows what other poisons and biological weapons manufactured, stored, and corroding their containers underground. So, thought Wolfe. Maybe *not* so environmental. He smiled.

Andrew Wallick was not pleased to see Terri, and showed it. "What the hell are you doing, Wolfe?" he said as they walked into his office.

"Helping you with your investigation," Wolfe responded innocently.

"Who's she?" he said, nodding in Terri's direction.

"Terri Sommers," she said, offering her hand.

Wallick looked at the offered hand, then at Wolfe, then back to Terri. "Will you excuse us for a minute?" he said to Terri, ignoring her outstretched hand.

"Certainly," she said icily. She withdrew her hand but made no move to leave the room.

Wallick walked out of his office into the hall. Wolfe followed, closing the door behind them. "What the hell's going on Wolfe? What'd you bring her here for?"

"She's part of my investigative team," Wolfe said calmly.

"I didn't hire any damn investigative team, Wolfe. I hired *you*."

"I needed additional resources. The problem seems to have expanded."

"Expanded, hell," said Wallick. "It's gone to the moon!"

"That's why I need her," Wolfe continued, humoring him. "I can't be everywhere at once. In fact, I might need to bring in even more assistants if this continues."

"The hell you will! I've already gotten my ass in a room full of slings over getting you involved in the first place! Now *you're* gonna find out who the hell's killing my people, and you're gonna do it without bringing in any damn investigative team!"

"Sorry Andy," Wolfe said matter-of-factly. "She's in. Now we can either keep yelling at each other in the hall—actually, you're the one who's doing the yelling . . ." Wallick's face was crimson by now. "Or we can get down to the business of solving this nasty mess you've gotten yourself into."

Wallick started to say something but Wolfe cut him off. "And you can start by leveling with me. Who took a dive off Presque Isle into zip feet of water, and why didn't you tell me about it?"

"You want her to know all this?" Wallick was incredulous.

"Not only that," Wolfe continued mercilessly, "I want her to know everything about your 'inadvertent' exploding ELF terminals, and anything else you've been withholding from me."

"So you're telling me she's in," Wallick said with resignation. "All the way in."

"That's right Andy. All the way in. You're intuitive as hell. You know that? This must be what they mean by military intelligence."

"Cut the cracks, Wolfe. If circumstances were different . . ."

"Oh, but they're not," said Wolfe casting his eyes at the ceiling. "And we can thank all that's holy for that."

"You win," Wallick, said, opening the door to his office. "But so help me if word of this gets out . . ."

"It already is out, Andy," Wolfe cut in. "You're living on borrowed time right now."

"Warren Beaks," Wallick said as he sat in his government-green chair. "He was the one who dove onto the rocks."

Terri looked at Wolfe, then Wallick. "He left a note," Wallick continued in monotone. "Said he couldn't stand the isolation of living in the wilderness. Navy wouldn't let him transfer, so he dove into oblivion. End of story." He leaned back in his chair, took a deep breath. "That's why I didn't tell you. Nothing to tie in the others, and a note, to boot. Case closed." Wallick was getting his confidence back now.

"Case *not* closed, Andy," said Wolfe. Wallick grimaced every time Wolfe called him that—which was why he did it. "You've got three apparent suicides of top researchers in less than two years. Doesn't that seem a little high? A little out of the ordinary?"

"Maybe," Wallick said, trying to gain control. "But there's still no proof . . ."

"And that's what we're here to find—if it's there. Proof. A

conspiracy. Or nothing but coincidence. Whatever comes up. But first we need all the facts. That's *all* the facts, Andy."

Wallick grimaced, mumbled something that sounded remotely like an affirmative response, and then stomped away.

"What happened in the hall?" Terri asked when Wolfe returned to the room. "I could hear him shouting, but I couldn't hear what he said."

"He's going to give us the information we want."

"I see," she said. "And are you going to share this information with me?"

"Absolutely," he said, making it a point to look around the room. Catching on that the room might be monitored, she played along."

"Where'd he go, anyway?"

Just then Wallick came back in the room and threw two, one-inch thick files in manila folders plus a third half-inch thick file on the desk in front of them. "There they are. All the files. Go to it. Have a party."

"Thanks, Andy, we will," Wolfe said. "Anything else you might have overlooked?"

Wallick glared at Wolfe, then stormed off, returning moments later with another, newer file on the terminal sabotage. "That's it. Now you have everything I have. If anybody finds out you have these, I'm dead. Does that make me part of your team now, Wolfe?" he said, dripping sarcasm.

"Not yet, Andy," Wolfe said, standing as he picked up the files. "You have to prove yourself first." Wallick's jugular veins began protruding from his neck. Wolfe turned in the doorway as they were leaving, and smiled. "We'll be in touch."

Wallick started to say something, but Wolfe shut the door and cut him off mid-sentence.

chapter 47

They left the building and headed to the car. "Don't you think you were pushing him just a little hard back there?" Terri said once they were in her car and safely off the base.

"Not in the least," Wolfe said, flipping through the first file. "He's been playing games with me for some time now. Just a little of his own medicine. He'll get over it."

They drove in silence while Wolfe looked at the files, making mental notes. "Anything interesting?" she said finally after he closed the last folder.

"I think Wallick's right," he said staring straight ahead. "I think if they find out he gave us these, he's dead."

"Good stuff then, huh?" Terri said, smiling sardonically.

"The best. Raw material," said Wolfe. "Unedited, uncensored data collected by skilled investigators. We can draw our own conclusions without an olive-drab cast to it."

"Where to?" she said as they neared the cut-off to town.

"Let's check out Presque Isle, then see how Eino and company are doing."

"OK," she said as she punched the 289 engine and accelerated past the rock-cut toward the upper harbor.

The wind blasted Terri's hair as they drove in silence. Wolfe wondered how long he could hold the pieces together. And hoped it was long enough.

Terri pulled in to the parking lot near the rocks, and they got out. They walked over to the rocks that protected the shoreline, which was about eight feet below. Terri looked at the large, angular rocks. Most of them weighed a hundred pounds or more, and their dark, foreboding color matched the dark blue-green waters of Lake Superior, especially when the storms came and twisted the water into a swirling caldron of power and destruction.

Looking over the rocks along the shore, she stopped and looked closely at one spot that was different than the others in appearance.

"Looks like he must've hit here," Terri said, kneeling next to a large, bolder at the bottom of the cliff on the north side of Presque Isle. "See this dark spot?" she said, pointing to an oval, dark stain that started just off-center at one of the jagged edges that sloped down toward the water. "It would have been hard to get all the blood off," she said, looking around for other evidence of the violent death. "Especially at night."

"I believe you're right," said Wolfe. He bent down closer to look at what Terri was point at. "Looks like a blood stain for sure. A large one at that. It's far enough up from the waterline that it would have had time to set and dry in the pores of the rock. It'll have to be sand-blasted out now."

"I guess they just had to hope nobody noticed, or if they did, didn't realize what it might be," she said as she stood up and looked out over the lake.

"Why don't you check around here while I go up top," Wolfe said as he started to climb back up.

"Right," she said, and began examining the cracks, crevices, and sand. Wolfe checked the top of the cliff, not expecting much. It was heavily traveled by sightseers and families on picnics.

Then, between a weather-worn white pine and the encroaching edge of the cliff Wolfe saw something that made his stomach tighten. Pressed into the soft dirt between two clumps of grass was a marble. Wolfe picked it up and examined it. It was clear with a red cat's eye in the middle.

Wolfe had seen it before. It was the calling card of a man who made his living killing people—people Wolfe knew. It was the man who killed Mary.

"What's the matter?" Terri asked as she reached the top of the cliff. Wolfe was looking out over the lake, staring at some unseen, distant place.

"We've got trouble," he said without changing his gaze.

Terri walked over to him, taking in his somber face. "What is it?"

"Warren Beaks did not go willingly to his death."

"What?" Terri asked.

"Our scientist didn't take the plunge on his own."

"He was murdered?" she asked, still watching him. "How do you know?"

Wolfe showed her the marble. "The man who left this is cold-blooded and ruthless. And if he was out here for any reason at all, it was not to enjoy the native outdoors."

Terri looked at the marble. "It's a cat's-eye," she said, puzzled. "What's so significant about that?"

"Nothing," Wolfe said, "unless you know the history of the man who left it. That's the beauty of it. It only has meaning to him, and a few, select individuals who know his work."

"And you are one of those select individuals, I suppose?"

"Unfortunately, yes," he said.

"Well, why did he leave it here?" Terri asked, handing back the marble. "What's its significance?"

"It's like carving a notch in your gun for each person you kill," Wolfe explained. "Except, in his case, he leaves a red cat's-eye as a symbol of his victory."

"Like the Pink Panther."

"Yes, I guess it is like the Pink Panther. Except he doesn't just steal from his victims."

"What's his name?"

"Malcolm Draco," he said. "Definitely not the sweetest sound you'll ever hear."

"Where do you know him from?" she asked.

"We knew each other in another time."

"Part of your dark, mysterious past?"

"Government work," he said with resignation.

"Of course," she said. "The enigmatic *government* work."

"Look," he said with exasperation, "I can't tell you everything I've done in my past. There are limits to what I'm allowed to reveal."

"Are you telling me you worked—or work—for the CIA?" she said, her reporter's instincts honing in for the kill.

"No. I'm not saying that at all. But I have worked for government agencies whose activities are classified, and I can't say much about what I did, or for whom, or why."

"But you can tell me that you worked with Draco."

"Yes."

"And that he is cold-blooded."

"That's correct."

"And that he worked for the government."

"Yes," he said, taking in her eyes, then looking away.

"So how can they let such a man work for the government?" she asked. "I mean, don't they know about his methods? Aren't there some kind of moral standards about spending taxpayer's money on such a person?"

"They thought they knew him," he said, looking out over the edge of the cliff again. "The government occasionally has need of such a man."

"To do what? Throw people off the edge of a cliff when they get in someone's way?"

Wolfe stared silently, took a deep breath and let it out slowly. "The world isn't a perfect place, Terri," he said softly. "Nor is it fair, nor just. But it's here and it's all we have, with all its warts and scars. What matters is what we do with it—no matter where we live or under what government."

"Are you saying all governments are equal? That it doesn't matter what freedoms people have or don't have?"

"It matters," Wolfe said, trying to make her understand. "Even the best governments have their flaws—serious ones. But you live within the system and do the best you can with what you're given."

"So we've been given Draco, and the need for Draco's talents."

"We're not all like the people who hired Draco," he said, tossing a pebble off the cliff into the frigid lake below. "There are limits."

Terri began to speak, then shivered and turned toward the car. "Let's go see if the Sheriff found anything."

chapter 48

They drove in silence to the damaged terminal, or as close as they could get—neither wanting to continue a conversation which might lead to more arguments. They got to the closest point to the terminal and then parked the car on the side of the road.

Sheriff Josephs met them at the shoulder while Eino stayed at the crime scene, processing what he could find.

"Gonna have to hoof it from here," Josephs said. Wolfe nodded, as they walked into the woods. They both had donned hiking boots before meeting the Sheriff, to make their journey a little easier and to protect themselves against snakes and other hazards.

Terri looked at the terrain as they walked. To her it looked wild and untamed. What a place to put a military terminal, or anything, for that matter, she thought. The locals called it God's County, but to her it just looked desolate. At least this part. She thought about her research as she walked. UPers, pronounced "you-pers," were those residents who were born in the Upper Peninsula of Michigan, she had found, and they were proud of it. Some residents were unhappy when the Mackinaw Bridge was built. They thought that their home would be invaded by the Neanderthals from downstate who would ruin its pristine beauty.

There was also long-standing talk about blowing up the bridge, not only to keep the invading hordes from getting in, but also to keep the onerous DNR regulators at bay. To the UPers, the deer and bear and other wildlife belonged to them. They didn't need anyone from the Lower Peninsula, as the rest of the State was called, to be telling them what to do.

Terri had even heard stories of Department of Natural Resources Officers and game wardens suffering fatal mishaps as they tried to enforce 'their' laws. In one such incident, UPer hunters killed one enforcement officer and then blew him up with dynamite to cover their crime. Terri shuddered when she thought of it. What a horrible thing to do. This area is truly a strange place, she thought. She suddenly longed for city life.

When they arrived at the scene, Terri's trail of horror was not over. Eino and Josephs were sticking two-foot-long wires with little yellow flags on them into the ground around the terminal.

"Planning a miniature golf course?" Wolfe shouted. Terri walked with Wolfe over to where Eino was inserting another wire in the ground. They stood over him, watching as he struggled to insert the wire into the rocky soil.

"Nope," Eino grunted, as he finished and stood up. "Just marking body parts. Wanna give me a hand?" Eino pointed to a spot on the ground a few feet to the right of where they were standing. Their gaze followed his finger until coming to rest on a tuft of wild grass. There, nestled in the center, as if in some macabre display, was the thumb and forefinger of a human hand, just barely attached.

"Eeeeewwwww," said Terri, turning away from the sight. "You guys are sick! How can you make jokes about that stuff?"

"Wolfe started it with his golf course crack," Eino said in defense.

"Never mind that," Josephs shouted. "I think I found his ID."

Suddenly Terri felt ill. A wave of dizziness and nausea passed over her. Nothing seemed real, and she thought she was going to pass out. Then, as suddenly as it began, it stopped. Must be the scene, she thought. The smell of death must be affecting her equilibrium.

Josephs was about fifty yards away bending over something near the base of a large, white pine. Terri didn't want to go. She didn't want to see any more blood and gore—enough was enough. This time she might really pass out. But her reporter's curiosity was too strong. Plodding along, as if on some invisible track, she followed Eino and Wolfe over to where the Sheriff was, carefully watching out for anything that might warrant a little yellow flag.

Half-looking away, Terri could see Josephs carefully removing a wallet from the right hip pocket of the victim's blue jeans. There was no left hip pocket because there was no left hip, nor anything else resembling a human being. "Who is it?" she said, squinting at the sun's intense rays.

"If the owner of this wallet is the person we've been collecting," Josephs began dramatically, "then his name is Kenneth Henson."

"Know anything about him?" Terri asked, studiously not looking at the body.

"Actually, I do," he said, thumbing through the wallet. "He's a local environmentalist—radical-type."

"Think he was radical enough to try something like this?" Eino said, motioning toward the obliterated terminal.

"Yes," Josephs said hesitantly, "I do."

"But you have some doubts," Terri said.

"Maybe," he said, putting the wallet in a plastic bag. "Could be someone killed him knowing his background, then planted the body here and blew it up along with the terminal. The terminal gets destroyed and Henson gets the blame."

"You think that's what happened?" Eino asked, looking around the area.

"You tell me, Eino. Think you can handle it?" Josephs said.

"I can tell you whether or not he was alive when the terminal blew up, if that's what you mean," Eino said confidently. "Beyond that . . ."

"That'll do nicely," Josephs said as he walked back toward the cruiser. "Let me know."

Josephs started to pull out, then stopped and got out of the cruiser. "Wolfe," he shouted motioning him to the car. Terri came with him, glad to be away from the yellow flag area. "Just got a call on the radio," he said. "Had a rash of accidents a few minutes ago. Bad ones. Got fifty passengers trapped inside a bus that went out of control and hit an abutment. I got multiple car accidents, at least two of which are probably fatals, and three mining accidents." He stared at Wolfe for a moment, then said, "What the hell's going on, Wolfe? What the hell's going on?"

"I don't know," Wolfe said. "When did this happen?"

"Few minutes ago. Everything suddenly went nuts." He bent an ear to the radio. "Calls still comin' in. I gotta go."

"Sheriff," Terri cut in as Josephs shut the car door, "did anything happen to you a few minutes ago? About the time of the accidents?"

"What do you mean 'happen to me'?" he said. Wolfe looked at Terri, his thoughts clicking.

"Did you feel strange, like you were going to pass out, or did you get real dizzy?"

Josephs looked at Wolfe and then back at Terri. "Now that you mention it, I did. Felt sick to my stomach, too. Thought I was going to lose it for the first time in my law enforcement career."

"What about you, Clay?"

"Pretty much the same thing. Almost like in a dream where everything is spinning. Thought maybe I'd passed out for a minute."

By this time Eino had come over and caught the tail end of the conversation. "Same with me," he joined in, "but I didn't want to admit it. Doesn't happen to coroners, but nobody would understand. I'd never live it down."

"Then that may be it," she said.

"What?" said Josephs.

"The cause of the accidents," answered Wolfe. "It all happened at about the same time. If the drivers of those vehicles or the injured workers felt the same symptoms we just felt, that could account for the accidents."

"The question then, is what caused the symptoms," Josephs said. They all looked at the destroyed ELF terminal, then back at each other.

"Can it work with two of the terminals out of commission?" Terri asked Wolfe.

"It's designed with massive redundancy," he said. "To withstand a nuclear attack. It could still function with eighty percent of it blown away. Maybe more."

"Could it do all that?" Eino asked. "Those symptoms over such a wide area?"

"It could," said Wolfe. "I think Terri's right. I think we're seeing some of the effects of testing the ELF system."

More calls came on the Sheriff's radio. "Gotta go," he said putting the car in gear. "We'll meet up later after I get this mess straightened out—*if* I get it straightened out."

chapter 49

Terri and Wolfe walked back to where Eino was still examining the crime scene. The weather had gotten warmer, and the sun was bright in a clear blue sky, which normally would have been nice, except for the fact that body parts would be heating up with the inevitable consequences.

Terri decided to focus on non-biological clues. "How could it do those things, Eino?" She asked. "I mean, all those symptoms?"

"Don't know, Terri," he answered, scratching his buzzard-like nose. "Cells communicate through a complex electro-chemical process. The central nervous system—the brain—they're all connected through minute electrical impulses. My guess is that the electromagnetic wave sent out by ELF disrupts this process—scrambles our signals, so-to-speak."

"No wonder they're trying to cover it up," Wolfe said squatting down to examine something in the dirt. He scooped up a handful of soil and let it sift slowly through his fingers. "The Navy's got a communication system that screws up people's minds—causes horrible disasters. The environmentalists are right. This damn thing's dangerous."

"What are we going to do, Clay?" she asked.

Wolfe let the remaining dirt fall from his hands and turned to Terri. "Find out who's killing the scientists," he said. He took hold of her hand and led her back to the Mustang.

"You don't think it's the environmentalists, I take it?" she said, pulling closer to him.

"That's right. There are more pieces to the puzzle."

"Like the guys trying to kill us," she finished.

"For starters, yes. They try to kill us, then they just watch us. They've got to keep this thing under wraps at any cost. But how they would ever get funding for such a system is beyond me."

"Unless funding was requested for something else," she added. "Like a simple communication system that was not hazardous, according to EPA studies."

"Of course," said Wolfe. "Kevin. He found out, and they killed him. We've got his notes, and now they're afraid of what we'll do with them. They took care of the first victims, but now it's too widespread. Maybe the cat's out of the bag."

"The jig's up?" she said, smiling at the cliché war.

Wolfe shot her a worrisome glance. "Or maybe they just don't care anymore."

Andrew Wallick's mood was less than genial when they arrived back on base at his office. "Good to see you again, Andy," Wolfe said innocently.

Wallick glared at him from behind his desk piled high with papers. "You see these?" he said, gesturing to the stacks in front of him. "I got a mess I'm never gonna get out of. And you've been one hell of a big help, Wolfe."

Wolfe started to say something but Wallick cut him off. "No. I mean it," he continued sarcastically. "You're one impressive investigator. I ask for some help and bamm! There you are with all the answers for me just when I need 'em."

Wolfe stiffened perceptibly. "Well, maybe if you were straight with me we'd have something by now."

"Straight with you?" shouted Wallick. "I gave you every damn piece of . . ."

"Cut the crap, Andy," Wolfe said. "You've been holding back critical information and don't try to tell me otherwise."

Wallick's face was red. He started to say something, then thought better of it. "I need some air," he snapped. "That convertible of yours got any punch to it?" he said to Terri.

"Enough," she said warily. "Why?"

"I need to clean out some cobwebs," he said, heading for the door. Terri looked at Wolfe, but he just nodded and they followed him out of the room.

No one spoke until Wallick was behind the wheel of Terri's Mustang and they were blasting along the open road, top down. Terri peered over Wallick's shoulder from the back seat, her eyes wide as the speedometer needle slid past ninety.

"So what the hell's going on?" Wolfe shouted over the rushing air, barely audible even then.

"I'm screwed," Wallick shouted back. "We're all screwed." Wolfe looked at the speedometer needle. It hovered around ninety-five.

"Slow down!" Terri shouted. "You're going to kill us all!"

"Doesn't matter," Wallick shouted, pushing the accelerator even deeper into the floor board. "We're already dead."

Wallick finally slowed and then, inexplicably, pulled into an A&W. "I'm famished," he said with unexpected enthusiasm. He ordered enough food for a battalion, then dove into it like a starving lion. "Have what you want," he said through a mouthful of food. "There's plenty."

Terri and Wolfe looked at each other, then passed around the

Coney dogs, onion rings and root beer, eating silently until it was gone. Finally, Wallick wiped the remnants from his face with a napkin, belched, and turned to Wolfe. "You want the straight story? Well, I'm going to tell you everything. And her," he nodded to Terri. "Everything I know. It means committing treason, but what the hell. My career—my life's down the toilet anyway, so you may as well come along for the ride—right?"

"We're waiting," Wolfe said, unsympathetically. Terri looked at Wolfe, a little surprised at his coldness.

Wallick looked at Wolfe too, for the same reason. "That's right. I forgot," he said finally. "You're the *wolf.* Nothing gets to you, does it? The cool, calculating hunter. No mercy for its prey. Shit. What do I care? We're all dead anyway."

"Why do you keep saying that?" Terri asked in frustration. "Why are we all dead?"

"Because there's a cancer in the operation," Wallick said. He was suddenly depressed again.

"Let's have it from the beginning," Wolfe said, the edge in his voice diminished.

"From the beginning," Wallick began, settling back in the bucket seat, staring up into the clear, blue sky, "it was intended to communicate with submarines. The first research was done in the forties and fifties. That's how long this has been going on, you know. Since World War II." They said nothing, so he continued.

"They started out with a need to communicate with the subs without having them surface where they were vulnerable to attack. Well, the need got greater when satellites began having the capability to spot subs even under the surface, and radio their positions to waiting destroyers. The very low frequency waves could penetrate the water a little ways so the subs didn't have to surface all the way, but they couldn't be very deep.

"Experiments were done in the Appalachians with above-ground antennas, but this produced problems with radio, and then television reception for people within a hundred or so miles of it. It would induce electrical currents in wire fences, screw up electrical appliances, and so on.

"Now these were frequencies above one hundred Hertz—you know what a Hertz is?" Wallick said, looking over at Wolfe then back over his shoulder at Terri. Neither said anything. "One cycle per second," he said. "That's one sine wave of the electromagnetic spectrum per second. One Hertz." Wallick drew a wave in the air with his finger, going up, then down, then back again. "One wave per second, he repeated. A *sine* wave." To Wolfe, Wallick seemed drunk, but he wasn't.

Wallick continued. "Electric lights, etcetera, operate at sixty Hertz, or sixty cycles per second. All frequencies below one-hundred cycles per second are considered extremely low frequencies, or ELF," he said. "The human brain operates on frequencies well-below sixty Hertz," he finished. He took another slurp of his root beer and ate a cold French fry.

Wolfe finally responded. "We pretty much know all this, Andy. Tell us something we *don't* know."

chapter 50

Wallick turned to look at Wolfe, his eyes kind of glassy, as if in a daze. He heard Wolfe, but apparently didn't process what Wolfe was saying.

Wallick turned his head back forward, stared off in the distance, and lumbered on.

"Anyway, they kept dropping the test range of the frequencies lower and lower until they were in the frequencies that the human brain operates on." Wallick paused, took a long drink of root beer, belched again.

"Problems started when the researchers came on board."

"What researchers?" Terri asked.

"Contract guys," he said. "Experts. Specialists. Sent from overseas. They were standoffish from the beginning. Knew it all. Wouldn't let anyone see what they were doing. Top secret stuff. Hush, hush. Eyes only, and all that crap," he finished.

"And then our people started dying. Replacements had to be brought in from the outside. Pretty soon, there was an air of paranoia around here. Personnel who didn't get along with these scientists suddenly were transferred. Some were demoted."

"And some died," Terri added.

"Yes. And that's where Wolfe came in. I didn't know who to trust. We'd worked together before in other countries, and I knew his talents and his loyalties. I could trust him, so I secretly hired him to find out what was going on."

"Which brings us here," Wolfe summarized.

"Not quite," continued Wallick. "When I was pulling together the files for you, I came across a file I had never seen before. It looked like it had been hurriedly stuck in with the other files. It wasn't in a folder, and some of the papers in it were sticking up in disarray. When I looked to see what was in there, I found documents that made my hair stand on end."

Terri brushed her hair from her face. "How do you think the documents got there?"

"I don't know," said Wallick, "but I have my suspicions. It may have been one of the scientists who was murdered. They were very close to the inside workings of the ELF program. They may have come across the information and were trying to get it to me before they were killed. They might have stuck it in the file in the hopes I would find it, or maybe they had planned to retrieve it later when things were safer."

Wolfe set his glass down. "So what was in the file you found?"

"You're not going to like it," Wallick began. "This group of renegades has been deliberately lowering the ELF operating frequency and conducting tests on human subjects—without the knowledge of the Navy authorities."

"But why?" Terri asked.

"I don't know," Wallick said, "but when you hear the results, you'll know it's not for motherhood and apple pie."

"Tell us," said Wolfe.

Wallick stared into space as if reciting a homework assignment. "Subjects at forty-five Hertz began showing signs of decreased psychomotor functioning."

"That's the same thing we found," Terri said to Wolfe. Wallick was surprised at the comment, but Wolfe gave Terri a disapproving look, then said, "Some independent research we did. Please continue."

Wallick went on. "Yes. Well. As I said, psychomotor functions deteriorated. Hand-eye coordination—you know—putting the square peg in the square hole? That kind of stuff. Went downhill at forty-five Hertz. Below that frequency, things really started to get interesting. Under ten Hertz people got headaches. They complained of a tightness in their chests. They experienced fatigue, sweating palms, and paranoia. The experiments were dangerous. Before they knew what they were really doing, two subjects became violent. Nearly killed each other. In another instance, a subject attacked the experimenter, blinding him, and a third killed himself—although they weren't sure whether or not it was intentional."

"How awful!" said Terri.

"That's not the end of it," Wallick said, finishing his root beer, followed by the now obligatory belch. "Lower frequencies produced even stranger effects. Below one Hertz, subjects slipped into another reality. Their minds became fuzzy—unreal—their thoughts vacillated between reality and fantasy."

"Wow," said Terri. "Is there any more?"

"Afraid so," said Wallick, grabbing for his now empty root beer glass. He examined the glass, as if he were trying to figure out what happened to the root beer, then put it down. "Sometimes the dreams turned into nightmares and the subjects did awful things to themselves—and others—much the same way people get when overdosing on hallucinogens."

"Self-mutilation," Wolfe said knowingly.

"Right," Wallick said, fishing the last French fry out of its greasy paper container. "One subject thought his penis was a snake trying to bite him. So he cut it off with a rusty tin can top."

"Eeeyuck," said Terri, visibly upset. Wolfe's knees clamped together reflexively.

"Another had visions so horrible he gouged his eyes out trying to remove the sight from his mind. Problem was, that's where the visions came from—his mind. He went permanently insane."

"Any of this reversible?" Wolfe asked.

"Some seemed to return to normal once exposure to the field was eliminated. Others seemed to flip out permanently. But the file didn't refer to any long-term studies. I think you can see why. No one knows whether or not there could be a spontaneous relapse as with hallucinogenic drugs."

"Are we at the end of the horror story *now*?" Terri asked, her hand attempting to shield her eyes from her own nasty visions.

"Not quite," he continued. "When you reach frequencies under one Hertz, another phenomenon occurred."

"And what's that?" she asked, now looking at the floor, not wanting to hear his answer.

"This one didn't make sense to me," Wallick said as he watched a puffy white cloud slowly drift across the sky. "After the things I just described, it didn't seem to be that important. Yet, it was circled and underlined in red."

"What was it?" Terri demanded, unable to bear the suspense.

"It seems," Wallick continued finally, "that when you reach that frequency with a sufficient level of intensity, the subjects lapse into unconsciousness—and they stay that way until the field is turned off."

They sat in silence as the impact of what they had just learned sank in. Finally, Terri spoke.

"You're right. It doesn't seem as serious. In fact, it seems preferable to the results at the higher frequencies."

"That's how I see it," Wallick responded.

"How wide-spread is the effect?" Wolfe asked.

"It's fairly localized as far as I can tell," Wallick said. "At least that's what's indicated by the test results I've seen. It seems to cover about twenty-five miles in each direction from the grid, plus all the area in between. That's at fifty percent power. What full power would do, is anybody's guess."

"What about the communication effect of the system then?" Terri asked. "It would have to have a global effect to be effective in communicating with subs."

"Oh, it'll do that too," Wallick said, adjusting the rearview mirror. "I thought you were talking about the effects on humans. The waves are so long they oscillate within the cavity between the ionosphere and the earth. They'll travel around the world at the speed of light. But they won't have much intensity. Enough to send a weak signal to a submerged sub, but not enough to affect humans the way I described."

"How far up the line do you think knowledge of this goes?" Wolfe asked.

"I don't know," said Wallick. "It's hard to tell because everything is on a need-to-know basis."

chapter 51

"How about the President?" Wolfe asked carefully.

"I doubt it. I don't see him condoning such research for any reason."

Wolfe looked at Wallick carefully. "Do you know who is in charge of this group of renegade scientists?"

Wallick breathed a sigh of resignation. "If you knew the man in charge, you'd know why I'm scared. He has a mission, and he's going to carry it out regardless of the consequences."

"Or maybe because of them?" Wolfe came back.

"What?" Wallick said, surprised.

"I think I know who you are talking about."

"You couldn't. I never said a word . . ."

"You didn't have to," Wolfe cut in. "I know his style. I should have seen it before—must be getting old."

"Who is it?" Terri said impatiently.

"It's Malcolm Draco," said Wolfe. "I've had dealings with him before. *Unpleasant* dealings."

Wallick's shoulders drooped visibly. "If you know Draco, then you know why I'm a dead man. Why we are all dead." Wallick's mind drifted to an unhappy place. "We know too much," he added. "He's the kind of guy who's obsessed. He has to know everything that's going on. Hell. He probably knows we're having this conversation right now. I don't know how, but he probably does. And that means we're finished."

"Can't you take it to his superiors?" Terri asked.

"Don't you think I'd like to do that?" Wallick said, exasperated. "But I can't. I don't know who his superiors are. This is a top-secret project. It doesn't go through the normal channels."

"But isn't there someone you could . . ." she started.

"Even if I could identify someone above him," he cut in, "I couldn't tell him. And for all I know, he could be in on it too. This project is on a need-to-know basis. I violate that and I go into the stockade for life. Maybe even the firing squad. So no matter what I do, I'm doomed. I do nothing and Malcolm gets me. I try to go around him and the military gets me. I'm screwed. We're all screwed."

They drove back to the base. Their mood was somber, as if they were on the way to an execution—theirs. Wallick was morose, Terri depressed. Only Wolfe's mind was racing. He considered the various options they might have—then discarded each, one by one. Things looked bleak.

Then, as they neared the base Wallick suddenly pulled off the road and stopped. "There's one more thing," he said with renewed energy.

"What's that?" Wolfe said, suddenly attentive.

"I wasn't going to say anything about this because I wasn't sure. And I figured I was in deep enough with you two anyway. But I guess it doesn't matter one way or the other now. Besides. I'm kind of curious myself."

"Curious about what?" Terri asked.

"That road we just passed. On the left."

"I don't see anything," Terri said, looking back where he was indicating.

"It's not much of a road. But it's there," Wallick continued. "I've seen trucks pull down there before. Military trucks. But what's more interesting, I've seen civilian vehicles go in there too. At least they looked like civilian vehicles."

"So?" said Terri. "What of it? What's down there?"

"That's just it," continued Wallick. "Nothing's down there. At least not according to the military. It's supposed to be vacant land. But I think there's some kind of building in there—surrounded by trees. I've seen it from the air and occasionally there's a reflection of light off of something in the area. Something metal. I have my hunches, but since we're in deep anyway, why not take a peek?"

"I'm game," said Terri looking at Wolfe. "What do you say?"

"Let's do it," said Wolfe, pulling strength from resources deep within—preparing for the unexpected.

The road was almost invisible, the hard-packed ground yielding little to the weight of the car and its passengers. Dust swirled behind them as they came up to the wooded area Wallick had spoken of.

"Looks a little desolate," Terri said as the woods grew thicker. The road wound around like a serpent, then the building came into view. "There it is," she said, pointing to the nearly invisible brown and green building dead ahead of them.

"Typical military," said Wallick as they drove up and stopped. The building was painted in traditional military camouflage colors of tan and brown, green and dark green. The paint was flat, and seemed to reflect very little light. It was about fifty feet square and twelve feet high, and had no discernible features, save the front door.

"Turn the car around, Andy," Wolfe said as he got out of the car. "I'm going to look behind the building."

Wallick did so, and by the time he and Terri got out, Wolfe was back with them. "You're right," he said to Wallick. "Typical military. Let's see if it's open."

"You don't think it's going to be unlocked, do you Wolfe?" Terri said as she tried the front door.

"No," he smiled, "but one can always hope."

The door was locked tight, its metal frame matching the building covering. There were no windows, and no visible vents. "What kind of building is this?" Terri said, giving up on the front door. "How can there be no windows? Whatever's inside must be really cooked in this sun." Suddenly a motor kicked on, its muffled sound concealing its location.

"What's that?" Wallick said, jumping back from the building.

"Sounds like a compressor motor," Wolfe said, backing up so he could better see the flat roof of the building. "My guess is it's an air conditioner of some type. Probably on the roof. I'll bet that's the reflection you saw from the air."

Wallick backed up further, as did Terri. "I think you're right, Wolfe," he said, his hand attempting to shade his eyes from the sun's rays as they poked through the trees. "Nothing on the rest of this building would reflect enough to be seen from the air."

"Is there a door in back?" Terri asked.

"There is," answered Wolfe, "but it's probably locked too."

"May as well check it out," Wallick said as he headed around back. The others followed until they came to the door. It was just like the front door, with a handle and deadbolt lock firmly embedded in the steel-clad door and frame.

"Try it," Terri said. Wallick turned the handle and pushed. The heavy door swung open—to absolute darkness.

chapter 52

A gust of ice-cold air struck them as it escaped from the building, mingling with the warm outside air. Certainly answered the air conditioner question, thought Terri.

"Damn, that's cold," Wallick said as he peered into the pitch-black interior.

"Well?" Terri taunted, "Are you going in?"

Wallick clearly would have preferred to do anything else but that, but his male ego forced him to show he had the right stuff. Reaching in, he felt for the light switch. Finding it, he flipped it up. The fluorescent lights gave their standard flicker, then came full on, illuminating the flat black interior with their stark, unforgiving glare.

Terri peered in and gasped. In the middle of the room, laid out on examination tables, were what appeared to be half a dozen bodies covered with black plastic sheets. "I don't like the looks of this," she said turning away from the entrance.

"You better stay here, Terri," Wolfe said motioning her back. "We'll check it out. You keep an eye out for visitors." Wallick was grateful Wolfe was willing to go first. He would have been even more grateful to be working as a short order cook in Baton Rouge.

Wolfe stepped into the frigid room and looked around. Aside from the six stainless steel examination tables with their mysterious cargo, there was nothing else in the room except a stainless steel cabinet. Wolfe walked over to the cabinet and tried the handles but it was locked.

Wallick entered the room and stood just inside the doorway, not pleased at all with what he saw. "This is not good," he said, giving new meaning to understatement.

"Looks like a temporary morgue to me," Wolfe said walking over to the closest black sheet. "What do you think?"

"I think this makes me very nervous," Wallick said, not moving from his position. "Why would the military have such a building out in the middle of nowhere? I mean, they couldn't perform autopsies here. There are no facilities. No drains, sinks, nothing."

"Probably just storage," Wolfe said, taking hold of the corner of the black sheet. Wallick grimaced, terrified that whatever was under the sheet would be too much for him to bear.

Wolfe suddenly whipped the sheet back, startling Wallick into an involuntary shriek.

"What is it?" Terri said, suddenly scared. She ran to the edge of the door but could not quite bring herself to look in. "What's going on?"

"Just a familiar face," Wolfe said as he gazed into the frozen, dead eyes of Babyface. "Well, that's one mystery solved," Wolfe said as he replaced the sheet.

"You know him?" Wallick said astonished, still riveted to the same spot by the door.

"We've met under more favorable circumstances—for me that is."

"Who is it, Wolfe?" Terri demanded.

"Babyface."

"Babyface?" she exclaimed. "What's he doing in there?"

"Not a lot," Wolfe quipped.

"I mean, how'd he get there? Isn't he supposed to be in the county morgue?"

"Doesn't Eino have him?"

"Offhand I'd say not," Wolfe continued. "Looks like one got away." Wolfe whipped back the second sheet. "Make that two," he said as he stared down at the face of the John Doe who had disappeared from the cemetery.

"What now?" Terri said, not really wanting to know.

"The John Doe," he said softly, knowing what was next. "He's here, too."

Terri's heart was pounding. "Is he in there, Clay? Please tell me. Is he there?"

Wolfe walked to the next table and pulled the sheet back. It was a young man—college-aged student. His features, even though blue like the rest, left no doubt as to his parentage. It was Kevin.

"He's here, Terri," Wolfe said, as softly as he knew how. "With the rest."

She let it all out then, tears finding their way down her cheek as she left the building to sit on the ground outside the door. Wallick accepted the opportunity to comfort Terri, happy to leave the room without discovering what was behind doors four, five and six.

Wolfe quickly looked at the remaining three bodies, discovering by their wounds and appearance that they were likely the three scientists who had committed suicide. "Andy," Wolfe shouted out the door. "I need your expert skills for a minute."

Wallick was in no mood to go back in the room, but when Terri said it was OK, he had no alternative. "What is it?" he asked cautiously as he re-entered the room.

"See if you can I.D. these three for me will you? I think you know them."

Wallick looked quickly at the three blue bodies then turned away, his lips pressed tightly together.

"Our deceased scientists?" Wolfe offered.

Wallick nodded and without saying a word, left as quickly as he came. Wolfe followed, turning off the light and shutting the door behind him.

"What are you doing?" Terri said to Wolfe, a shocked look on her face.

Wolfe looked startled, then said, "I'm leaving. Just like you."

"Not without my brother I'm not," she said defiantly.

"You're kidding," Wallick jumped in. "We can't take that body out of there. If Draco finds out we were here it'll be the end of us for certain. Besides," he said as an afterthought, "How'll you get the body back? I don't think the convertible's going to make it. Do you?"

"No," she continued stubbornly, "probably not. But I'm *not* leaving without him. I lost him twice and damn it, and it's not going to happen again."

"You won't reconsider?" Wolfe said, more as a statement than a question. Her look gave him his answer.

"All right then. How about if I stay here while you go get Eino? I'll make sure Kevin doesn't disappear again 'til you come back. Fair enough?"

Terri thought about it for a moment. "You won't leave 'til I get back?"

"Promise," he said, crossing his heart.

"What about you?" she said to Wallick.

"I should get back to the base as soon as possible. I'm sure I've been missed already, and the last thing I need right now is an audience with Draco. I'm sure it will come soon enough."

"OK," she said. "I'll drop you back at the base on my way to get Eino. You try to stall if you think someone might be coming out here. And you stay put 'til I get back," the last directed at Wolfe.

"I'll be here," Wolfe said, "but don't dally. Our friends won't be gone forever."

"I'll hurry," she said. "Let's go."

chapter 53

The wait seemed interminable. Wolfe scouted the area more thoroughly now that he had time. Finally satisfied that there was no one else nearby, and no electronic counter-measures he could detect, he settled down to await the arrival of Terri or Draco—whoever came first.

Forty-five minutes had gone by with no sign of anyone when, from inside the building, he heard the muffled sound of a telephone ringing. Damn, he thought. I don't remember seeing a telephone in there. Getting to his feet, he tried the door, but it was locked. The phone was on the third ring by now.

Wolfe quickly removed his lock picks and opened the door, the same way he had done when they first arrived. He followed the sound to the wall opposite the door and saw what he had missed before—a flat black grillwork in the wall, behind which was a speaker, and a key pad just below it with the traditional telephone letters and numbers on it. To the left of the grill was a spring-mounted toggle switch. Wolfe pulled the toggle down and held it. It was the tenth ring.

"Yeah?" he said in his most neutral voice, letting up on the toggle when he had done so.

"Wolfe?" came the half-whisper. "That you?"

"Wallick?" Wolfe said into the speaker. "Of course it's me. Who else did you expect to answer the phone? And where'd you get this number?"

"Skip the black humor, Wolfe, and never mind where I got the number," the voice rasped. "There's no time. Draco and his henchmen are coming your way. They left a couple of minutes ago. I tried to stall. If they find you there, you're done."

"They won't find me," Wolfe assured. "It's Eino and Terri I'm worried about. If they should cross paths . . ."

"I know, I know," he croaked. "I tried. I really tried . . ."

"Forget it, Andy. I know you did. Just go back to what you would normally do and try not to worry. The less attention you draw to yourself the better."

"Don't I know," Wallick rasped. "Good luck, Wolfe. I mean that."

"Good luck yourself, Andy," Wolfe said as he released the toggle and walked out of the room. He did not lock the door this time, banking that Eino and Terri would get there first. He found a good vantage point halfway up a white pine behind the building and began watching for company. It was not long in coming.

Within minutes he saw the telltale dust rising in the distance. As the cloud got closer, he could see that whoever was coming was not on a Sunday drive. Wolfe could see he would not be able to recognize which vehicle it was until it came around the last turn, so he climbed down from the tree and positioned himself behind the tree where he could clearly see the turn.

His stomach tight, his senses alert, he listened as the sound of the engine grew closer. Suddenly Eino's black limo wagon slid into view, tires spinning as he gunned it for the home stretch. Sliding to a stop at the back door, he backed the hearse up to the door and jumped out.

"Let's go!" he shouted at Wolfe, but Wolfe was already in the building, wheeling the table with Kevin on it toward the door.

"What took you so long, old man?" Wolfe said as they wrestled the frozen corpse into the back of the hearse.

"Old man, my ass," Eino shot back as they finished strapping the body in and slammed the door shut. "I'll never see the day you can do better."

"Hurry," Terri said from the front seat. "You never know when they might show up."

"I know when they're going to show up," Wolfe said as he hopped in the passenger side next to Terri. "They're on the way right now."

"The hell you say!" exclaimed Eino as he jumped in and threw the transmission into drive. "Then we'd better git."

The heavy hearse slid first one way, then the other as Eino kept the accelerator down. The powerful engine seemed more worthy of a Grand Prix than the leisurely pace of a funeral procession, thought Wolfe. "What've you got in this thing anyway, Eino?" Wolfe shouted past Terri over the roar of the engine.

Eino was busy throwing his shoulders into it, trying to avoid the bumps and the trees at the same time. "Four-twenty-nine," he shouted back with the trace of a grin on his face. "With a few extras on it."

"I *guess*," said Wolfe, smiling. "I didn't know you had it in you."

"We're not all gloom and doom, you know," he shouted, suddenly swinging wide to avoid a deep hole.

"Shit, Eino," Wolfe said, grabbing the courtesy strap to keep from squashing Terri. "Get us out alive—will you?"

"Quit your bellyachin'. We'll make it, or I'm not the coroner."

"That's what scares me," Wolfe said under his breath to Terri. She did not find the exchange amusing because as they turned onto the highway, she saw a three-car caravan slowing about three hundred yards down the road, preparing to turn in.

"Damn," she said. "That looks like them."

"Sure does," said Wolfe, watching the caravan in his rearview mirror. "Apparently they saw us as well," he said as Eino punched the big engine, pulling away from the caravan which was by now, completely stopped in the road.

"They seem to be a little upset," said Eino, watching in his own mirror. The drivers of the cars jumped out and shouted at each other in a flurry of confusion. Then they split up, the first two going after the hearse, while the third went to the building.

"Looks like they made up their minds. Eh, Wolfe?"

"You'd better kick this thing in the ass, Eino," Wolfe said, his eye still on the mirror. "Those cars are movin' up fast."

"Hang on, folks," Eino said, mashing the pedal to the floor. "It ain't over 'til the skinny coroner sings."

The hearse surged ahead, its big engine gradually pulling the heavy vehicle away from its pursuers. "Grab the radio in the glove box," shouted Eino as the hearse swung wildly around a car driving less than half their speed.

"What?" said Terri.

"The radio," repeated Eino. "There's a police radio in the glove box. You can use it to call the Sheriff. I think we're going to need his help."

"I think you're right," echoed Wolfe as he watched the rearview mirror. The hearse was no longer pulling away from the pursuers.

Wolfe opened the glove box and turned the radio on. Grabbing the microphone he pressed the transmit button. "This is Clayton Wolfe with the coroner's office calling for Sheriff Josephs. This is an emergency." He released the button and waited.

"Sheriff's office," the voice quickly came back. "This is the dispatcher. Who's calling?"

"This is Clayton Wolfe. I'm calling for Eino Loukkala. We

have an emergency situation and need to talk to Sheriff Josephs immediately."

"Stand by," the voice said, sounding confused.

Then, "Wolfe? This is Josephs. What's going on?"

"We have a hot package and are heading towards town from the air base. We have two pursuers and it's definitely not friendly."

"Where are you now?"

"We're on 553 coming up on 480," Wolfe shouted into the mike. "We're doin' over a hundred." Tires screeched and a horn sounded as an angry motorist was forced off the road.

"Shit. OK. I'll try to intercept them at the Carp River."

"Better hurry, Ed. If we slow down any they'll be up our tail pipe."

"I'm gone," he said. A staccato of calls went out in rapid fire over the radio, the Sheriff shouting orders to his deputies. Wolfe put the mike back in the glove box, but left the radio on.

"Think he'll make it?" Terri said anxiously.

"Don't know," said Eino. "It'll be close. I gotta put some more distance between us and them or he's never gonna have time to cut them off after we pass." Eino jammed the pedal as far into the floor as it would go. The big hearse once again began pulling away from the cars behind.

chapter 54

"There's the sign for 480," Terri said, pointing. "One mile."

"Should take about thirty seconds," Eino said, his eyes glued to the road. Terri looked at the speedometer. It was pegged at one-twenty. She closed her eyes, then opened them again—afraid to look, afraid not to.

County Road 480 definitely came up quickly. "Watch out!" Terri yelled as a yellow van began pulling across the road in front of them.

"I see it," Eino shouted as he deftly applied the brakes and accelerator. The tires screamed as the hearse started sliding sideways. But the van stopped half-way across, leaving Eino just enough room to counter-steer and slide by the horrified occupants.

"That was close, Eino," Wolfe said soberly. "Let's get there—OK?"

"Almost there," Eino shouted, half-acknowledging Wolfe. "Sixty seconds to Carp River."

"You sound like a damned tour guide, Eino," Wolfe chided. "Watch out for that sharp curve just before the river," Wolfe warned. "We'll never make it at this speed."

"I know, I know," snapped Eino. "Don't you think I've been down this road a few times before?"

"There it is," Wolfe said, indicating the ninety degree turn up ahead. Eino hit the brakes but they weren't slowing the car fast enough.

"Slow down!" Terri yelled.

"I'm trying," shouted Eino, both feet now jammed on the power brake pedal. The smell of burned brake linings filled the car. "These brakes weren't designed for this. Hang on."

"Einooooo," Terri said as the car slid too fast into the turn. The hearse went into a four-wheel drift across the road into the oncoming lane. Suddenly the two right tires lifted off the road and the vehicle began to roll over. They seemed to stay like that, rolling along on two wheels, for an eternity. Terri was screaming, and both she and Wolfe had slid across the seat pressing Eino against the driver's side door.

Then, just as quickly, the wheels snapped back down and the car straightened out. Terri's jaws were tight. "Eino," she screamed, "so help me if you ever do that again . . ."

"There he is," yelled Wolfe as they saw the three sheriff's cruisers positioned on either side of the road. Josephs waved them on by, then pulled his vehicle across the road behind the other two.

Seconds later the lead pursuit car appeared, accelerating away from the sharp turn toward the cruisers. The second car was right behind, not to be outdone. Suddenly they slowed, but not all that much. Moving quickly up to the cruisers they squealed to a stop. A man dressed in a dark blue suit got out of the first car and walked briskly over to Josephs.

"Military business," the man said, holding up credentials as he approached. "I order you to let us pass immediately."

"Order me?" Josephs said, giving Draco a withering look. After several seconds, Josephs took the black leather ID case and looked at the picture studiously, eating up as much time as he could. Then he looked at Draco. "Malcolm Draco, eh?" he said, sizing him up. He was not tall—about five-nine—and trim, with thin, dark hair combed straight back. He looked more like a banker than a military official, thought Josephs, but his penetrating eyes told another story.

"Hurry!" Draco ordered. He clearly was not used to *asking*. "We must get through. It is of utmost importance."

"Movin' along pretty fast, weren't you, Mr. Draco?" Josephs said, ignoring the plea.

"We had reason enough," Draco came back quickly. "Valuable military property has been stolen. It is critical we get it back immediately."

"I'm sure it is," Josephs said slowly, deliberately agitating Draco. "But first I'm gonna need to see your driver's license—and your buddy's, too," he added, indicating the driver of the second car.

"You can't do this, Sheriff," Draco said in a very menacing tone.

"Oh, but I can, Mr. Draco. And I'm going to," Josephs said, walking back to his cruiser to move it off the road.

"You're in on this, Sheriff. Don't think I don't know it," Draco shouted after him. "You're going to pay dearly for this, I assure you."

"So you say," Josephs said.

Eino slowed down after seeing the roadblock take effect. "See? I told you we'd make it," he said with a mischievous grin. Terri's color had drained from her face, and she wouldn't even look at him.

"A temporary victory," Wolfe said stoically. "You're going to have to secure Kevin's body good this time, Eino. You know they'll be back."

"Don't worry," Eino said smugly. "They won't get him away from me again."

"I hope you're right," Terri said, looking at Eino.

chapter 55

They arrived at the morgue, and Wolfe and Eino transferred Kevin's body without incident. Then they joined Terri in the situation room in the Sheriff's department to await Josephs. He wasn't long in coming.

"This better be damn good, Wolfe," Josephs barked as he entered the room with a swiftness seldom seen of the Sheriff. "My ass is out fifty feet on a limb right now and you and that Draco fella are on each end of the saw. Now what the hell's goin' on?" Josephs slammed his bulk into the chair, lit his cigar, and started puffing furiously as he stared at Wolfe. "Well?" he barked.

Wolfe explained it all, with occasional interjections from Eino and Terri. "So you were right, Terri," Josephs said after they had finished. "That mess of dead and mangled people I got strewn all over this damn county is due to ELF. A few more days like today and we'll all be looking for a new line of work."

"Why don't you tell us what you've got in the way of effects of the last ELF test," Terri said to Josephs.

"*If* that was the cause of it," cautioned Eino. "We still don't know for sure."

"Well, we're going to have to go on the assumption that it is," Terri said. "The evidence points to it, and Malcolm Draco appears to be the renegade official behind it all."

"It does seem convincing," Wolfe offered. "Looks like Draco was the one who hired the thugs who were after us—like Babyface. Or at least he knew about it. And Kevin and the others. They were all in the building where Malcolm was heading."

"Maybe he was hired by higher-ups to keep the lid on ELF 'til the unauthorized experiments could be completed," said Eino, scratching his protruding Adams apple. "Kevin got in the way first with his environmental study. Then you came and started digging around and got hitched up with Wolfe. Two more liabilities."

"Then the obvious casualties of ELF testing were 'collected'—maybe for examination, or, more likely, just to keep them out of the way," said Josephs, jumping in.

"Like in the cold storage building," Terri said.

"Right. And it looks like the scientists were also victims of Draco," Josephs continued, now puffing on a cold cigar stub.

"I think they got in the way of the illicit testing," Wolfe said. "That's the impression I got from Wallick. The murdered scientists were good men. They probably became aware of what was being done, and refused to go along, or maybe threatened to go over Draco's head."

"No argument there," said Josephs, mercifully removing the soggy cigar from his mouth and placing it in the ash tray.

"So. Back to your casualties, Sheriff," Terri said. "Can we say they are most likely caused by a renegade ELF field test?"

"Well, everything seems to fit all right," he said placing his wire-rimmed spectacles halfway on the bridge of his nose. Pulling a notebook somewhere from the recesses of his clothing, he flipped several pages until he found what he wanted. "Bus driver got dizzy all of a sudden. Thought he saw giant vampires standing in the roadway. Swerved to avoid them and hit an abutment.

"Same for the drivers, with obvious variations. Dizziness, hallucinations, disorientation. Had the same with the mine workers who were hurt, only stronger. Maybe 'cause the antenna's buried in the ground."

"Any others seemingly affected?" Terri asked.

"Probably everyone was to some extent, just like we were. I did hear through the grapevine that a couple of doctors slipped up during surgery about that time. But you know them. They'd never report it if they did. They just bury their mistakes."

"How about other counties?" asked Wolfe.

"Nothing really," Josephs said, closing his notebook. "As far as I can tell, it's just this county. But then, they probably haven't got the whole thing hooked up yet. I guess there's no point making a bigger mess than they have to, at least for now."

"But the effectiveness of the antenna would be drastically reduced if they only had one section functional," said Terri, puzzled. "That's why the Navy wanted the antenna grid to extend from Marquette all the way to their test site in Clam Lake, Wisconsin. With waves hundreds of miles long, the longer the antenna, the better."

"She's right," Eino said. "The most efficient antenna is one where the antenna length is the same as the length of one wave. As the antenna length is shortened, it loses its efficiency, with maximum effects coming in multiples or fractions of the wave length."

"So if an ELF wave is two hundred miles long, the best antenna is the same length," Josephs summarized.

"Right," said Eino. "And the next most efficient length is one hundred miles, then fifty miles, then twenty-five miles, and so on," he finished.

"Or you could double it," Josephs said, not wanting to be bettered.

"Yes, you could," said Eino. "If you wanted to build an antenna four hundred miles long."

Wolfe turned to Eino. "Changing the subject, how are you coming on the body of the *terminal man*, Eino?"

"Ha, Wolfe, very funny," Eino said, all agitated. "I got eighteen hands and twelve legs, eh? If I didn't have to spend all my time tryin' to pull your ass outta the soup I might have time to do a little of my *own* work."

"You identified him?" Wolfe continued.

"Of course I did," Eino said, calming after his show. "I'm a miracle worker."

"And?" Terri prompted.

"He's the same guy as on the ID, all right. Get anything more on the name check, Sheriff?"

"Nothing local. But a criminal history check did show some affiliations with leftist groups out of state. Oregon and Washington, if I recall correctly. I've had about the same lack of time to do my work as you, Eino."

"And now for the main question," Terri continued. "Was he alive when the bomb went off?"

"He was," Eino said.

"I guess that makes him a prime suspect in the bombing," Wolfe said.

"Well, at least we can call Wallick and let him know who blew up his terminal. Maybe the military can find out more about his background," Wolfe said, getting out of his chair. "I'll call him," he said, and left to use the sheriff's office.

Moments later he walked back into the room, a somber look on his face. "So much for military assistance," he said quietly.

"What?" said Terri. "He won't help us?"

Wolfe shook his head. "More like, can't," he said. "He's dead."

chapter 56

"Dead?" Terri asked, incredulous. "How?"

"Suicide, of course," Wolfe said. "Draco knew he couldn't get at us right away. And we already figured Wallick was on the hit list. He just made it sooner than later."

"Your theory about the NSA monitoring our telephone conversations," Josephs directed to Wolfe. "You think Draco is involved in that?"

"It's possible," Wolfe said, tapping his fingers on the table. "Probably not officially, but yes. I think there's a good chance he knows someone there who would do what he needed done. Draco's that kind of guy. He's a great recruiter."

"What do you mean by that?" asked Terri.

Wolfe hesitated, not wanting to get too deep into his past connections with Draco. "He . . . uses people's weaknesses," he said finally. "When he wants something from someone, he doesn't just ask like a normal person. That might result in a negative response. Draco doesn't like negative responses and he doesn't like uncertainty.

"So he finds out the person's weaknesses—and we all have

them, be it sex, drugs, lust for power, love, whatever—and he blackmails them. Actually," he said, leaning back in his chair and reciting as if from personal experience, "he prefers the carrot-stick approach. That gets the person in even deeper. You do what he wants, and he'll reward you, thus you've accepted payment for a usually illegal act. That gives him even more blackmail material.

"On the other hand, if you don't do what he wants, then he'll ruin you—or worse—and he'll do it without hesitation."

"But doesn't that mean he's failed?" Terri asked. "I mean, he wouldn't achieve his objective in that instance."

"Not initially," Wolfe continued, "but it serves as a great object lesson for the next person he chooses, particularly if done in a dramatic way. It shows his power over people. It's very intimidating."

"I must admit," interjected Josephs, adjusting his spectacles, "that my short exposure to the man was less than cordial. I guess you could say I wouldn't care to meet him on his terms in a deserted warehouse."

"How is it you know so much about him, Wolfe?" Eino asked, leaning a bit closer.

"I've had . . . dealings with him in the past," Wolfe said, uncomfortable at the line of questioning. No one spoke, their attention directed at him, waiting for more. "Let's just say I used to work with him in a foreign country, and had the opportunity to observe his methods up close."

"Care to elaborate?" Josephs pressed.

"I can't, really," he said, knowing what was coming, unable to avoid it. "It's a . . ."

"Matter of national security," Terri cut in. The others looked at her. "I know," she said. "I've heard it before."

"What can I say," he responded in defense.

"Not much," she said. "But we've got to decide what to do now. I have a feeling we're running out of time."

Josephs nodded. "One, we've gotta find out the whole purpose of this thing—what its ultimate use is. Two," he pressed two fingers on the table," we've gotta find out how far this thing goes up the line—who knows about it—who's supporting it." He paused, slowly looking around the table. "And three, we've gotta stop Draco."

"That sounds like a good plan," Eino said, "But how are we going to do all those things? There're just the four of us against who knows how many people."

"I didn't say it was going to be easy, Eino," Josephs said condescendingly. "I just said that's what we gotta *do.*"

"Sheriff," Wolfe cut in, "it would be helpful if you could try to run down more about Henson. Since Wallick's not available anymore, we'll have to settle for what civilian law enforcement can come up with. It might help to know for sure what leftist groups he affiliated with and how long ago."

"I'll take care of it," Josephs said, making some notes.

"Fine. Eino," Wolfe said, turning toward the coroner, "It's still important to see if we can find out more about the physiological effects of ELF on the human anatomy, and what effects we are likely to see if the field intensifies. Maybe that will help us to answer the question of what it's really intended to be used for."

"I'll keep working on it, Wolfe," he responded.

"Great. And Eino?"

"What?" he said, looking up.

"Hang onto that body."

"Up yours, ya smart-ass," Eino said, his thin lips pursed.

"In the meantime," Wolfe continued, ignoring the outburst, "Terri and I will try to find how far up this thing goes. I may have some connections who will help us out."

"Do I have a say in any of this?" Terri said to Wolfe.

"No," he said, a twinkle in his eye. "You don't."

Terri nodded, smiled. "Just checking."

"Let's do it," said Josephs as he grabbed his soggy cigar from the ash tray and put it back in his mouth.

chapter 57

Wolfe drove Terri back to his cabin. Terri started a fire in the fireplace while Wolfe poured two glasses of Pinot Noir. He knew there would be lots of questions, but he knew he would not be able to answer them all. At least, not now. He sat by her on the couch as the fire took the chill of the air. They were both silent for a few minutes, then Terri turned to him and spoke.

"So, who are these 'connections' of yours, Clay?"

"I don't have any connections," he said casually.

"What? But you said back there . . ."

"I know what I said," he interrupted. "I just wanted to forestall any further questions as to how I was going to proceed."

"And I suppose it's for our own good."

"Actually, it is," he said. "The less you know about some things, the better."

"Well, I don't buy it, and I never will."

"I know," he said, the trace of a smile on his face. "But I love to tease you."

"I know," she said, a different look coming across her face. "And turnabout's fair play," she said, striking a provocative pose.

Wolfe looked at her, her eyes suddenly soft—inviting. "This is much more fun than fighting."

"Yes, it is," she said, inching closer to him.

"So why do we argue so much?"

"I don't know, Clay," she said. "You drive me crazy. Sometimes I hate your secretiveness—your distance. I admire your self-confidence and I respect you and what you're doing," she said, taking his hand in hers. "But other times," she said softly, slipping her arms around his neck, "like now . . ."

Wolfe kissed her, his powerful arms pulling her tight. Her pliant body responded to his strong tenderness.

"So if you don't have connections," Terri said to Wolfe, as they reluctantly pulled apart, "what do you plan to do?"

"Break into Wallick's safe," he said casually.

"What? Why his safe? What's in it?"

"More information than he was letting on, that's for sure," Wolfe said.

"He *was* panicking toward the end."

"So where is Wallick's safe?" she said, turning around.

"In his home, off-base."

"Don't you think Draco will have already been there?"

"He doesn't know it exists."

"The home?"

"The safe," Wolfe said, shaking his head.

"How could he not know it was there?" she said, still puzzled. "Knowing Draco's penchant for thoroughness, don't you think he would have searched it by now?"

"Undoubtedly," Wolfe said. "But it's hidden. Even Draco couldn't find it unless he knew where to look."

"All right," she said. "What if you do find some documents showing that ELF is being sabotaged? What then? Who are you going to report it to?"

"Not sure yet," Wolfe said. "We have to be careful what we say and who we say it to. Too many dead bodies piling up."

"How high do you think it goes, Clay?" She said.

"I don't know that either," he said. "It might not be a matter of how high, but more specifically, how high in what branch or agency. It might be that it is part of the government, or a civilian contractor agency, or a combination of both," he said. "Or it could be something completely different."

"You think it could be in the military? Maybe up to the joint chiefs?" she said.

"Could be," he said.

"And if you do find out who to take it to, how do you think you're going to get this information to them?" she said. "Just walk on in and say, 'Hi. I'm Clayton Wolfe and I have information that people under your command are about to create an Armageddon?'

"That might not be as difficult as you think," Wolfe said. "But it all depends on who we decide to go to. Don't worry. When the time comes, we'll get in."

"What if they already know about it?" she continued relentlessly.

"Then we're out of options," he said, "except to invoke our 'insurance policy.'

Terri sat bolt upright. "You mean the press?" she said. Then as the realization slowly hit her, "*My* wire service?"

"It would be a legitimate news source," he said, "that people would accept as valid. We could also feed it to the evening news programs. That would be literally impossible to stop. It'd be our last shot," he said, shrugging his shoulders.

"I think 'shot' is the appropriate word," she said, shaking her head. "I never intended that we'd actually publish the documents we sent. That would be risky—going public with military secrets."

"I just said it was our last option—I didn't say it was a good one," he responded.

"That's it then?" she said.

"That's it."

"Then we may as well get it over with," she said, pulling him up off the couch. "It's now or never."

chapter 58

They rode in silence as Wolfe moved the Mustang deftly through the turns towards Wallick's house. It was isolated from other houses, sitting far back along the Chocolay River. The tall pines blocked most of the sun, even during midday. Now, nearing dusk, they made it already dark.

"Pretty house," Terri said, as they drove up the long, sandy drive. It was natural wood and two stories tall with a large redwood deck along the side and back. "Not bad on military pay."

"He worked for Draco," Wolfe reminded. "Remember the carrot-stick school of management and mayhem?"

"You think he paid off Wallick?" she said as Wolfe brought the car to a stop on the circular drive in front.

"Most likely," Wolfe said, opening and closing the car door quietly. "That's his style."

"Think anyone's here?" she whispered, getting nervous.

"Not likely," he said, trying the front door. "But it pays to be cautious." It was locked, so he jimmied the door using a credit card. It looked easier than it was. Finally it opened.

The lights were all off, so Wolfe turned on a penlight and

walked in. "Looks like no one's home," he said, closing the door behind Terri. Finding the light switch, he turned on the lamp.

"What are you doing?" Terri exclaimed. "Someone will see us."

"There's no one within half a mile of here," Wolfe said, going into the kitchen. "Besides. It would look less suspicious if someone saw us in here with the lights on, than with a flashlight flickering around."

"I guess you're right," she said. "Let's just get out of here as soon as we can. It gives me the willies. Where is the safe, anyway?"

"In the kitchen," he said, going to the refrigerator.

"The safe's in the ice box?" she said as he opened the door.

"That's right." Lifting one of the shelves, he turned the plastic foot that held it in place. There was a soft click, then a small panel below the door swung open revealing a six-inch by two-foot cavity.

"Wow," she said. "That's impressive."

"Specially built from the ground up," he said, reaching inside.

"A safe disguised as a refrigerator," she said as he slid a metal, safe deposit-type box out of the cavity and onto the floor. "What'll they think of next?"

Wolfe lifted the clasp on the box and opened it. Inside was a hundred thousand dollars in cash, some loose diamonds, emeralds and rubies, and a black leather-clad folder marked, 'EYES ONLY.' Wolfe lifted out the inch-thick document and quickly flipped through the first few pages. "This looks like it," he said, then returned the folder to the box that he then shut tight.

Terri looked at him funny. "You're taking the whole thing? All the money and everything?"

Wolfe took the handle of the box and stood up, shutting the secret panel with his foot. "You want to leave it for Draco?"

"And what's so wrong with that?" said a cold voice from behind them. They spun around to find Draco grinning at them, a silenced machine pistol held at the ready. "I think that's a splendid idea."

"Fancy meeting you here," Wolfe said coolly, moving slightly forward and to the left in an effort to partially cover Terri.

"Oh, your gallant effort is quite unnecessary," Draco said of Wolfe's move. "I've no intention of harming either of you. What I would like, however, is the contents of that box you are holding."

"This?" Wolfe said, abruptly raising the box in front of him.

Draco stepped back quickly, raising the machine pistol as he did so. "None of your tricks, Wolfe," Draco said, smiling again, his composure in place. "I haven't forgotten the days of yore. You'll not get the drop on me again."

"I've no intention of doin' that, laddie," Wolfe said, slipping into a thick, Irish brogue. Apparently it meant something to Malcolm, because the smile vanished from his face along with any trace of civility.

"Put the case down," Draco said in measured words, "and let's get on with it. I've things to do."

"Oh, yes," Wolfe said. "I forgot. You're an important man. You've got defense systems to make operational. Scientists to kill. Witnesses to silence."

"Clay," Terri said nervously, "Let's give him what he wants so he'll go. We don't need that stuff anyway."

"My, my," Draco said, smiling again. "You two've been chummy with each other, haven't you?" Wolfe's jaws tightened but he said nothing. "Clay—not again," he said in a false fatherly fashion. "I thought you'd learned your lesson the last time." Then directing his words to Terri, "Wolfe has a fatal charm for women. He loves them and then they die."

Wolfe's eyes were burning now, his fists clenched. He started to take a step forward but Malcolm quickly raised the machine pistol to him. "Here and now," he said quickly, pointing the gun back and forth between the two of them. "Doesn't matter to me either way."

"Oh, I think it does, Draco," Wolfe said. "If you gunned us

down now, you'd be deprived of your sadistic pleasures. And I know you can't resist the temptation to get back at me."

"How true, Wolfe, how true. But there's more than one way to get back at someone, Wolfe."

"I'm sure there is," Wolfe said, "especially in that warped, twisted mind of yours."

Draco's smile faded again. "Enough idle chatter. Set the case down, Wolfe. Nice and slowly. Good. Step to the left please, three paces. Thank you. Now Terri, you bring that chair over here for Mr. Wolfe, and bring one for yourself, too. I have some rope you're going to use to tie him up with, then I'll tie *you* up," he finished in a sing-song tone. "That way no one has to get hurt. I get what I want, and you stay alive."

Terri did as he requested. "That-a-girl," Draco said in the most patronizing tone. "You catch on quick. She catches on quick, don't you think, *Clay?*" he mocked. Wolfe said nothing as he sat in the straight-backed wooden chair while Terri began tying his hands behind his back.

"And do make it tight, sweetie," Draco said. "I'm afraid I'll have to check when you're done. If it's too loose, there will have to be some sort of punishment. Wolfe knows about that, don't you Wolfe?"

"Don't worry about me," Wolfe said to Terri. "Do as he says. I'll be OK."

"See?" Draco said to Terri. "He'll be OK. So tie him tight so I can leave you two love birds alone."

When Terri had finished tying Wolfe, Draco tied Terri in the chair opposite Wolfe, so they could see each other. "There," Malcolm said, admiring his handiwork. "That should do. Now. Are there any questions you'd like to ask before the show begins?"

"Show? What show?" Terri asked. "You said you would leave us alone if we cooperated."

Draco laughed a humorless laugh. "Oh dear," he said, shaking his head. "You forgot to tell her—didn't you, Wolfe?"

"Tell me what?" Terri said, fear rising.

"Tell her, Wolfe," he said. "She should know, don't you think?"

"He's a liar," Wolfe intoned with no emotion.

"I'm a liar," Draco repeated, his eyes bright with anticipation. "Yes. You can't believe a word I say. Wolfe's absolutely right."

"He had no intention of letting us live from the very beginning," Wolfe continued in the same monotone.

"Right again," said Draco, calmly. "He knows. Wolfe knows me. Now. Back to my question. Is there anything you want to ask me before the show? Take your time. Think about it. Anything you want to know. Absolutely anything," he said as he removed a thin, black box from his coat pocket. "I'll just get ready while you think."

"What are you going to do?" Terri said, her voice wavering perceptibly.

"Oh please. Please," he said, taking several items out of the box. "There's time for that later. Plenty of time. Questions first. Then we'll play."

"I have a question," Wolfe said with no enthusiasm.

"Oh goodie. Let me guess," Malcolm said, like a little child guessing a riddle. "You want to know about ELF—am I right?"

"What's it for, Draco?" Wolfe said, with growing impatience.

Draco's face turned to stone. He walked over to Wolfe and jammed the barrel of the machine pistol in his ear. "I don't like your tone, Wolfe. Maybe I'll just send your brains for a ride right now."

"Go ahead. Do it," Wolfe barked. "Beats the alternative."

Draco smiled, regained his composure. "Yes it does, doesn't it?" He pulled the gun out of Wolfe's ear. "Then I guess we'd better wait. Don't want to spoil all the fun."

chapter 59

"So you want to know about ELF," he said, prancing around as if he were giving a lecture to a class of college students. "First you must tell me all you know about it. And don't spare the details. I really want to know how good our security's been."

Wolfe summarized what they knew, while Terri kept adding details, trying to stretch it out as long as she could. Finally Draco raised his hand. "Thank you class, you've really done your homework. But I'm afraid you don't get an 'A'. You see, you missed the real genius of the system. It does all that, like you say, but you're too narrow in your perspective. You've got to think big, like me."

"We thought big," Wolfe cut in, "but we couldn't figure out how it could be anything more than a local chamber of horrors."

"Well, I'll fill in the missing pieces, then," he said, prancing again. "Ever hear of something called 'The Schumann Response'?" Draco looked at Terri, then Wolfe. "No? Well then. How about sferics—or perhaps, resonance?"

"Yea, we've heard of resonance, Malcolm," Wolfe said. "So's every tenth-grader in America. So what?"

"That's where you missed the point," he said, leaning close to

Wolfe's face. "The concept of resonance allows us to expand the scope of the system."

"I see," Wolfe said.

"Yes, I'll bet you do, now that I've explained it," Draco chided. "You use the cavity between the earth and the ionosphere to capture the wave. As it makes its way around the earth at the speed of light, it comes in phase with itself, reinforcing each additional wave until its strength is magnified higher and higher until it reaches incredible power. "So you see, that lets us propagate the wave around the world at great strength, and cause the effects you described, world-wide."

There was silence as his words sunk in. Draco stood there, his hands clasped behind him. His head was tilted slightly back, his eyes focused on the vision he had described.

"But why?" Terri asked.

"To control the world," Draco said softly, not moving from his vision. "We can make and enforce a global policy from right here. Think of it. From here, we can turn the world into a madhouse. At the correct frequency and intensity we can make people the world over paranoid—suicidal—we can turn the world into a hellhole of bloodshed and disruption until the governments are toppled and the armies destroyed."

"But what about the civilians?" she said. "The innocent people?"

"There are no innocent people," he said, walking over to her. "There are just people. They would all be affected—men, women, children—they would all go crazy.

"The real coup de grace, however," he said dramatically, "is that when we crank the frequency down even lower, we can make the entire world go unconscious. We can then go in and take over what we want, where we want, who we want. We will be in control."

"But you'll be affected too," she said. "Where will that get you?"

"They've got protection from its effects, Terri," Wolfe said unceremoniously.

"To the head of the class," Draco said. "Yes, we've developed a shield against effects of the waves. And yes, it is something the opposing forces could do if given enough time. But they won't have enough time. That's one of the reasons for all the secrecy. But even then, there's no way to shield the entire population of a country. All you could do is shield your chosen leaders, and the soldiers necessary to keep them in power."

"Something you've already done," Wolfe ventured again.

"Absolutely astonishing," exclaimed Draco. "Right again. There is indeed a select group within this government and the military who have been chosen to participate in the new world order. In fact," he said, walking over to the safe box, "you actually had that list in your hands for a brief moment." Draco opened the box and pulled out the black folder. "I believe you'd be very surprised to see the people on this list," he said, flipping through the pages. "Unfortunately, there won't be time. I've answered your questions, and now it's time for the show to begin."

Draco took several incendiary devices and placed them strategically around the room. Then he took two more and placed one under each of their chairs.

"You're going to burn us to death?" Terri said, horrified when she saw what he was doing.

"Why, yes, Terri," Draco said condescendingly. "That is precisely what I'm going to do."

"You can't!" Terri said. "It's inhumane!"

"But oh, so effective," he responded. "This way, I get rid of you, the evidence, and everything. It all goes up in smoke, if you'll pardon the expression."

"Stop him, Clay!"

"Yes, Clay," Draco mocked. "*Stop* him."

"I'm afraid there's nothing I can do now, Terri," Wolfe said. "Don't give him any more satisfaction."

"Spoil sport," Draco said. He held up the detonator for them both to see. "I'm going to hang around to see the beginning of the fireworks, folks, if you don't mind."

"Be our guest," Wolfe said.

"Thank you," Draco said politely. "I will. And now, as they say in the theatre, let the show begin."

"Show's canceled," came the gravelly voice of the Sheriff from behind them. They turned and saw Josephs emerge from the shadows with a twelve-gauge shotgun pointed at Draco's chest.

"Thank god!" Terri exclaimed.

Draco jumped up with the instincts of a cat. Spinning around, he grabbed Terri's hair, pulled a switchblade knife from his boot, and put it to her throat. "Too bad you're so old and so stupid, Sheriff," Draco snarled. "Touch me and she's finished anyway. And now I have three victims instead of two."

"Not exactly," Josephs said, moving closer, the gun still aimed at Draco's chest.

"You can't shoot me, Sheriff," Draco said, his veneer cracking slightly. "You do and she'll die too. That shotgun's too powerful at this range."

"Maybe," Josephs, said calmly. "But the sniper outside's got your temple in his crosshairs, and if you so much as twitch, he'll aerate that demented brain of yours without so much as moving a hair on her head." Draco turned his head slightly to see out the window.

"Oh, you can't see him, but he's there, Draco. Trust me," Josephs said. "Now put down that knife and let's end this nightmare."

Draco's eyes were darting around the room, looking for a way out. "You'll kill me anyway," he said, his breathing rate increasing.

"Draco, you're an asshole," Josephs said, as he watched Draco's eyes spot the machine pistol two feet out of reach. "You've got to *three* to put the damn knife down or I'm gonna signal the sniper to take you out. One," he began, as Draco's eyes darted around the room. "Two," he continued, raising his left hand.

Draco lunged for the machine pistol, throwing his knife at Josephs as he jumped.

"Three," said Josephs quietly as Draco was still in mid-air, his arm extended toward the pistol. Josephs dodged the knife and let go a blast that caught Draco directly in the chest. Draco's body spun from the force of the hit, landing face up at Wolfe's feet.

A red, cat's eye marble rolled out of Draco's pocket and over by his head. "Now that's fitting," said Wolfe.

He looked down at the dead body. Draco had a hole in his chest the size of a fist where his heart used to be. "Bye Draco," he said, unemotionally. "Thanks for the show."

chapter 60

"Thanks, Ed. We owe you one," Wolfe said as Josephs untied them. Terri was still in shock.

"Thought there might be a problem up here," he said, "when I got the call on some prowlers."

"But there's no one within half a mile of here," said Terri, beginning to calm down.

"That's true, most of the time," Josephs said, walking over and looking out the patio door onto the deck. "Just so happens some fishermen were going down the Chocolay right behind here. Saw the lights on, knew the place was supposed to be empty. Neighbors of his, I guess," he said. "Heard about the suicide.

"Anyway," he said, lighting up a cigar, "when I heard it was Wallick's house, I figured it might be you two, or maybe Draco snoopin' around, and maybe I should take a look. Damn good thing I did, eh?"

"You can't begin to know, Sheriff," Terri said, giving him a hug. "Thank you."

"In the line of duty, Terri," he said. "In the line of duty."

"Maybe you'd better call your sniper in now, Ed," Wolfe said. "He might be getting chilled."

"What sniper?" Josephs said, puffing on his cigar, a twinkle in his eye. "You know I ain't got no sniper, Wolfe. Too damned expensive to keep the good ones trained—the rest aren't worth shit."

"What?" exclaimed Terri. "You mean to tell me there was no sniper on him?"

"Only in his mind, honey," Josephs said, getting folksy.

"What would have happened if the bluff hadn't worked?" she asked intently.

"Good question," Josephs answered, looking at Wolfe.

Wolfe smiled. "Guess we'll never know."

"And what about you?" she said, walking over to Wolfe. "You were just going to let him turn me to cinders, weren't you?"

"Us, dear," he said correcting her. "He was going to turn *us* to cinders."

"And you weren't going to do anything about it?" she accused.

"I had a plan," he said defensively.

"Oh yea, what was it?"

"Doesn't matter. Didn't need it," he smiled at Josephs. "I'll save it for another time."

"Sure. Right," she said. Then, she looked down at Draco. "What a demented man. You think his death will stop this madness?" she asked.

"I hope so," said Wolfe. "Draco wasn't a scientist. He couldn't have made any of the technical changes in ELF, but he could be the brains behind this new world order scheme. That's a twist that would have been right up his alley."

"Well, at least we have the notebook with all the names in it," Terri said reaching for the case. "It won't take long to find out who's involved." She took the notebook out of the box and opened it. The first half of the manual was a technical description of the modified system, and how it worked.

"That's the part I saw before Draco came," Wolfe said looking at the notebook. Terri kept flipping through until she came to part two. When she turned the divider, all she saw was page after page filled with nothing but numbers.

"Code," said Wolfe shaking his head. "All the names are in code. Damn!"

"How can we break it?" Terri said to Wolfe.

"*We* can't," Wolfe said. "This will require sophisticated ciphering computers."

"Great," she said. "And where do we find those?"

Wolfe looked at Josephs who just stood there puffing on his cigar.

"NSA?" Josephs said finally, his cigar making the letters sound like a new language.

"That's it," said Wolfe, letting out a deep sigh.

"So now what the hell we gonna do?" Josephs said, chewing hard on his stogie.

"Get the names decoded," Wolfe answered, "and get them to someone who can stop this thing before it's too late."

"You mean take them to the NSA?" Terri said. Wolfe nodded. "What about Draco's contact there? Aren't you taking a chance he'll get it and alert the rest?"

"Calculated risk we'll have to take," he said. "We don't have many other options. If we take a book of numbers to the Secretary of the Navy, he'll just have to do the same thing—get it to the NSA for decoding. And that's likely to take longer, with more chances of a leak than if we do it."

"How you gonna get in?" Josephs said. "That place's shut tighter than a spinster's knees."

"I'll work on it," Wolfe said, brushing the question aside. "In the meantime, you'd better get Eino over here. He's got some waste to dispose of," he said, looking at Draco's corpse one last time.

"I'll call him," Josephs said, going to the phone on the kitchen wall. He dialed the number, then waited. "Strange," he said after ten rings. "No answer."

"Maybe he's at home," Terri said.

"Possibly," Wolfe said, "but he always leaves the answering machine on if he's gone so people can get in touch with him if there's a need—like now."

"Could be he just forgot," Josephs said hanging up the phone. "I'd better go check to make sure."

"We're going too," Terri said, looking at Wolfe.

Wolfe looked at the body. "Guess he'll be all right for a while," he said, putting his arm around Terri. "His plans for the evening have been canceled."

chapter 61

The lights were on but no one answered the door when they arrived at the morgue. Wolfe tried the door, but it was locked.

"Eino," Josephs yelled as he pounded on the door. "Wake up, you lazy Finlander," he said, knowing that would get a response if anything would.

"I don't like this," Terri said nervously. "Maybe we'd better break in."

Josephs looked at her. "Well, he may be hurt or something," she insisted.

"It's the 'or something' that bothers me," Josephs said as he put his shoulder into the door. It popped open easily and they cautiously walked in, Josephs leading the way. The lab was a mess. Chairs tipped over, books and files strewn about—it looked like a hurricane hit it.

"Oh no," Terri said, dread creeping over her like a thick blanket. "Please, no. Not Eino." Tears started to well in her eyes as they walked towards his office. Just before they got to the door, she saw the blood.

"Better wait here," Josephs said, stepping around spots of blood on the floor leading to Eino's office. "I'll check it out."

His office was worse than the lab. Everything was out of place and upside down. The blood trail led around behind the desk which was tipped on its side. Josephs walked cautiously toward the desk, looking around the room as he did so, careful not to destroy any evidence. When he looked behind the desk he shouted.

"Eino!" he said, rushing quickly to the coroner. There on the floor was Eino, with blood on his forehead and face, and his glasses hanging off one ear, bent and broken. His head was tilted at an odd angle up against the bookcase wall. It looked like he wasn't breathing.

"Is he . . ." Terri began, afraid of the response.

"Don't know," said Josephs, quickly checking for a pulse. "He's so damned skinny—I can't find a pulse. Quick. Help me move him," he said, trying to get some more room. "I'm gonna start CPR." Wolfe and Terri helped move the desk while Josephs slid Eino away from the wall.

Josephs positioned himself, tilting Eino's head back as he pinched his nostrils. He bent over to blow into Eino's mouth when suddenly the coroner rasped, "you touch those ugly lips to mine and *you'll* need CPR." Josephs jerked back as Eino's eyes popped open.

"Eino!" Terri shouted. "You're alive!"

"Not for long, the way this rhino's going at it," he said, trying to sit up.

"Just stay where you are, you ungrateful old buzzard," Josephs said, placing his jacket under Eino's head. "I'm checking you out first."

"What happened?" Wolfe asked Eino.

"They came for Kevin's body."

"Kevin?" Terri exclaimed. "They got Kevin?"

"Who was it?" Josephs asked.

"Didn't identify themselves," Eino said, coughing. "Just walked in—started making demands. Wanted to know where Kevin's body was—kept mumbling something about stolen government property."

"It was them," Wolfe said, looking at Josephs.

"That's not all," Eino continued as Terri began wiping the blood from his face with a damp cloth. "They wanted to know where *you* were."

"Who?" Terri asked.

"You," he said to her. "And Wolfe. They wanted you real bad. Thought I knew where you were. That's when they started to rough me up 'cause I wouldn't tell 'em. Then they conked me on the head. Knocked me cold 'til buffalo breath here started to kiss me. That'd bring anybody back from the brink."

"So they got Kevin," Terri said, more angry than upset.

"I didn't say that," Eino said. "I said they came for Kevin's body."

"You mean they didn't get him?" she said, her eyes brightening.

"They got someone," he said, a smile cracking his thin lips. "But it wasn't Kevin."

"How do you know it wasn't Kevin, if you've been out cold?" Wolfe said.

"'Cause he's not here," Eino said smugly."

"What?" Terri exclaimed. "Where is he?"

"Let's just say he's safe for now," Eino said, sitting up. "I'm OK. Let me up," he said, pushing the cloth away.

"Who did they get, Eino?" Wolfe asked suspiciously.

"I'm not positive," Eino said, "but my guess is they've got Scott Frazier's body."

"And why would they take his body instead of Kevin's?" Wolfe continued, playing the game out.

"Maybe it's because he was in the cooler marked, 'Kevin Sommers'," he finished, brushing his clothes off. "They look a lot alike," he said, looking at Terri. "Just a case of mistaken identity."

Wolfe quickly checked and came back. "He's right. The door marked for your brother is open. There's no body inside."

"See?" Eino said. "I told you I'd take care of it."

"What I don't understand," Josephs began, "is why they need his body back now. I mean, it's not like it's a big secret any more. They know the cat's out of the bag about ELF."

"I asked them that—why they wanted the body," Eino said. "One of them said that it was none of my damn business. That's when they were still being civil. They didn't know I knew the whole story."

"That could explain it, then," said Wolfe.

"Maybe," said Eino, looking for the first time at his office. "Shit. What a mess. Probably doin' the same to Wallick's house right now."

"What?" they all said simultaneously.

"That's where they were going next," he said, surprised at their reaction. "Musta heard 'em say that just as I passed out."

chapter 62

Josephs stayed in town while the others went back to Wallick's. Draco's body was gone, as they expected. Wolfe looked at the mess. "Got the same treatment as you did, Eino," Wolfe said to the bandaged coroner as they surveyed the house.

"'Cept he don't have to clean it up," Eino said, squinting to see without his glasses.

"Well, now they know about Draco," said Terri. "Maybe they'll call this madness off." Just then the phone rang.

"Yea?" Wolfe said into the phone, wondering whether it was Draco's men checking up, or the Sheriff. It was the latter.

"Wolfe," Josephs began.

"What's up?"

"We got big problems."

"Remember, Ed. We're on the phone," Wolfe reminded.

"Yea, well screw the phone and the codes, Wolfe. It's too late for that stuff. One of my men tipped me off. The FBI wants me for questioning. They're also looking for you and Terri."

"What for?"

"They wouldn't say," Josephs continued. "But my deputy did

some checking, and it looks like it involves national security—espionage, most likely."

"Damn," said Wolfe. "They're working fast. I guess Draco wasn't the only key to this whole mess."

"Afraid not. Looks like it goes a lot higher, Wolfe," said Josephs.

"How much time do we have?" said Wolfe.

"Basically, none. If we don't turn ourselves in immediately, they'll issue a fugitive warrant for our arrest. I'm told the paperwork's already done, and you won't like the wording."

"What does it say?"

"*'Stop at any cost. Armed and extremely dangerous.'* It's going out nationwide as we speak."

"Where are you now?"

"I'm at the truck stop on US 41. Listen. This conversation's probably goin' straight to Maryland so I'll keep it short—and don't interrupt. I'm turning myself in right now. I'm going to the FBI office and try to convince them of the truth—what's really happening. I don't know if I'll be successful or not, but I'm gonna give it my best shot.

"I'll send one of my deputies to get Eino, so don't worry about him. As for you and Terri—what you two do is up to you. I've got the file they want hidden in a safe place, so don't worry about that. I'm gonna go now. Good luck." The phone went dead before Wolfe could say anything.

"That doesn't sound good," Terri said, listening to his half of the conversation.

"It's not," he said hanging up the phone. "Draco's group has the FBI on our tail. They must have convinced them we're responsible for all these deaths—and maybe the sabotage of the ELF installations. Probably told them we're spies."

"Super," she said.

"We're not finished yet," he said, grabbing her arm. "Let's get out of here. We've got work to do."

"What are we going to do, Clay?" Terri asked once they were back in the car.

"First thing is we're going to ditch this car. They'll be looking for it and it's easy to spot."

"What do you mean, 'ditch'?" she said warily.

He laughed. "Don't worry. Nothing will happen to your precious car."

"You seem in a good mood," she said, looking at him curiously. "Considering all that's happened."

"The choice has been made," he said. "Now it's a race against the clock. We know our objective, and they know theirs. We'll see who wins."

"This isn't a game," said Terri. "There are lots of lives at stake—ours included."

"I work best under pressure," Wolfe said stopping the car. "Get out. We're going to change cars."

"Here?" she said. "In the middle of a used car lot?"

"Lots of rentals here," he said, checking out the cars. "No one will know 'til morning. By then we'll be long gone."

"But what about my car?"

"It'll get towed to the police impound lot," he said. "It's been there before. It'll feel right at home, and be protected at the same time."

She followed him to the back of the lot. "What are we going to 'buy'?"

"A nice, innocuous car. Something that doesn't draw attention to itself—like this Chevy Impala," he said, walking over to the beige, ten-year-old sedan. "This'll do nicely."

"The plate's expired," she said, looking at the rear of the car.

"That's one reason it's a good car. At least it has a plate, and it's not yours. They'll be looking for your car or your out-of-state tags. Besides—trying to spot an expired sticker's almost impossible at night."

Wolfe quickly jimmied the lock and they got in the car. "You're pretty good at that," she said. "Looks like you've done it before—a lot."

"Hope this baby has gas," he said, ignoring her comment. Twisting the appropriate wires under the dash produced the desired results. "Damn," he said. "Our luck. Eighth of a tank. That's about twenty miles tops in this gas hog. I was hoping we could get farther before we had to stop."

"How far we going?" she asked.

"Green Bay," he said, putting it in gear.

"We're going to Green Bay?" she said. "Wisconsin?"

"Well we can't drive this all the way to D.C.," he said. "It's a twenty-hour trip, at least. They'll have a description of this car by morning." He checked his watch. "In about ten hours. So we've gotta be where we're going by then."

"But why Green Bay?"

"We'll catch a plane from there."

"But won't they be watching all commercial flights for us?"

"Who said we're going commercial?"

"Not again," she said, shaking her head. "Now you're going to steal a *plane*?"

"I know. It's quick and dirty—but effective. By the time they find out it's gone, we'll have landed. They probably won't know it's us if we ditch the car on the outskirts of the city and take a cab to the airport. It's far enough from here that I doubt they'll make the connection. Besides," he added, "Josephs is helping throw them off our trail."

"How do you know that?"

"Because when he called, he told me he had the box from Wallick's house and that he would keep it safe."

"But we have the box with us," she said, looking down at the steel case under her feet."

"Right. It was a two-sided message. One to those on our trail, if they were listening in on the conversation, that he had the box. The second was to us, to let us know that he'd try to throw them off our track."

"Pretty clever for a hick sheriff," she said, obviously impressed.

"He's no hick, I can tell you that," he said.

chapter 63

Wolfe began looking for a place to stop and get gas. He tried to find one where there wouldn't be a lot of chit-chat with a station attendant. Finally he spotted one with the electronic pumps where you could use a credit card at the pump and not have to go inside.

He pulled in cautiously, checking for any signs of police or military. He made a quick drive around back, in case there were cars or officers there. Seeing none, he pulled back around front, and up to a pump. He kept watch as he inserted his credit card, selected the grade of gas, and started the pump. As he pumped he kept his eyes open for anything suspicious.

Then, as he about finished, the station attendant ambled out towards his car. He looked to be in his fifties, thick grey hair, about five-ten in height, two hundred pounds, and walked with a slight limp. Wolfe kept eyeballing him as he approached. He might be a ringer, you never know, Wolfe thought. Put the word out to everyone to be on the lookout for . . .

But he just wanted to talk. Probably bored, thought Wolfe.

"Really somethin 'bout them war games, eh?" the man with the blue shirt said to Wolfe. His name Ralph was written on his shirt.

Wolfe finished filling the gas tank, put the cap on, and closed the cover. "War games?" he said, as he returned the pump handle to its proper slot.

"Yea. You know," said Ralph. "The bulletin 'bout half an hour ago on the radio. How the military's conducting some kinda surprise war game in the area. Settin' up road blocks and all. Jest like we was at war and fearin' an invasion from a foreign country. Guess it's 'cause we're on a foreign border with Canada, you know?"

"I know," said Wolfe, carefully looking around as he talked with Ralph, his new buddy. "What else did this bulletin say?" he asked, trying to appear casual."

"Jest that there might be some shootin' and not to worry. They won't be usin' real bullets. Kinda excitin' if you ask me."

"I'm sure it will be," Wolfe went along. "They say when these games were supposed to start?" he said, still looking around.

"Sure," the man said, sticking a big wad of chewing tobacco in his cheek. "That's the surprise part," he said, smiling. "They all ready started."

chapter 64

"What's the matter?" Terri said as Wolfe got back in the car. "You look like you've seen a ghost."

Wolfe started the car and pulled out of the gas station back the way they came.

"What are you doing?" she said. "You're going the wrong way."

"It's worse than I thought," he said, driving slowly as he looked from side to side. "The military's in on the hunt." He explained the conversation with the gas station attendant.

"I don't believe it," she said, shaking her head. "You think this is all a maneuver to get us?"

"I believe it is," he said soberly.

"You think they'd shoot us on sight?" she said, "under the ruse of a war game?"

"I think that's a distinct possibility," he said, turning north on the road toward his house.

"Where are you going now?" she said as he started up the street. "You're not going home, are you? That's the first place they'll look."

"No, but all the roads out of the county will be blocked by now. Plus the airports and bus stations."

"Then we're trapped," she said with utter resignation. "They're going to kill us and take over ELF anyway."

"Maybe not," he said with what sounded to Terri like a note of hope. "There's still one place left to go."

"Where's that?" she said, not comprehending.

"Where they won't think to look 'til it's too late."

Terri didn't push him anymore. The way he said the last, she wasn't sure she wanted to know. They rode in silence until they approached the entrance to Wolfe's house. As they passed, he pulled a small, black transmitter out of his shirt pocket, aimed it in the direction of his house, and pressed the button in the center. He then threw the transmitter out the window and accelerated.

"What was that all about?" she said.

Wolfe said nothing for long seconds. Then, slowly, deliberately, "You remember our conversations about my secret past? About how I never tell you what I really do for a living?"

Terri looked at his face, high-lighted in the eerie glow from the dash lights. "Yes?" she said expectantly.

"In a few minutes some very unusual things are going to occur. They're necessary for us to stay alive—to complete our objective." He paused. She said nothing, waiting—not wanting to destroy the moment so long in coming.

"What you're about see," he continued, "will answer some of your questions, raise others. The ground rules are, you don't ask me any questions about what you see, you don't talk to anyone you meet unless asked specifically to do so. Whatever you learn from this experience is yours, but I won't elaborate on it, or clarify any questions you may have."

"Is that all?" she said, upset that it was not the expose she had hoped for.

"No," he said with finality. "You must never reveal what you learn to anyone for any reason."

"And if I don't agree?" she said defiantly.

"Then you stay behind."

"But I'd probably be killed! You wouldn't do that!"

"If I didn't, others would," he said, his voice controlled, masking his real emotions. "The only way they'll let you come with me is if you agree to these conditions."

"If I agree, how will they know I'll keep my word?"

"Because I'll vouch for you," he said, eyes fixed on the road.

"And that's enough for them?"

"That's enough."

"And what if I change my mind when it's all over?"

"You won't."

"And how do you know that?"

"Because," he said carefully, "if you do, they'll kill *me*."

Terri stared at Wolfe. She couldn't believe what she was hearing. "You mean they—whoever 'they' are—would kill you if I revealed any of the things I learned?"

Wolfe nodded.

"Why, that's crazy," she said. "You're not responsible for my actions."

"Are you saying you don't agree to these conditions?" he said carefully.

"No Clay, not necessarily," she began in frustration. "But it's not reasonable to expect . . ."

Suddenly she stopped. His face seemed to turn to granite. She looked away. The trees marched by as the car pulled smoothly down the road. One after the other they marched, like obedient soldiers—not knowing their destination, not caring.

Terri took a deep breath and slowly let it out. "I agree to the conditions," she said softly.

The approaching car slowed. It was a large, four-door sedan with an antenna mounted on the trunk. As it passed, someone inside flashed a bright spot light inside their car, illuminating Wolfe and Terri against the dark forest, nearly blinding them.

Terri shielded her eyes from the brightness. "What's that?"

Wolfe diverted his eyes immediately when the spotlight hit them, allowing his vision to recover quickly. "Judging from the way the car just did a U-turn in the road, I'd say offhand that it's a police car—or the FBI."

"They're chasing us?" she asked, turning around in time to see the car accelerate towards them.

"Looks that way," he replied, watching the big car narrow the gap between them.

"But how do they know it's us? They couldn't know the car was stolen yet, could they?"

"Probably not," he said. "But they saw a man and a woman together not far from my house. And it's pretty late. My guess is they're not sure. They're going to try to check it out."

"Aren't you going to try to get away?" she said as Wolfe maintained his speed.

"Not yet," he said, watching his speedometer. "We need more time. I'll string him out for a little longer—see what he does."

The big sedan closed quickly on them, then stayed about two car lengths behind. "They're awfully close," said Terri. "What're they doing?"

"Checking our license tags, I imagine," he said. "Strap yourself in. It won't be long now."

It wasn't. The big car suddenly accelerated and tried to pull alongside their car. Before the car could pull abreast of them, Wolfe mashed the pedal to the floor and the big Chevy surged ahead, barely holding its own against the advancing vehicle.

Suddenly around the curve came a pickup truck. The driver of the big sedan slammed on his brakes and pulled in behind them, just missing a head-on collision. "That was close," said Terri, twisting to see if the car made it. It did. "They're even closer, Clay," she said. "What are you going to do? We can't outrun them."

"We're going to have an accident," he said calmly.

"What?" she said, puzzled.

"An old demolition derby trick," he said, accelerating as fast as the car would go. "Make sure you have your seat belt on. After I slow down for the next curve I'm going to begin to accelerate, and as they do the same, I'm going to hit the brakes as hard as I can. They won't be expecting it, and they should crash into the back of our car."

"Wonderful," Terri said, snapping her seatbelt in place. "And we go up in flames as the gas tank ruptures."

"Hopefully not," he said. "Our car should still be drivable, but, if things work out, theirs won't."

chapter 65

The next curve came. Wolfe slowed the car barely enough to make it and then accelerated. As the big sedan did the same, Wolfe suddenly jammed on the brakes, locking all four wheels. The driver of the sedan never had time to hit the brakes. The big car crashed into the back of them, crushing their trunk about two feet in.

Wolfe and Terri were jammed up against their seatbelts as their tires screamed against the blacktop, shedding rubber and smoking like they were on fire. When the big sedan struck their car, they were slammed back against their seatbacks. Then Wolfe quickly accelerated away from the scene.

The new sedan fared far worse. "Jeez!" said Terri, turning to see what happened. "Look at that!" *That* turned out to be the sedan with its front grill smashed back and the hood buckled up in front of the windshield. Radiator fluid was spewing out all over the road as the driver fought for control of the car and lost. The sedan swerved across the road a couple of times, then came to rest in the ditch on the side of the road, plowing up a mountain of sand as it did so.

"You OK?" Wolfe asked as he assessed the damage.

"I guess so," she said, "other than a little whiplash." She turned to look back behind them and saw the disaster as they were pulling away. "Looks like that takes care of *them*."

"It does," said Wolfe. "Now let's hope we make it the rest of the way."

"What do you mean?" Terri asked.

"I mean they probably radioed to everyone and his brother that they had a vehicle in hot pursuit. They don't know for sure it's us yet, but they're likely to think it's a good bet. In which case, it won't take long for them to head this way. But I'm gonna give them something else to take their attention away from us."

"What do you mean, Clay?" said Terri.

"Do you remember when we passed my house that I clicked that garage opener, then threw it out the window?"

"Yes," said Terri. "I was wondering when you were going to tell me about that."

"Well listen." Wolfe looked at his watch. "In about ten seconds you'll understand why."

Just about ten seconds later there was a loud explosion behind them from the direction of town. A few seconds later, there was another explosion, even louder, from another direction, and then a third, even louder explosion.

"What's that," exclaimed Terri. "Did you . . ."

"We needed a diversion," Wolfe said. "That should dry up some of the resources that are pursuing us."

"I guess," she said. But what did you blow up?" Terri said. "I hope nobody . . ."

"Got hurt?" said Wolfe. "Hardly. The first was an old house that was uninhabited, and the second and third were in spots that were hard to get to, but consisted of abandoned buildings. They were both wired so that if someone were to get near either one, it would activate the explosives."

"Alright," said Terri. "I feel better now."

"Don't get feeling too comfortable, Terri," Wolfe said. "The worst is yet to come, I'm afraid."

They made it through Big Bay, without further incident, then pushed on up through the tunnel of trees they had been through once before. Wolfe mashed down on the gas pedal as far as it would go, pushing the Chevy to maximum speed as it blasted along the narrow road.

As they neared the end of the road, Terri saw the guard shack come into view. Wolfe slowed again, flashing his lights in some kind of code. Suddenly a guard appeared and opened the gate arm, lowering it immediately as Wolfe pulled passed.

As they started down the narrow, winding dirt road, Terri saw nearly two dozen more men come out of the woods and fan out near the entrance. What shocked her even more than their number was that each was carrying a machine gun and other heavy armament. She even thought she heard the sound of a tank's diesel engine and the clatter of its tracks climbing through the forest. Could that be? she wondered.

The car bounced and slid as Wolfe pushed as fast as he could through the heavily wooded trail. "Who were those men?" Terri asked. Wolfe didn't reply. "Oh. I forgot," she said grabbing the dash as they hit a bump that launched her forward. "No questions."

"Sorry," he said, smiling slightly. "Part of the deal."

Finally the road opened into a clearing. Though the headlights illuminated only a small area, she could still see large, wooden houses and other buildings she had seen before—and she could hear the roar of the lake as the waves crashed up on nearby rocks. This was the top of the Upper Peninsula, she thought, recalling her last visit. This was the end of the line.

Wolfe turned off the engine, then the lights. It was almost pitch dark as the cloud cover completely obscured the moon and stars.

"Let's go," he said to Terri as he opened his door and grabbed the steel case.

A man appeared and walked over to Wolfe. He was Wolfe's height and weight, but seemed older. Terri couldn't see his features in the dark. "Lupo," he said, shaking Wolfe's hand, clasping his arm. "Long time."

"Too long," said Wolfe, as he greeted the man.

"The girl?"

"Cleared," Wolfe said.

"By who?"

"By me."

"Good enough," the man said, throwing his arm around Wolfe's shoulders and walking him toward the sound of the waves. Terri followed.

"I see you got my message," Wolfe said.

"Did you doubt?" the man said as they came to a building by the edge of a cliff. Terri could hear the breakers roaring now. "Turned to shit, eh?" he said, smiling.

"You could say that," Wolfe said as they stepped into a building made entirely of wood. As rustic as it seemed, it was fully updated with modern furnishing, electronics, and state-of-the-art communications and monitoring equipment. Terri would have had more time to be impressed if they were not running for their lives.

As they walked through the building, low-level floor lighting came on in each room as they entered, and turned off as they exited. Like in movie theaters, thought Terri. She continued following closely along, taking in as much as she could. They walked down some steps, came to a landing, then walked down some more. Terri could hear the waves crashing loudly on the rocks. They sounded like they were right outside the wall.

chapter 66

"Chewtoy should be here any minute," the man said, now shouting to be heard over the sound of the waves. "He's been on standby just in case this happened. We all hoped it wouldn't."

"I understand," Wolfe said, clapping his hand on the man's back.

"I just hope you can get through," he shouted at Wolfe. "I'd hate to think this was all for nothing." The man seemed to want some assurance.

"Don't worry. We'll make it."

"That's what I wanted to hear, Lupo."

Lupo, thought Terri. That's twice she'd heard the man call Wolfe that. She knew it sounded familiar. Then she remembered. Lupo. Italian for 'wolf.'

Suddenly Terri heard the faint sound of something else mingled with the sound of the waves. At first she couldn't make out what it was. Then, it became more distinct. It was the sound of an airplane.

"Sounds like Chewtoy," the man said. "Better get going. Not much time left." The man opened a door and Terri could hear the sound of water lapping gently. A light came on and she could see they were in a large boathouse. Nestled safely inside was a huge speedboat, its windshield and canvas top breaking what otherwise would have been a straight line from bow to stern.

"Nice," said Wolfe, admiring it as he they stepped in.

"Twin engine," the man said proudly. "It'll do ninety on smooth water."

"Not today," Wolfe said. The roar of the engines got louder. The man pressed a button and the door to the lake slowly rose, revealing the break wall which shielded them from the angry waters. Terri looked for the plane, but couldn't see it. The sound from the plane seemed to get louder, then the engines cut back.

"That's him," shouted the man over the sound of the wind and the waves. "We'll have to take this to meet him out there a ways. Too dangerous close in." The man started the boat. "She's already warm," he shouted. "Hang on." The boat pulled out smoothly, still under the protection of the break wall.

Suddenly Terri heard what sounded like gunfire. A moment later, she was sure. The staccato of automatic weapons was unmistakable, even as the man gunned the engines and launched the boat crazily into the churning seas.

Terri didn't know how the man could see where he was going. Then she saw the radar mast. Of course, she thought. This boat would be outfitted with everything. The cold spray stung her face as the boat charged against the forces of nature.

Soon, she could see the outline of a large seaplane bobbing in the heavy swells. As they got closer, she could see it had no markings, and was painted a flat black. Even up close it was almost invisible. Its twin engines were facing into the wind, turning just enough to keep the plane stable.

"It's gonna be rough," the man yelled as he cut the boat's engines and pulled alongside the planes pontoons. A man on the plane tossed a rope to Wolfe who grabbed it, and pulled the boat closer.

"You first, Terri," Wolfe said taking her arm. "I won't let go until he has hold of you." Terri stood on the edge of the boat, trying to keep her balance between the two moving surfaces. The man on the plane was reaching for her, trying to time their grasp with the action of the waves. Finally they gripped and he pulled her aboard.

Wolfe turned to the man. "I owe you," he shouted, hugging him briefly. "Just stay alive until you can collect!"

More gunfire erupted as Wolfe stepped onto the side of the boat. "You bet your ass, Lupo," the man shouted as Wolfe made the jump and cast off the line. "Just get there!"

Wolfe waved as the plane's engines revved. He stood in the doorway and watched the plane pull away from the boat, then shut the door. He sat next to Terri, and strapped himself in. He looked at her in the dim, red glow of the plane's interior light. She sat there quietly, staring straight ahead, her unasked question filling Wolfe's head.

"Thunder Bay," he said into her ear as the plane's engines crescendoed into a deafening roar. Terri looked at him. "Canada," he said, smiling. His voice was inaudible as she read his lips.

The plane bounced and pitched until she thought it would tear apart in the heavy seas. Finally it lifted, but not far. "Got to stay under the radar," Wolfe shouted. She nodded. Then, for the first time, she noticed a man sitting across from her, staring at her. Wolfe followed her gaze. "Don't worry about him," he yelled. "He was elected Mister Congeniality of his high school class—he just doesn't know it yet." She looked away from the man. Wolfe's attempts to put her mind at ease failed miserably.

chapter 67

After what seemed like hours, the plane finally landed. The waters were just as choppy near Thunder Bay, if that's where they *really* were, thought Terri. The same exercise in reverse put them on shore in what appeared to be a well-appointed vacation home.

Terri looked at their escort and the other two men who greeted them inside the lighted cabin. Their escort was over six feet tall, ruddy complexion, with a soup bowl haircut. He appeared to be in his late twenties and wore dark brown clothing. He was the same grim man who had sat across from them, staring at her on the plane.

The older man in the cabin appeared to be in his fifties or sixties and had thick, gray hair. His paunch was accentuated by his tight, black, turtleneck sweater—an obvious carryover from leaner years.

The third man was thin, almost emaciated. His sunken eyes indicated he had not gotten much sleep lately. His clothes hung on him like hand-me-downs.

"Sit down," the older man said, ignoring the usual amenities. Everyone sat except Soupbowl, who stood at parade rest behind them. "Now I want to know what the hell's going on," he said, his eyes burning. "I've just lost a lot of good men because of you, and now I find out that both your military and your famed FBI are out to get you at any cost.

"I've saved your asses like I was supposed to," he said glancing at Terri, his eyes offering no apology, "because this was a top priority INTEROP mission. Now before I waste one more minute of my time, you're gonna tell me what the hell's going on!"

"I suggest you follow the remainder of your orders, General," Wolfe said stiffly. "I'll answer no questions per INTEROP directives."

"The hell with INTEROP directives!" he shouted. "And I'm not your General! By god, you'll tell me what I want to know, or you won't leave this room!" he said, waving his finger at Wolfe. Soupbowl took a step forward.

"Not a good idea, General," Wolfe warned, ignoring his disclaimer. "I suggest you call off your dog before we have some unpleasantries."

The General glared at Wolfe for a moment, then finally nodded to Soupbowl to stand off. "Maybe you want to show me what's in that case," he said, more under control.

"No one's going to see what's in this case, General," Wolfe said icily, "except the authorized person. And none of you are him."

Soupbowl's eyes lit up at Wolfe's tone of voice. He couldn't contain himself anymore. He grabbed Wolfe by the shoulders and spun him around, and drew his fist back. "No one talks to my . . ."

But that's all he got out because Wolfe had already driven his own fist deep within Soupbowl's solar-plexus. Doubling over with a whoosh as every ounce of air exited his lungs, he reached in his boot for a knife. But before he could use it, Wolfe gave Soupbowl an uppercut directly to his nose, which drove him back against the Franklin stove. A nasty cracking sound indicated that Soupbowl would not be getting up soon, if ever. Wolfe looked back to see the General smiling.

"Now isn't that a bad turn of luck," he said, turning to the thin man. "He was your pilot out of here."

"No loss," Wolfe said indifferently. "Just get us to the plane."

"I'm sorry," the General said, obviously not. "Regulations, you know? Only authorized personnel can fly . . ."

Wolfe pulled out his nine millimeter semi-automatic and put it up under the General's nose. "No time to pussyfoot around, General," Wolfe said, his nose one inch from the General's. His teeth were clenched tight and Terri could see his jaw muscles tight. The thin man took a step furtively back towards the desk drawer.

"And tell the Grim Reaper here," he said motioning toward the thin man, "that if he moves one more muscle he's gonna meet the real one first hand." The thin man froze.

"You're gonna pay for this, Mister," the General said, fury rising in his voice. "You're gonna pay!"

"Take it up with my accountant," Wolfe said as he motioned toward the door. "Let's get in the car. Both of you."

chapter 68

"Nice plane," Wolfe said as they arrived at the small airstrip. "No control tower. Good," he said as the Jeep came to a stop. "Get out, one at a time," he said handing the gun to Terri. "If either moves, shoot 'em," he said, watching her reaction.

"Done," she said coldly, surprising him.

Wolfe tied them up with twine taken from the cabin. "Thanks for the lift, boys," he said as he opened the door to the sleek, twin engine jet. "Tell the queen I said hello." The General yelled some expletive but Wolfe didn't hear. He helped Terri in first, then he grabbed the steel case and climbed in. Then secured the door.

"Where do I sit?" Terri said, admiring the sumptuous accommodations in the cabin.

"Up with me," he said, motioning her toward the pilot's seat. "Today, you're a co-pilot."

Terri watched as Wolfe deftly handled the controls, going through the checklist. Then he moved the throttle forward and she felt the power of the jet engines pressing her back into the luxurious seat. Wolfe took off smoothly, climbing until they were at cruising altitude.

"Aren't you worried those guys back there will get loose and call you in?" she asked.

"What? And admit they violated a strict INTEROP directive? Not likely," he said, leaning back in his seat and closing his eyes. "They were completely in the wrong. They could be court martialed for what they did. No. They'll come up with some cock-and-bull story to cover themselves, and pretend they followed orders. They know I won't say anything about it either."

"Why's that?" she asked.

"Because I could be shot for what I did."

Two hours later, they found some cold roast beef sandwiches and lemonade in the fridge, both of which tasted like manna from heaven. After consuming enough for four, Wolfe laid in a course change, notified the appropriate tower, and settled back to watch the sunrise over the clouds.

"That's indescribable," she said, watching the deep purples turn to red over the cotton-like mounds of clouds. "It's like being in fantasy land."

"It is beautiful," he said, his hand resting on her shoulder. "Hard to believe something so gorgeous up here could cover such ugliness down below."

They sat silently until the sun was up, then Wolfe handed her a pair of aviator's sun glasses while he donned a pair of his own.

"Are we going to make it, Clay?" she said looking at him, her glasses still in her hand. "Are we really going to make it?"

Wolfe looked at her eyes, now vulnerable and soft. The pain of the past now mingled with the present. His different lives over-lapping, emotions invading each other, Wolfe closed his eyes behind the dark glasses, and tried to sort out the confusing feelings and sensations. He stayed like this for several minutes. Then he took off his glasses, leaned over and kissed her. "Yes, we're going to make it."

chapter 69

As they approached Washington National Airport in Washington, D.C., Terri popped a question at Wolfe out of the blue. "You're Canadian, aren't you Clay?"

Wolfe kept his eyes focused on the gauges in front of him, occasionally answering the control tower. "What prompted that question?" he asked finally, trying to be casual.

"Back there—at Thunder Bay," she said. "You kept calling the older man 'General'. He seemed to be bothered a lot by that—as if he really *was* your General, but you weren't supposed to acknowledge that."

"A figure of speech," he said minimally. "Besides—that falls under the conditions. Remember?"

"It was an innocent question, Clay," she said simply. "It had nothing to do with those circumstances falling under the 'conditions'. I just wondered, that's all."

"Right. And I'm JFK," he said, making the final approach.

Terri began to get nervous. "What are we going to do when we get there, Clay? Who are we going to see?"

"I'd intended to try to get to NSA to get this thing decoded," he said, indicating the steel box. "But I'm afraid that's where they'll expect us to go. I think they'll be waiting."

"So what do we do?" she said. "Right now all we have is a box of meaningless paper and a whopper of a story."

"And some dead people," he added.

"Which will probably be hushed up or explained away," she replied.

"And we most likely will, or have already gotten, the blame for any problems back there," Wolfe said. "I'd sure like to know who's pulling the strings, and how they're doing it."

"So?" she said, waiting for an answer.

"So I guess I'll have to play my final trump card."

"Which is?"

"Go directly to the President."

Terri's mouth fell open. "You're going to do what?"

"He's the only one I can trust. Anyone lower might be involved. I mean, think about it," he said. "We know what kind of power Draco had, yet after he was killed, the program didn't miss a beat. Someone else higher up knew exactly what was going on and they jumped in and took control instantly. And they had to have high authority to suddenly have the FBI and the military join forces to catch two foreign spies—which is what they must have been told we were—even if we were supposedly a threat to national security."

"But how're you gonna get in to see him?" she asked. "You don't just walk up to the White House, ring the doorbell and ask his mommy if you can speak to the President."

"Very funny," he said. "Hold on. We're landing." The plane came in smoothly and they taxied over to the general aviation area. "When we get out, act as if we are the passengers," Wolfe said. "I want to get out of here as fast as we can."

"I'm right with you," she said as he opened the door, let down the steps and climbed down. "Thank you, sir," she said, smiling at him as he took her hand and helped her down the steps.

They walked briskly out and hailed a taxi. "Here's one," he said as a Yellow Cab pulled up. "The White House," he said as they climbed in. "And step on it." Wolfe turned to Terri. "I always wanted to say that," he said.

The cabbie turned around and looked at Wolfe like he was from Mars. "Seriously," Wolfe said. "Take us to the White House. We're in a hurry." The cabbie shook his head and pulled out into traffic squealing his tires.

"I'm sure he needed the encouragement to speed," she said, shaking her head.

A block from the White House there was a public phone. "Stop here," Wolfe said to the cabbie.

"But we're not there yet," the cabbie said turning to look at him.

"That's OK," Wolfe said reaching into his pocket for the money. "This is close enough. Here," he said, and handed him five hundred dollars.

"Clay?" Terri said, bewildered by the large sum of money.

"Pull around the corner and wait for us over there," he instructed the cabbie, pointing to a parking place. "We're going to make a phone call, then we're going to walk the rest of the way," Wolfe said. "Don't answer your radio, and don't take any runs 'til we get back. For every hour you wait, I'll give you five hundred more. Understand?"

The driver nodded. "Five hundred dollars. For every hour. You're crazy mister, but I'll wait. Crazy money spends the same."

"I thought you'd understand," Wolfe said, more to Terri than the cabbie.

"Well I'm glad he does 'cause I sure don't," she said after the cab pulled away.

As they walked toward the phone booth he explained. "Two reasons, really. One, if anyone is trying to track us down, it'll be damn hard to get hold of that cabbie for the next hour to find out where his fare went.

"Two, I thought it might be nice to have a handy escape vehicle that blends in with the other ten thousand yellow cabs in the city should we need to make a hasty departure."

"And do you expect that to happen?" she asked.

"No," he said, digging out his change, "but I like to be prepared. Throwback to when I was a boy scout," he finished, a twinkle in his eye.

"You were never a boy scout," she said, more to herself than to Wolfe.

chapter 70

They found the phone booth, and after looking around to see if anyone was watching them, Wolfe dialed a number and waited. "White House," the soft female voice said at the other end of the phone.

"I have a coded two-twenty-eight priority blue message for the President," he said. There was some whispering which Wolfe couldn't hear, then an older, more seasoned female voice came on the line.

"May I help you?" the woman said officiously.

"I gave my message," Wolfe said firmly. "I'm waiting."

"Could you please repeat it?" she said, not as a question but as an order.

"One doesn't repeat priority blue messages. Play it back on your recorder," he said. "I'm sure you've got one." More whispering followed.

"One moment please," the voice continued. Then, "from where are you calling?"

"I'll wait one more minute," he said coldly, "then I'm hanging up and you can kiss your job goodbye, whoever you are."

"One moment," the voice said in defeat. Thirty seconds later a man's voice was on the line.

"You have a coded two-twenty-eight priority blue message for the President," the crisp voice said, exactly as Wolfe had given it.

"That's correct," he said.

"You have a name," the voice went on.

"Lupo," he said.

"For?" the voice came back cryptically.

"Wagonmaster," Wolfe finished. There was silence for ten seconds.

"You know this is a highly irregular procedure," the voice said, relaxing a little.

"This is a highly irregular circumstance," Wolfe said, getting irritated. "And I suggest you get on with it before I'm speaking with your new replacement."

The man got the message. "A black Chrysler sedan, license number 3031 will be at your location within five minutes," the voice said finally. "The driver will bring you in."

"I have a spare," Wolfe said to the voice, referring to Terri. More silence.

"I'm sorry," the voice began. "We can't allow . . ."

"Code blue," Wolfe cut in abrasively. "*Replacement*?" he finished, driving home the point.

"Five minutes," the voice said tersely, then hung up.

"I'm gonna have to teach them some manners," Wolfe said, hanging up the receiver.

"Well?" she said, expecting the worse.

"Look for a black Chrysler, license number 3031," he said.

The Chrysler pulled up in exactly five minutes as stated by the voice on the phone. There was no one else in the car except the driver, who made no move to get out and open the door for them.

"This is it," Wolfe said as he opened the back door for Terri. She got in, then he went to the passenger side next to the driver and got in. The driver pulled away from the curb quickly, saying nothing, looking straight ahead. The cabbie watched with interest, making no move as the car pulled away.

Within minutes they were inside the White House gate, then the White House itself. Once inside, they were met by a Secret Service agent who inspected the metal case, took his gun, then escorted them to the Oval Office.

"I don't believe this," Terri said in a whisper after he had gone. "Do you realize where we are?" she said, looking around like a kid in a candy store. "This is *the* Oval Office."

"That it is," Wolfe said quietly, watching her reaction.

"How . . . ?" she started. He just smiled. She gave up.

Just then the door opened and in walked a tall, distinguished man with gray hair and slightly stooped shoulders. "Wolfe," the man said, his gruff voice belying his soft heart. "How the hell are you?" he said, shaking Wolfe's hand. "And this beautiful young lady?"

"Mister President," he said formally, "I'd like you to Meet Miss Terri Sommers. Miss Sommers, President Thomas Masterson."

"Very pleased to meet you, Mister President," Terri said, barely audible.

"The pleasure's all mine," said the President. "Please be seated." They all sat.

"Now. What's this all about, Wolfe?" he said, business back in his voice. "I understand this was a code blue?"

"Yes sir, it was," Wolfe said. "Let me explain. After you had asked me to find out why those scientists were dying on the ELF project, I ran into Miss Sommers whose brother had mysteriously disappeared and was later found dead." Wolfe related all of the events up to that moment, in detail. When he had finished, the President sat there for several minutes, saying nothing.

Finally, he spoke. "Wolfe, you've got to believe me," he said looking right into Wolfe's eyes, "I knew nothing of this . . . this renegade ELF system. As far as I was told, and believed," he continued, "its purpose was to communicate with submarines." He cleared his throat, took out a handkerchief, removed his glasses, wiped his eyes, and replaced each item in turn.

"This is very upsetting," he said, getting up and walking to the window. Standing there looking out, his hands clasped behind his back, he continued. "I had a feeling something was wrong, Wolfe. That's why I sent you. The budget was swelling. Scientists were dying. I couldn't seem to get a straight answer from anyone. 'It's OK, Mister President,' they'd tell me," he said. "'Everything's fine, Mister President,' they'd say. 'We need the system.' Well now I know what for." He turned and faced them. "You say they had orders from the highest level?"

"Yes sir," Wolfe said. "Supposedly signed from the very top."

"Well that would mean it would have to have been the Secretary of Defense, or . . ." he paused, turning to look out the window again. "Or me," he finished. "Did you think it might be me, Wolfe?"

"No sir," Wolfe said. "Wouldn't have made sense to send me to uncover a secret system you had already set up—would it, sir?"

"I suppose not," Masterson said, shaking his head. "But I can't imagine my Secretary of Defense doing something like that, either," he said, obviously bewildered. "Who the hell signed the orders?"

"We don't know, sir," Wolfe said. "We were hoping you could tell us."

"And you tell me that the names of these conspirators are in code on papers in that case over there?"

"We believe so sir. That's what Draco said when he planned to kill us."

"Then if that's where the answer is," he said, reaching for the case, "I guess we'd better get it decoded.

"Get me Randall," he barked into the phone on the desk of the Oval Office. "I don't care who you have to interrupt," he shouted at the hapless secretary who was unfortunate enough to get this once-in-a-lifetime call. "This is President Masterson and when I want to talk to the head of the damned NSA, by god I'm going to or heads will roll!"

"Right away sir . . . uh, Mister Presid . . ."

"Just get him!" Masterson snapped. It sounded like the phone was dropped on the floor on the other end.

Seconds later an out-of-breath Ralph Randall, head of the NSA was on the line. "Tom," he said, trying to be congenial. "How are you? You don't usually call me on this . . ."

"Never mind," the President said, cutting him off. "I'm coming over with a couple of people. We've got a code to break and you've got a damned mole in your operation. A big one! Now I want your most trusted person on this code, as if your job depended on it, Ralph. Because it does."

"Right now?" Randall started to say, but he never got the chance to finish. Masterson had already hung up.

He then hit another button on his phone. "Get me Tim Deerfield and tell him to get to my office pronto!"

chapter 71

Less than a minute later, Deerfield appeared. "Yes, Mister President?" Deerfield said as he entered the room. Terri sized him up. Late thirties, strong, alert and handsome. Her appraisal of him was not lost on Wolfe.

"We're going to NSA headquarters—the three of us. Now. Set it up will you?"

"Yes sir. Right away," said Tim. "They know you're coming?"

"They damn well better," he said gruffly. "We've got some hot documents to decode and they're gonna do it right now." Deerfield eyed the metal case in the president's grasp.

Masterson turned to Wolfe. "Tim used to be a Secret Service agent assigned to protect me," he said, somewhat boastfully. "Did such a good job, I hired him as my aide. Handles a lot of the grunt work for me that none of my other staff seem to feel is dignified enough for them. Still packs a rod, though," he continued, smiling. "Drives the Secret Service wild, but I want him to have it. Besides. He was one of their own, once."

Wolfe looked at Deerfield, who seemed to be avoiding his gaze.

"Here," Deerfield said, reaching for the case. "I'll carry that for you."

"Thanks," Masterson said, handing him the case. "See what I mean?"

Wolfe continued watching Deerfield. He looks uneasy, thought Wolfe. Something was not right.

"What other types of things does this extraordinary aide do for you, Tom?" Wolfe asked innocently. When Masterson looked at him quizzically, he continued, "I may be interested in a job like that myself someday."

The President laughed. "Somehow I can't see you in this role, Wolfe," he said as he reached for his coat. "He takes care of paperwork for me," he continued finally. "Routine stuff, you know."

"Yes," said Wolfe carefully. "I know what you mean. Screens paperwork for you—only sends you the important stuff."

"Exactly," Masterson said, moving toward the door. By this time, Deerfield was not looking well at all. Wolfe had been eyeing him constantly during the conversation, and he seemed very nervous.

Wolfe instinctively made his next move. "Why don't you let me carry that," he said to Deerfield, as he reached for the case with the coded documents. Wolfe smiled disarmingly as he did so. "Be good training for my future position."

Deerfield hesitated, looked at Wolfe, then at Masterson who was now looking at him.

"Well?" Masterson said. "Give him the case, Tim."

Suddenly Deerfield took a step back and quickly drew his gun. Wolfe was watching for the move and lunged at him as the gun cleared his holster.

"What the hell?" Masterson yelled as the two fell to the floor.

Terri yelled. "Clay!"

Deerfield was quick. Wolfe tried to grab the gun, but got his wrist instead. One round of the powerful .357 magnum went into the ceiling as they struggled. Another went into the wall near the entrance door.

"Watch out!" screamed Terri as she and Masterson ducked away from the shots, one narrowly missing the president's head.

Deerfield broke free of Wolfe's grasp and brought the gun down hard on Wolfe's head. Wolfe went down and didn't move. Swinging his aim at Masterson, Deerfield again started firing. Masterson ducked behind his desk just before several more rounds went off.

Suddenly, Wolfe jumped up behind Deerfield and kicked the backs of his knees, sending him to the floor. As Deerfield was falling, Wolfe grabbed Deerfield's revolver around the cylinder and held it tight. Deerfield was futilely trying to pull the trigger, but the cylinder wouldn't turn in Wolfe's grasp. Deerfield twisted around to face Wolfe, which was his fatal mistake. Wolfe pulled back and drove the knuckles of his free hand deep into Deerfield's throat.

They both went down to the floor just as the door to the office burst open and four Secret Service agents with guns drawn charged into the room. "Tell 'em!" Wolfe shouted at Masterson.

"It's Deerfield!" the President shouted. "He tried to kill me!" The agents quickly moved in. But Deerfield was no threat. With his windpipe nearly crushed, his attention was totally focused on getting air to his lungs.

"Get EMTs now!" yelled one agent while the another agent cuffed Deerfield. Within seconds the on-duty EMTs rushed in, assessed the situation and began treatment.

"Get that traitor out of here!" yelled Masterson. Surrounded by Secret Service agents, the EMTs quickly removed Deerfield and began prepping him for a tracheotomy.

Wolfe slowly got to his feet, breathing hard. "Not as young as I used to be," he said. "I think we've found your problem, Mister President," Wolfe said to Masterson. "At least one of them."

"I don't understand," Masterson said after Deerfield was removed. "He was one of our best agents."

"I think you'll also find," began Wolfe, "that he was paid a lot of money to forge your signature on the orders for the renegade ELF system."

"Forge my name?" Masterson said, with disbelief.

"Think about it, Tom," Wolfe said. "The Secret Service agents are trained to detect forgery. It's part of their professional training. Not a great step from there to becoming an expert forger himself— particularly when the stakes are high."

Masterson shook his head and walked over to his desk. "So, who's the brains behind this mess? Deerfield?"

"My guess," said Wolfe, "is that it was Draco. He used Deerfield for his own end, but it was Draco who engineered the world take-over scheme. He was brilliant enough, and just crazy enough to pull it off."

"And he almost did," Masterson said.

"He may yet," Wolfe said seriously, "unless you take some steps quickly. May I suggest that you contact the FBI and the military as soon as possible? I've got some friends in a tough situation who need your assistance badly."

"That's easy enough," Masterson said, picking up the phone. He barked the necessary orders to the Director of the FBI, then called his Secretary of Defense and did the same. "They should be in good shape very soon."

"Thanks," Wolfe said.

"No. Thank you," Masterson said sincerely. "I owe you one, Wolfe. As you know, I can't publicly recognize you for your assistance, although I wish to hell I could."

"No need, sir," Wolfe responded.

"Well, I just want you to know that this country owes you a debt of gratitude. If there's anything I can ever do . . ."

Terri looked at Wolfe at the mention of 'this country', but said nothing.

"Thanks for your kind words, sir," Wolfe said, ignoring her

penetrating look. "I'll keep that in mind. Now to more pressing matters."

"Right," Masterson said. "The list. I'll get it decoded and take care of the rest of the conspirators."

"We'll help," Wolfe said.

"Let's do it," Masterson said, in charge again.

chapter 72

The night air was cool, but warmer than it had been in Marquette. Wolfe and Terri sat on the steps of the Lincoln Memorial looking up at the thousands of stars visible in the clear night sky.

"So Eino and Josephs are back in business," Terri summed up. "The conspirators out of business, and your mission is done. My boss still wants me back, so I guess it's a return to things as usual. What about you?"

"Do some more teaching, I guess," Wolfe said. "Maybe some investigations—to help out, you know," he said with a twinkle in his eye.

"I don't suppose you'll answer any questions I have about these last few days, would you?" Terri said.

"Like?" Wolfe said, taking a deep breath of the fresh air.

"Like what INTEROP is," she said, "or what country you're really from?"

Wolfe smiled, kept looking at the night sky.

"I didn't think so," she said. "Will I see you again?" she said, looking at down at her feet.

"You're a part of my life now," Wolfe said. "As much as

anything. We'll see each other. No question about that as far as I'm concerned."

"Good," she said, shivering in the cold. Wolfe noticed, and put her arm around her. "Now I have a question I know you can answer."

"Shoot," he said.

"Where's Kevin's body?"

Wolfe smiled. "Eino said not to worry, and he meant it. But he told me, in case anything happened to him, so you'd know."

"Well?" she said, waiting.

"He knew you wanted it done," Wolfe began, "so he took care of it for you himself."

"What?"

"He had him cremated. He had completed all his tests, so he made the arrangements. Kevin's ashes are there in a beautiful urn, whenever you want to pick them up," he said.

Terri thought for a minute, then finally spoke. "No, don't save them," she said. "He would hate being all cooped up. That's why he didn't want to be buried. No. Set him free. Spread his ashes over the North Country. After all," she said. "That's what he died protecting. That's what he loved. I'm sure he'd want it that way."

"I'll see to it," he said. "Anything else?"

"Yes," she said, turning to him, her lips close to his. "There is. But we need to go somewhere private."

He pulled her to him and kissed her. Then, standing, he took her hand and helped her up. "I know the perfect place," he said.

"That's good," she said, "because I know the perfect cabbie."

"The cabbie!" exclaimed Wolfe. "I'd forgotten all about him." Then he thought about the money and smiled. "I bet he's still there."

"I bet he is, too," she said, laughing. "Hope you have enough for the tip," she said as they walked arm in arm to the cab.

epilogue

Wolfe sat by the fire in his remote cabin. It was evening and there was a new moon. There was no road to his cabin, the closest being over twenty miles away. Wolfe liked it like that. Total solitude, unreached, and unreachable. Here, he had no phone, no TV, no electronic device or wire of any kind. In fact, he had no electricity at all. He lived off the grid entirely. He even built the place himself so there was no record of his cabin anywhere. It was the peace he needed after his increasingly difficult missions.

On his property was a small lake that he also owned. It was well-stocked, and was a favorite place for him to go fishing, and to contemplate the universe. Maybe he was through with this life, he thought to himself. Maybe he needed to retire. He doubted 'they' would be pleased. But screw 'em, he thought. He didn't owe them anything. His performance over the years was always well above and beyond. Nobody knew about his place, and he was damned if he was going to tell *anyone* about it. He just might never leave, he thought.

Wolfe was feeling very comfortable as he contemplated his future of peace and tranquility. He gazed into the flickering fire and watched as the flames danced their hypnotic rhythm.

Then there was a knock at the door.

Printed in the United States
By Bookmasters